# *TWIN*

## *By Deborah Dunlevy*

# Other Books by Deborah Dunlevy

*The Book of Sight*

*The Broken Circle*

*The Secret Source*

*The Poisoned Cure*

*The Shattered Heart*

# TWIN

## By Deborah Dunlevy

Digital Edition ISBN: 978-0-9966556-8-2

Print Edition ISBN: 978-0-9966556-9-9

Madison House Publishing

www.madisonhousepublishing.com

Quantity sales. Special discounts are available on quantity purchases by corporations, associations, and others. For details, contact the publisher at the web-address above or call 317-797-9993.

# Contents

*For David*

*who can't read my mind*

*but always has my back*

"Some of what you are about to hear will be confusing. Some will be shocking. Some will be difficult to understand or even to believe. All of it will be the truth, at least as understood by the speaker, and though there is still so much we do not know, nothing that we do know will be omitted. We are committed, as always, to full disclosure. No secrets. No lies.

"Whatever you feel about what you hear, we would ask, as we always do, that you listen fully before drawing conclusions. We would ask, as we always do, that all discussion remain calm and reasoned. And we would ask that you be patient. The Charter taught us to prepare for the unexpected, and the events of the last few weeks have taken us further into that territory than we ever dreamed possible. Navigating our path will not come without false starts and stumbling. As long as we continue in our commitment to patient progress, we will find our way together as we always do."

-Governor Cal Mayland
Address to the full gathering
Colony of Mayland
L.D. 81

# Chapter 1

# *Home*

Tom was home.

He hadn't sent them a message, and the perimeter chimes hadn't sounded yet, but Cara knew he was at the east gate.

She always knew.

When you've shared every minute of your existence with someone, there are some things you don't have to question.

He must have pushed his group hard to get back in time. She would have to find the heart to reprimand him. She had told him not to hurry. He was the leader of an exploration team, and they were looking for the site for their second settlement. Compared to something that historic, their twentieth birthday wasn't important.

Being Tom, though, he knew she didn't mean it. Celebrating her birthday without him would be like playing football without any ball. She could go through the motions, but there wouldn't be much point.

She made a note to share that metaphor with him. Tom would find the idea of pantomime football hilarious. Of course, he'd also probably take the opportunity to tell her they were twin-tastic and follow it up with the song he invented, called "Double the Trouble." He liked to wait until she was focused on something important and then sing it over and over to drive her crazy. He had a terrible singing voice.

A bubble of happiness filled her. Stars, she had missed him so much she actually wanted to hear that ridiculous song.

Cara repressed the grin that wanted to escape. Kim, the chief agricultural engineer, was explaining the difficulties he was having with the new strain of maka grain. It was important to show that she valued his work and the time he took away from it to communicate with the governor's office. Interrupting him, or even looking distracted, would have implied that she had more important things to do. Never mind that this grain problem would be solved by his experts with no need of her help. Never mind that she hadn't seen her brother in two months.

*A leader's life is not her own*, her father's voice lectured in her head.

Cara ignored the tingling in the back of her mind that told her Tom was anxious to see her. Why wasn't there a perimeter alert yet? Were the chimes broken? She tried to focus on Kim's words.

"...be trying a new modification starting next week. The chemists think..."

A soft ding, repeated several times, interrupted the chief's words. Kim smiled. "That'll be the explorers, won't it?" The twinkle in his eye made Cara think of her grandmother. She and Kim had been good friends. "You'd better get over there and greet them. Apprentice governor's duty."

Kim had always been one of Cara's favorite people.

He gave her a pat on the shoulder. "Tell him happy birthday for me."

Cara felt like running, but she didn't want anyone to think there was an emergency.

*Leaders must never seem anxious*, her father's voice cautioned, *or they will breed anxiety in those who follow them.*

She held herself to a brisk walk, trying to focus on her usual delight in the order around her. She loved the strategic arrangement of the buildings and the tidy gardens surrounding each one. Mayland Settlement, the first human home on the planet Una, was the model for future settlements. Everything was laid out for maximum efficiency and aesthetic appeal.

Today, though, each well-designed feature felt like an obstacle. Why were the greenhouses so ridiculously far from the gates? And was it really necessary to plant that many trees?

Cara kept on her friendliest smile, greeting the people she passed by name. If she didn't pause to chat, no one seemed offended. Probably, they all knew where she was headed. Her father had been the governor of Mayland since he took over from his mother. Her family had no private business. It was a burden sometimes, but it had its advantages, too.

With every step, Cara's excitement rose. She couldn't wait to hear how far Tom and his team had gotten. She couldn't wait to see if he had grown the beard he had been threatening. She couldn't wait to find out what the team's big new discovery was.

Cara's step faltered. How did she know they had made a big discovery?

With a swoop in her stomach, Cara realized that not all of the excitement she was feeling was her own.

She shivered. It had been a long time since she had felt Tom's emotions strongly enough to confuse them for her own. She had hoped that she had stopped that for good.

It was one thing to have a vague sense of his location; science had documented that phenomenon for centuries. It was something totally different to have him take over her head.

When she came around the corner of the archive pavilion, her discomfort fled. The team of explorers clustered around her father, all talking at once. Cara barely had time to take in Lin's striking red hair in the center of the group before a tall, lanky figure broke away and ran toward her, grinning.

"Six! What took you so long? Too busy filling out checklists to come see your long-lost twin?"

Cara laughed as he crashed into her and wrapped her in a suffocating hug. "You were gone?" she said into his shoulder. "I didn't notice."

That brought on a flurry of tickles which made her shriek and push away. "Tom! Stop it!"

She saw her father glance over, felt his disapproval. She stepped back and fended Tom off with both hands. "Stop! I mean it. People are staring."

"The only people here are the ones who have been missing their families just as much as I have. They won't judge." He stopped, though, giving her long black ponytail a tug before stepping back. He looked good, healthy and tan, his dark hair overgrown and disheveled, a few days of scruff on his face instead of a full beard. "Happy birthday."

"Happy birthday to you. I can't believe you made it back."

"Are you kidding me? You knew I wouldn't miss it. But where were you? I thought you'd be waiting for us."

"Kim was giving me the grain report."

Tom nodded. "Yes, I can see why that would be more important than your brother. It's not like grain reports happen every day."

"They don't," she said with a sniff. "They only happen once a week." She kept her smile hidden under a prim face.

"Honestly, I don't know how you stand the excitement, Six."

Cara grinned. Her father didn't approve of nicknames, so naturally, she didn't have one. Only Tom called her Six, a reference to the number of minutes that had passed between her birth and his.

The Charter required the first two children in each family to be apprenticed to their parents. By the time Tom and Cara were born, their sister Bree was seven and had already shown an aptitude for her mother's job as a doctor. That meant the next-born Mayland would be apprenticed to their father, while any other children would be trained as explorers and colonists to found future settlements.

"Those six minutes are very important to me," Tom always said. "Those six minutes are the difference between a life of paperwork and the freedom of life outside the fence."

Of course, he only said things like that when their father wasn't around.

"Are you available now? Or are there more urgent reports you need to file?"

"A leader always knows when to interrupt her routine for matters of pressing concern," she quoted sternly.

"Good," he grinned. "Because I have something amazing to show you."

"A birthday present?"

"Better than that."

He took her hand and dragged her over to the group, which parted to allow them in to where their father stood with the red-haired Lin, studying the clear bottle she held up.

"What is it?" Cara asked.

"Something of importance, according to Lin," her father answered, "but I have yet to receive a full report from the team leader." He looked up at his son, and the warmth in his eyes softened his dry tone. "Perhaps now you are ready to bring us up to speed, Tom?"

"I thought it was important that your apprentice be here to receive the report at the same time," Tom answered glibly. "Efficiency is a virtue."

"Naturally," his father said. "But as she has arrived, please proceed."

Tom planted his feet and straightened his back formally.

"Per our mission parameters, the team travelled northwest after leaving Mayland, following the Vita River. As our early scans had shown, the river passed through one small fresh-water lake with no suitable ground nearby for the establishment of a new colony. To the south, we could see a forest in the distance, but we stayed with the river as instructed. After two weeks, we came to a place where the Vita split into two courses. One stayed in open grassland and the other headed directly into the forested area. We took a week to explore the first, then returned and followed the other branch into the forest. Lin has the logs which contain all of the geographical data.

"The day after we entered the forest, we sighted a herd of yesela grazing along the river. Since we had exhausted our stores of fresh food and were down to camp packs, I authorized our two best hunters to take down a pair of yesela for us to eat. Pel got hers with a clean shot through the head. Rik was not so accurate. He clipped his yesela in the hindquarters, and it ran off through the trees."

"Please stick to pertinent data, Son. We'll have time for hunting tales over dinner."

Tom raised a brow at his father. "This is pertinent data, as it leads to the most important part. The rest of the herd was, of course, frightened off by the shots. They ran straight into the river and away on the other side, but the injured yesela stumbled into the forest. We chased it. One yesela wouldn't feed us all, and we didn't want to lose our dinner. Even wounded, those things are fast. The yesela followed a well-trampled path through the trees and up over a steep hill. When we got to the top, the trees had thinned out, and we saw the yesela plunging into a flat lake at the bottom of the incline.

"If I hadn't seen what happened next with my own eyes, I wouldn't believe it. The yesela was limping badly, blood running down its back leg, but the minute it submerged itself in the water, it began to walk normally again. After a few moments, it came out of the lake, completely healed, and darted off before we could get over the shock of what we had seen."

Cara watched her father's face. He showed no sign of surprise or wonder. His eyes studied his son thoughtfully. "Who witnessed this healing?"

"There were four of us who made it to the top of the hill in time to see it happen. Myself and Rik, Lin and Grish. Several others arrived just after and saw the yesela running away. We were all amazed at what we had seen."

"I'm confident that your amazement didn't hinder you from taking appropriate precautions however," his father said.

"Of course not," Tom answered. "Lin took charge of collecting a sample of the water for scientific study, and we were careful not to touch it. No further tests were conducted in the field, but we did survey the land surrounding the lake, and the results were extremely favorable. A well-watered plain surrounded by forest, reasonable proximity to the river. Our full evaluation will be in my report." Tom dropped his formal commander stance and grinned. "Basically, it's perfect. I think we've found our new settlement."

"As long as this water doesn't turn out to be dangerous," Lin said, holding up the bottle. Cara noticed she was wearing gloves even though the bottle was firmly capped. Lin may have been an explorer, but she wasn't the kind who took unnecessary risks.

"It's not dangerous," said Rik. He was older than Cara, but he still had the gangly arms and legs of a teenager and the idealism that went with them. "It's healing water! We're going to live by a lake of healing water!"

The governor quelled him with a look. "You will have time to make your own report later this evening, and your report will include only the facts of what you observed. The safety of the sample and its effects will be determined by our scientists, and the eventual location of our second settlement will be decided by our leaders. Is that clear?"

Rik turned bright red as he bobbed his head.

"Excellent. No doubt you would all like to see your families and clean up from your journey. I would ask that you keep the details of your trip confidential until we've compiled enough data to ensure accuracy. I understand your excitement about what you've experienced, but we don't need wild rumors about healing water. That will only breed confusion. Once we have solid facts to share, the whole colony will hear them. For now, keep your stories to the more mundane aspects of the mission. I'll expect written reports from everyone in my office by tomorrow morning, and we'll start the interviews at noon. In the meantime, enjoy your well-earned rest. You appear to have done exemplary work on this expedition. The whole colony is proud of you."

Someone let out a whoop, which made the others laugh as the knot of explorers broke up, each in a hurry to get home. Cara noticed that Tom grabbed Lin's hand and squeezed it briefly before she slipped away. The smile Lin gave him made Cara feel giddy until she furiously pushed her brother's emotion away. What was wrong with her? She must have gotten lazy while Tom was gone, forgotten how to maintain control.

"...which is why it would be better if you accompanied him," her father said.

Cara refocused. Her father couldn't know what she had been thinking. He was just telling her to escort Tom to the medical center to hand over the sample and give the report. The staff there would want to get to work studying the water right away.

"After that, you may have your rest, as well, Tom. Cara, meet me in the office. We will need to finish as many of the weekly reports as possible in order to be free to handle interviews with the exploration team tomorrow."

"Of course," Cara said, quashing her disappointment not to have the afternoon with Tom. Her father was right. The arrival of the explorers, not to mention this new discovery, was going to put pressure on their already tightly-scheduled week. At least that night was their birthday dinner. They would get to be together then.

"I don't know how you do it," Tom said as their father walked away.

"Do what?" Cara asked.

"All of this: the schedule, the reports, the rigidity, him."

"He's an incredible leader and a wonderful mentor."

"Oh, I know."

"I'm lucky. I couldn't be happier."

Tom shook his head. "I know you're happy. I can feel that. But there's something else there, too. Admit it."

"You aren't supposed to be feeling my feelings, Tom. You're supposed to be blocking me out."

Tom just looked at her with eyebrows raised.

Cara shrugged. "Nothing is perfect. Everything has challenges. It would be unreasonable to expect my life to be any different."

"Right. We wouldn't want to be unreasonable."

She didn't like the way Tom was watching her, like he could see inside her head. It was dangerous. She didn't want to ruin his homecoming with a lecture, but she made a mental note to talk to him about it later.

"No, there isn't any point in being unreasonable, and we can't all be blissed out in love like some people," she said with a raise of one brow.

Tom grinned. "Too bad. It would be good for you."

"I take it things progressed while you were gone."

"You could say that."

"I did say that."

"Yes, but did you say we're officially together?"

Cara stopped walking. "I didn't say that. Should I have said that?"

"Only if you wanted to beat me to the good news."

Cara felt a foolish grin on her face that matched his. "You and Lin are a couple."

He gasped. "How did you know?"

Cara wanted to jump up and down, to throw her arms around him, but she just stood there with that stupid smile. "You guys are perfect for each other."

"You really do have to say everything first, don't you?"

"Well, I am older," Cara said, starting to walk again.

"Six lousy minutes, and now I don't even get to tell my own good news."

"I promise I'll give you at least six minutes to tell Bree before I jump in."

*10*

"That should be enough."

Cara stopped at the door to the med center. "You know I really am…"

"…happy for me. I know." He pulled the door open and ushered her inside. "Like you had any choice."

*Twin-tastic*, Cara thought.

"I prefer twin-riffic," Tom said, "but whatever."

Cara's heart skipped. "Did you just…?"

"Did I just what?" Tom asked. He was already heading toward the office where their mother would be waiting.

"Nothing," Cara said. "Never mind."

She hurried to catch up.

# Chapter 2

# *Family*

Cal Mayland never said much at the dinner table, but everyone listened to him anyway.

Tom's mother, Jul, handed him his favorite dishes without being asked. Cara pumped Tom for all the information she knew her father wanted. Even Tom restricted his exuberance to a few fidgets and told his stories with the preciseness that Cal required.

"So Hy was singing these songs every night that he had made up himself. They were pretty entertaining, but the songs were the only thing he had contributed the whole trip. He forgets everything and spends so much time daydreaming that we have to remind him to watch where he's walking. It was Lin who suggested we have him work with Grish, cataloging flora and fauna. We told him to set the lists and descriptions to music. It worked like a charm. Not only did he start paying more attention, but his songs are really catchy. By now we can all tell you the names of every plant we saw along the way."

"Lin's a genius," said Cara.

Tom knew he was grinning goofily. Which was why she had said it, of course.

"She would make a good governor," Cal said.

Tom's grin faltered, but he brought it back. "She really would," he said.

When you had an amazing woman, you appreciated her. Jealousy wasn't on the table.

It wouldn't hurt to change the subject, though. "When, exactly, did Bree say that she and Jak were going to get here?"

"Sooner than you might think," said a voice from the doorway. "Happy birthday!"

"Bree!" Tom jumped to his feet and hugged his oldest sister.

She laughed, the same full-bodied laugh their mother had. "Let me breathe, not-so-little brother!"

Tom let go and turned to bestow a more restrained hug on Bree's husband, Jak.

"Good to see you, Tom," said Jak. "I have a million questions."

"A million?" Tom said. "It's usually just thousands."

"Well, this is the first time you've brought home the scientific discovery of a lifetime," said Bree, taking her seat at the table and reaching for the bread. "That's why we're late. I could barely tear Jak away from the lab."

"I just needed to get the samples running. This way the data will be ready in the morning."

Jak was a biochemist and one of the most brilliant minds in Mayland. Though Bree was a medical doctor like her mother and spent most of her time with patients, they often worked together in the lab after hours. They had fallen in love over test tubes and centrifuge machines.

Tom would have called them adorable, but Cara said that the word wasn't suitable for two highly-respected scientists.

"There isn't much to say that I didn't already put in the report," Tom said. "You guys are the ones who can find all the answers."

"Yes, but…"

"Jak, it's their birthday. We should at least let them eat before we start the interrogation," Bree suggested.

Jak looked at her like a guilty puppy as she handed him a glass of pale wine.

"A toast!" she said. "To Tom and Cara, and their big 2-0!"

"To Tom and Cara," the others repeated.

Tom grinned at Cara. "They put my name first this time. They really must have missed me."

She raised one brow, then turned to the others. "There is one thing that Tom didn't put in the report."

"Yes!" he said, nearly leaping out of his seat again. "I was just waiting for everyone to be here." He cleared his throat dramatically. "I have an announcement to make!"

"You and Lin are together!" Bree squealed.

He groaned. "Not you too!"

"I'm sorry!" Bree clapped a hand over her mouth. "I just got so excited."

Tom put on a mock sorrowful expression. "No one knows how painful it is to have intelligent sisters."

"You're officially a couple?" His mother asked.

"Yes," he said. "We talked about it on the trip. We're not in any hurry to get married or anything, but we both feel the same way."

Jul beamed. Bree abandoned her dinner for another hug. Even Cal nodded approvingly from the head of the table.

"Congratulations," he said. "She's an admirable young woman. You'll want to be careful not to rush things, though. You're both very young."

"Thank you," Tom said, forcing his smile to stay in place. "Like I said, we're not in a hurry."

Cal nodded gravely but didn't answer.

Cara jumped to Tom's rescue. "Another toast!" She said, raising her glass. "To Tom and Lin and a bright future!"

Everyone clinked glasses with the person next to them. As Tom's touched Cara's, he felt her twinge of sadness and realized that if he married Lin, Cara's would be the extra glass. If she was interested in any particular man, she had never told him about it. She never took enough time away from work to fall in love. He was going to have to work on that before he moved away.

"Next week at family dinner, we should invite Lin's family to join us," Jul said.

"That would be very appropriate," Cal agreed.

Tom was pretty sure Cara was the only one who heard him snort.

"I'll extend the invitation," Jul said, "I assume you and Cara can speak to the kitchens about having their family's food delivered here along with ours that night?"

Cal nodded and raised his little finger toward Cara in their usual sign. She took out her tablet and entered a note. Tom could never understand how she didn't resent the assumption that she would jump into action every time her father twitched a hand.

"So tell me all about the yesela that got healed by this water," Jak said. "How bad was the injury? How long was it in the water? Could you see the skin knitting itself back together or did it just wash the blood away?"

Bree laughed and put a restraining hand on her husband's arm, but Tom leaned forward, happy to focus on something else.

"The arrow sliced deep," he said. "We tracked the yesela for nearly two kilometers, and it lost a lot of blood. We caught up to it just in time to see it hobbling into the water. I thought it was going to collapse and make our job easy. We were maybe a hundred meters away, so I couldn't see the healing in process. That animal was in the water for less than a minute, though, and when it came out, it leapt away as good as new."

"Incredible," Jak said. "There must be something in the chemical makeup of the water that accelerates the healing process. Or maybe some kind of microscopic bacteria. It looks pure and clean enough, and the pH is the same as regular water, so only the tests will show where the differences lie."

"How will you know if it's safe to use on humans?" Tom asked.

"Hopefully once we understand the chemical makeup, we'll have a clearer picture of how it might interact with human physiology."

"It's critical to proceed with caution," Cal said.

"Of course," Bree said. "If the tests show it to be compatible, we'll try it on a variety of life forms before any human testing takes place."

"There is always some risk, though," Jak said. "There's no way to truly know how a new substance will affect us until we've tried it."

"Understood," said Cal. "But we need to do everything possible to reduce those risks."

Jak waved a hand dismissively. "Sure. In this case, though, the benefits outweigh the risks by a nearly infinite factor. Healing water? This could change everything. And if we discovered that it healed more than injury? What if it also heals sickness? What if it could strengthen weakness or slow aging? We're talking about a whole new world here."

Tom had spent the last couple of weeks thinking about it. This water opened up so many possibilities. He and Lin had already discussed how it could move up their timeline in founding the new settlement. He tried to hold his excitement in check. It was too early to make assumptions. But the thought of starting to build something, of finally putting all their training into practice, of getting out from under his father's thumb....

A trickle of fear ran through him, and he looked over at Cara. For a minute, he set aside his own excitement and saw the situation as she would. This level of change was risky. As wonderful as it was to have a cure for injury, introducing a powerful unknown agent could endanger the future they were carefully building here.

Mayland Colony had been established on the planet Una with meticulous preparation, the Plan for its structure and growth designed to ensure that it would be ordered and sustainable and would avoid the pitfalls of violence and overpopulation that led to the devastation of Earth. For three generations, they had been carrying out the Plan, and it was working beautifully. Mayland was peaceful and prosperous, and its people were happy. They were finally a few good years away from being able to found their second settlement without damaging the first.

Even minor changes had to be carefully considered. Tom could respect that. He would respect that. For Cara's sake, if nothing else. He wouldn't be in such a hurry to go that he left her with a mess to clean up behind him.

"It's vital," Tom's father said, "that you keep all information about this water confidential for now. Between your team at the lab and the leadership team, we have enough input to make initial decisions about how to move forward. Speculation will only cloud the issue, and speculation is exactly what will happen if this is discussed widely."

All of Tom's good intentions fled. "You can't keep something like this a secret!" he said. "Everyone on my team knows what happened, and though they'll try to follow your orders about confidentiality, things are bound to slip out."

"Then I expect you to encourage them to be discreet," Cal said. "It is not a matter of keeping secrets but of dealing in facts once we understand them rather than possibilities we do not understand."

Before he could respond, Cara jumped in. "It's only for a couple of days. We'll study this water, and once we understand it better, we can all work together to find a way to work it into the Plan, just like we always do."

"This isn't like anything else," Tom said.

"No," she answered. "But 'we expect the unexpected, and with thoughtful deliberation turn surprises into assets.'"

"Is that from the apprentice governor's handbook?" he snapped.

"No," Cal said. "It's from your great-grandfather, and his wisdom has served us well so far."

It was the hurt on Cara's face rather than his father's words that made Tom drop the subject. It wasn't her fault that she couldn't see how shortsighted Cal was. She was practically chained to his side.

After dinner was finished and the containers returned to the kitchen building, the family gathered in the common room around the cozy heating unit while Tom played his viol for them all. As usual, the music drained away Tom's frustration. He watched Cara listening with her eyes closed. He could feel her contentment. As hard as it was to be back with Cal's unspoken disapproval, being close to Cara again brought a peace to his own mind that he hadn't realized was missing.

When he finished, the married couples wished them both happy birthday again and left for their sleeping areas.

Tom set the viol aside. "Finally."

Cara smiled. "In honor of your return, I'll let you go first."

"Nice try. You always want me to go first."

Tom couldn't remember the first year they had secretly stayed awake until their parents were asleep, but they couldn't have been more than four or five. It had felt daring when they were little. A small rebellion, which Cara only went along with because it was their birthday. She had been so sleepy those first few years that Tom had invented the birthday game.

He put his fingers to his temples, adopting a wise expression. "I predict that this year…your team will lose the football tournament to an unexpected outsider."

"You wish," she said. "If you want to win, you're going to have to accept my offer."

"If I join your team, you'll never learn the important lessons of a humbling loss. Your turn."

Cara skipped the playacting, but she had hers ready. "I predict that this year…you'll start talking about dates for marrying Lin."

"Wrong already," he groaned. "You are so bad at this."

She raised an eyebrow. "I know you don't mean that you don't plan to marry her. You'd better not…you said you guys weren't in a hurry."

"We're not. The dates we talked about are all a couple of years away."

She shook her head. "If Dad hears you talking about marriage…."

"He won't. My turn. I predict that this year…you'll finally meet the man of your dreams."

Cara rolled her eyes. "Speaking of being wrong from the start…I've already met every human being on this planet. And I really don't have a dream man anyway."

"There's the problem then. It's not that you haven't met him; it's that you haven't dreamed about him enough."

"Moving on. I predict that this year…you'll officially name the site of your new settlement."

"And I predict that this year…you'll come and watch me break ground on my new settlement."

Cara went still. He could feel her sudden tension.

"Tom, you can't let yourself start thinking that."

"You heard Jak, Cara. He's right. This water changes everything."

Agitated, she stood up and walked to the window. The birthday game was finished, and he knew it was his fault, but he couldn't just let it go.

"Not everything can be controlled, you know," Tom said. "He can't make everything fit into a Plan made hundreds of years ago." He picked up his instrument and focused on wrapping it and storing it in its traveling case. He would let her pretend the comment was casual if she wanted to.

This was Cara, though. She could feel the intensity behind it.

She waited until he put the viol away and then waved him over, gesturing out at the dark sky with its streaks of autumn orange. The bright light of Dua, Una's sister planet, could be seen just above the horizon.

"You remember Hiram Mayland's speech when they founded this settlement?" she said. "'Look where you stand. In the first human colony outside Sol system. An achievement for the ages. Look, and be proud, and remember that our greatest accomplishment is also our greatest risk. We are one thousand humans living on a planet that is not our own, far beyond the reach of anyone who might care to help.'"

When she met his eyes, she was smiling but her voice was dead serious. "Nothing has changed. We're still all alone here. So we'd better hope he can fit this into the Plan. If he can't, we won't survive."

# Chapter 3

## Discovery

"The problem with Lane Tomson is all taken care of," the nursery leader said. "I spoke to his father, and he agreed to take an hour each evening to play more active games with the boy and distract him from his drawing. He has been much calmer and more centered since that routine began."

"That's a thoughtful solution," Cara said. She tried to ignore the headache behind her eyes. She had spent most of the night lying on her bed holding imaginary debates with Tom and her father. At the time, it had felt like she was forming coherent arguments and had won them both over, but in the light of day it all seemed like garbled nonsense.

"Honestly, it was Jem's idea. For an agricultural engineer, he is remarkably insightful into child development." Shar had been the leader of the nursery staff for twenty years, and she was known for being fair-minded.

Cara forced her mind back to the nursery. "Maybe children don't develop so differently from plants," she said with a smile.

Shar nodded, but her eyes were now on two teenage girls, huddled in a corner whispering to each other. "Neglecting their duties again," she muttered. "Please excuse me, Cara."

Cara watched as the woman strode over to where the two apprentices were lost in their own gossip. She stifled a laugh at the look of horror that came over their faces when their mentor suddenly grabbed their shoulders.

Cara couldn't hear the conversation, but whatever Shar was saying, the two girls bobbed their heads quickly, faces red with shame. Cara checked her tablet. Pol Mondberg and Lil Savari. Both 16, both apprenticed one year ago. Other than a few late arrivals to work, neither had any negative reports. That meant their mentor was kind as well as exacting. A good combination in the nursery.

Shar returned, shaking her head. "They're good girls," she said. "The children have taken to both of them. But they do like talking more than they like working."

"You'll get them on the right track," Cara said. "It's clear that they respect you."

"I had them here as infants. They just need a little nurturing along the way," Shar said. "But I don't want to take all of your time. I think we covered everything except the numbers. You can see on the report that we are up 20%. Lots of people having babies in the last few years. But the buildings still have plenty of capacity, and with our new apprentices we're maintaining a three to one ratio of workers, so we're keeping up with the demand nicely. As long as my apprentices do their work," she added with a quirk of her eyebrow.

"Excellent," Cara said. "Is there anything you need from us? Any way we could make things easier on your staff?"

They discussed a few alterations to the laundry schedule and a reservation of the meeting hall to do a family gathering. Cara made notes of everything on her tablet and then said goodbye, checking her schedule to see if she had five minutes to visit Tom before the next meeting.

She had eight. It had been a good morning.

Outside, the cold air nipped at her face. Dua was a half-circle in the sky, which meant everything would freeze tonight. Cara grinned. Cold weeks were her favorite, probably because they slowed everything down.

Halfway to the practice field where she hoped to find Tom, Cara's tablet chimed urgently. Code red. Medical emergency.

Heart pounding, Cara turned on her heel and hurried toward the med center as fast as she could without all-out running.

She burst through the double doors of the clinic lobby, and a blast of warm air hit her already flushed face. Cara skidded to a halt when she saw her family clustered around the reception desk.

Everyone was there. They all seemed fine.

Her father raised one eyebrow. Cara swallowed her panic and walked toward them with measured steps.

"What's the emergency?" She asked, thankful for the evenness of her voice.

"You have to see this!" Bree said. She held her tablet like it was a baby.

"There is no emergency," Cal clarified. "Just urgent information to be shared."

"I'm sorry. I really am," Bree said. "I sent out the wrong protocol. But at least you're here now, so you can see this."

She held up the tablet, and a video started. It was a recording of the lab. Cara saw Bree and Jak and two other scientists moving back and forth. Jak was showing some reports to the others. Then Bree used a syringe to take a few drops of the water sample and place them onto a slide for study.

Cara noted a few animals in cages on the long counter. She assumed they were there for testing later. She felt a brief pang at the idea of unsuspecting animals being endangered, but she pushed it away. In order for their colony to survive, they couldn't take chances with human life. The native flora and fauna of Una was held in highest value, and the long-term plan to care for every creature more than offset any that were used for food or scientific study.

"There it is!" Bree said.

"How did that happen?" Cal asked.

Cara jerked her attention back to the video. She must have missed something because the scientists on the screen were all clustered around Bree, who was on the floor.

"I slipped," Bree said. "I guess I was hurrying too much. I don't know. It's never happened before. But did you see my hand?" She skipped the video back and zoomed in on her hands.

The Bree in the video took a step and then stumbled. The syringe she was holding jabbed into her hand. For a moment, a bloom of red showed under her sheer gloves. Then she was on the floor, stripping the gloves off, and her hand was smooth and unmarked.

"It stabbed me," Bree said. "It hurt like crazy and I saw the blood, and then two seconds later the pain was gone, and when I took off the gloves there was no injury at all. There were only about two drops of water in that syringe, but look." She held up her hands. The skin was smooth and flawless. "Remember the scar I had from when I fell into the giant gashi? It was right here on my thumb."

The scar was gone.

Cara felt a chill.

"Whoa," Tom said.

"How far did the healing extend?" Cal asked. "What about the scar on your shoulder?"

"That's still there," Bree said. "We checked it right away. I guess a couple of drops can only do so much."

"Even so, this is astonishing," Jak said. "The water is more powerful than we thought. And Bree's accident saved us several days of testing. Now we know it's safe for humans."

"Perhaps," Cal said. "But we need to continue with caution. Just because there were no ill effects immediately does not mean we can be sure it is safe. I would like you to keep Bree under observation for a few more days before you proceed with any more human testing. And I would like you to request rubber-soled shoes for use in the lab. Let's not have any more accidents of this kind."

Bree and Jak traded a look. Bree took a deep breath.

"You already tried the water on someone else, didn't you?" Cara said.

"Jak wanted to verify that it wasn't an anomaly," Bree said. She was talking to Cara, but her eyes flickered over to her father. "It may not have been the wisest course, but we did only endanger ourselves. No one else has been exposed."

"And it worked," Jak said. He didn't share any of Bree's shame. "I cut open my hand, and one drop was all it took to heal it in seconds. Other than a slight itch, the process was painless, and now my hand is as good as new." He held it up in demonstration.

Cara and Bree watched their father. He showed no sign of emotion.

"I'll want to see all the video of that experiment as well," he said. "And I'll ask that you both stay quarantined in the medical center under your mother's care for 48 hours. If there are no other side-effects in that time, we'll meet to discuss further testing."

He gave Cara the sign, and she quickly made a note of that meeting on their schedule in two days.

"Forty-eight hours is a long time for quarantine," Jak said.

"Not under the circumstances," Cal said. "Please use the time to review the lab safety policies and make sure they are all stated explicitly enough to prevent these sorts of accidents in the future. We can go over that with all the scientific staff when we are ready to show your findings. For now, this needs to remain internal information only. Cara and I will speak to your coworkers when we leave here."

Bree dipped her head. "I'm sorry," she said.

"There is no need to apologize for an accident," he answered. "But for the well-being of everyone, we need to ensure that it isn't repeated in the future."

Bree and Jak nodded.

"Let's get you settled in the lab wing," Jul said. "Those patient rooms in the back have beds that are actually comfortable, and you can still work on the research from the work station there."

She led them away, leaving Tom and Cara alone with their father.

"I know you aren't happy about how it happened," Tom said, "but you have to admit this is an amazing discovery. Just think of how it can help our exploring and colonizing teams. We never have fully qualified doctors with us, but if we traveled with some of this water, we wouldn't have to worry about injuries along the trail."

"One step at a time," Cal said. "First we make sure it is truly safe. Then we can assemble a team to discuss the appropriate ways to use it. There are more implications than just a boost to first-aid in the field."

Cara knew what he was thinking. How would the colony react when they knew there was a substance that could heal anything? Suddenly that lake would be the most valuable resource on the planet, and historically, valuable resources were the cause of strife and violence.

Tom shook his head. "Fine. You two do what you do. Stars know you're good at it. I'll just keep training for the next trip."

He turned to go, but his father put a hand on his arm. "Tom, tell no one what happened in the lab today. Not even Lin should know until we have all the data."

Tom shrugged off his touch without answering and strode away. Cara could feel his resentment bubble up in her chest, but she pushed it down immediately. She wanted to say something, to help her father understand Tom's reaction, but he had already moved on.

"Shift our schedule. We'll need at least a half hour to explain things to the rest of the lab staff. And find me the full list of their current work. They're better off kept busy here until the observation period is over."

For a moment, Cal let his shoulders droop, and his worry showed on his face. Then he squared up again, the mask of serenity back in place.

Cara gave him a smile, and he nodded. She was the only one, except for her mother, who ever got to see the cost of the calm decisiveness he showed the rest of the world.

*A leader bears burdens without complaining.* But to Cara, at least, he had never sugarcoated things. The burdens existed. They were heavy. And one day they would be hers.

She hoped she could bear them with as much strength as her father did.

# Chapter 4

# Experiments

Tom was leading the team in a yoga break on the practice field when he felt the sting on both knees. A quick look told him nothing was wrong with his legs.

Something had happened to Cara.

Lin raised a brow as she stood on one foot, gracefully holding tree pose where he had left them in his distraction.

"Take over for a minute?" he said. "I'll be right back."

Because she was Lin, she asked no questions. As he jogged away, she was already talking them through the rest of the practice. She was better at it than he was. He probably should have had her leading it in the first place.

When he found Cara, she was limping along the path toward the med center.

"Stupid," Cara muttered as he came alongside. Her pants were shredded, and both knees bore bloody scrapes with bits of gravel stuck to the edges.

"Reading reports while walking again?" he asked.

"Maybe." She said, biting her cheek against the pain as he pulled her arm around his shoulders. He would have just had her lean on him for support, but their height difference made it impossible. Instead he picked her up.

Cara shook her head. "I'm so pathetic."

"Yep, you are."

"Hey! You aren't supposed to agree with me! You're my brother. Brothers aren't supposed to say their sisters are pathetic. They're supposed to say, 'You're way better than you give yourself credit for.'"

"Mmm, I think you're thinking of boyfriends. Brothers are definitely supposed to think their sisters are pathetic. Especially when they are."

"Now you're just being mean."

"Also a part of the brother's job description."

Cara pursed her lips. "What would you do if I started being mean to you?"

"My guess is I'd laugh, but you can try it, and we can find out for sure."

She sniffed. "No, I don't think I'll sink to your level."

Tom grinned. "I didn't think so. 'A good leader does not resort to petty retaliation.'"

He had many years of practice in imitating Cal's voice. A snort of laughter escaped her, followed by a sigh of relief as the med center doors opened.

Tom grinned in triumph. He had successfully distracted her from the last few meters.

"You're going to be a great leader, Cara," he said as he put her down to save her pride. "And the only pathetic thing about you is that you sometimes doubt it."

Inside the med center, everything was quiet. Usually at least one of the nurses or apprentice doctors was at the reception desk, but today the little receiving room was empty.

"Hello?" Tom called. "Anyone around?"

When there was no answer, he helped Cara hobble through the door behind the desk and into the triage area. Several long metal exam tables were lined up throughout the room, where nurses could evaluate those who came into the med center and treat minor injuries and illnesses. Along the back wall was a row of doors leading to the private rooms used for those who needed more care.

Tom was surprised to see one of those doors open and what looked like the entire staff of the med center crammed inside.

"Hello?" Cara called.

One of the young apprentice nurses looked over her shoulder and then said something to the rest of the room. The crowd parted, and Bree hurried out.

"What happened?" she asked, concern all over her face.

"Skinned my knees," Cara said. "Like a toddler."

"Reading while walking again?" Bree asked.

Cara tried to look innocent but she was terrible at it.

"Those reports aren't going to process themselves," Tom said.

"Well, it's your lucky day. Those skinned knees are going to give you a front row seat to all the excitement," Bree said, putting her arm under Cara's shoulder and helping her move toward the crowded exam room.

Tom trailed after them. "What's going on?"

"The water is safe. We've tried it out on every species we have available. There were no ill effects for Jak or me. So…"

"So today you are using it on patients?"

Bree beamed. "Yes. And wait until you see our first one." She stopped in the doorway and called out to her staff. "Make room, guys. If you've already had a chance for a closer look, it's time to get back to work. Miracles like this are about to be commonplace, so life has to keep moving. Remember that until the public announcement is made, all of this is staff knowledge only. I know it's hard to hide the excitement from your families, but the announcement should be coming in two days at most. You can hold onto a surprise until then, right?"

As she talked, the med center staff filed out of the room: one physical therapist and his apprentice, a surgeon, two nurses, two lab technicians, and three brand new apprentices whose specialties Tom couldn't remember.

When the room cleared, Tom could finally see the person sitting on the exam table against the wall. He didn't know him well, but his father had made them all memorize the personnel files, so he remembered the basics.

Oz Demar. Age 23. Mechanic. He would only be two years out of his apprenticeship, but he already had the patch on his shoulder that indicated he was in charge of his shift. Tom had played a few pickup games with Oz and his brother over the years, but they were just enough older that his path didn't cross theirs very often.

Oz was sitting on the uncomfortable table at perfect ease, his right hand resting in his lap. There was blood on his shirt, but Tom didn't see the source.

Bree led Cara to one of the two chairs that faced the exam table and helped her sit.

"Oz, you know my sister Cara and my brother Tom," she said. "Tom and Cara, Oz Demar."

Cara used her welcoming smile. "Sure. We talked for a while at your advancement, I think."

Oz nodded. As Tom recalled, the guy wasn't much of a talker.

"Today, Oz had an accident in the machine shop," Bree said. "His hand got caught in one of the machines and two fingers were sliced cleanly off."

Cara tried to keep her face as smooth as her father's would have been, but she couldn't keep her eyes from widening.

Tom made no attempt to hide his flinch. "Agh! That's brutal."

"An apprentice was able to retrieve the fingers and bring them, along with Oz, to us quickly. There was a good deal of blood loss, though fortunately, it seems that Oz knows how to tie a very tight bandage, even with one hand." Bree gave him a nod of professional approval.

"The water reattached his fingers?" Cara asked.

Bree wouldn't be rushed. "We asked his permission for the experimental procedure, and when he gave it, we sterilized the wounds, aligned the severed digits, and applied a few drops of the lake water. Within minutes, both fingers were completely healed. Can you show them?" she asked.

Oz held up his hand and bent his fingers into a fist, then lifted one finger at a time. Tom couldn't tell which ones had been healed. There were no scars.

"As you can see, full function appears to have been restored," Bree said formally, then she grinned. "Jak is going to die that he missed this. He's been buried in the lab all day."

Cara was smiling, but Tom could feel her fear. His own reaction was more like awe. The healing power of this water was overwhelming. The implications were staggering.

Oz had put his hand back in his lap and was now studying Cara's face. Tom took note of his scrutiny.

"That is incredible," Cara said.

"And now it's your turn," said Bree, grabbing a pair of scissors and beginning to cut away the torn fabric around Cara's knees. "It'll only take one drop on each of those legs, and you'll be as good as new."

Cara's tension wasn't visible on the outside. "Is that a good idea? We only have a limited sample of the water, and these are just scrapes. There's nothing new to be learned."

Bree raised her brows. "I think that it would be very valuable for someone on the leadership team to have experienced the healing effects of the water personally, as you will be actively helping to make decisions about its use. This is an opportunity."

"She's right, Six," Tom said. "Think of it as hands-on experience. Or knees-on, as the case may be."

Cara rolled her eyes. She looked over at the carefully packaged vial of water on the counter, and he saw the moment her curiosity overcame her fear.

"Okay," she said. "Do you need to call the others in to watch?"

"This is all being recorded for future study." Bree gestured at the camera attached to the ceiling. "Jak will be a little jealous, but I wasn't joking when I said that these miracles are about to become commonplace. We can't stop work for every little scrape we heal. My guess is that someday soon, it won't take a doctor to do this any more than it takes one to spread bunta sap on a rash."

While she talked, Bree put on gloves and carefully extracted some water with a tiny dropper. She gestured for Cara to lift her right knee.

When the water hit the open wound, Tom could feel Cara's relief almost immediately. He realized he was clenching his hands together and forced them to relax as he watched his sister's skin grow back before his eyes. Twenty seconds later, her knee was as good as new. Even the skin pigment matched perfectly.

A buzz of excitement electrified Tom. He had seen that yesela, had believed in what this water could do, but none of it seemed real until this moment.

"Ready for the next one?" Bree asked. She was beaming like a parent whose child had shown off a new trick.

Cara nodded tightly, and Tom studied his two sisters. Bree was so much like their mother. She had a quick mind balanced by a compassionate heart. Like Jul, she was born to be a doctor, and probably a mother, too. Cara had always been different. She was kind, but she had a core of steel that she had inherited from Cal. The ability to make hard decisions was a good trait in someone who would one day be the governor of Mayland, but it didn't leave much room for personal consideration.

Tom wondered where he fit. He had never been particularly like either of his parents. If they went forward with this new settlement, he might be a governor one day, too. What kind of governor would he be?

"Not even a little impressive?" Bree said, and Tom realized that the healing had finished while his mind was wandering.

Apparently miraculous healing really could become so common that it didn't hold your attention.

Cara flexed her knees. "Good as new," she said. She stood and raised up on her toes.

"Any pain?"

"None."

"So there you go," Bree said. "Healing from a drop of water. Painless and complete."

"I don't believe it," Cara said, "even though I felt it happen. Do you need anything from me to follow up on this?"

"Not today. You're free to go, with the understanding that if you feel anything unusual, anything at all, you'll come straight back here. And we're asking that everyone come for a quick follow up in twenty-four hours."

Cara pulled out her tablet and made a note on the next day's schedule. Tom saw that Oz was still watching her as she shuffled her appointments around to make room for the med check.

"Same goes for you, Oz," Bree said cheerfully. "If you've got ten minutes to do those hand exercises for me, I can let you get back to the rest of your life. I'll just need you to drop by tomorrow for the follow up."

"Sure," Oz said. It was the first word he had spoken since Tom and Cara entered the room. His voice was low and gravelly, maybe because it didn't get used very much.

"It was good to see you again, Oz," Cara said. "And wow." She gestured at his hand. "I'm glad we got that water when we did."

He flexed it again. "Me too," he said.

Her father would have said something about the accident in the machine shop, but Cara wasn't that cold. The man had just lost his fingers and then had them miraculously reattached. He didn't need to discuss safety procedures right now. Her ability to understand that is what would make her a better leader than Cal had ever been.

Cara set her tablet down to give Bree a proper hug, pulling Tom in, too. It only lasted a second, but it felt good to have an arm around each sister, to share the wonder of what had just happened for just a moment.

Then Cara pulled away. "Ready?" she asked Tom.

He suddenly remembered his team. They would have finished their stretches and moved on to the fields where they had ag duty for the rest of the day.

"Congratulations on the fingers," he said to Oz.

Oz nodded his thanks.

They were already out the door when Oz said, "Cara!"

He held out her tablet. "Don't forget this," he said with a half-smile.

"Thank you," she said. "I'd be lost without it."

The half-smile turned to a whole, and Cara returned it.

Tom hid his smirk.

Cara said nothing as they passed through the lobby and out the front door, but Tom thought he wasn't the only one wondering if they should make a point to socialize with more mechanics.

# Chapter 5

# *Rain*

"This won't take long, right?" Cara hopped up on the exam table and began rolling up her pant legs.

"Tight schedule today?" Bree asked absently. She tucked her dark curls behind her ears as she turned to put on gloves.

"It wouldn't have been, but the rain is supposed to come any minute, and if I want a shower this month, I only have the next half-hour to enjoy it."

When their great-grandparents had discovered binary habitable planets circling a star very like the Earth's sun, their decision of where to land the first colony had been an easy one. Though both planets had livable climates and abundant flora, Una had fresh water and natural fauna, neither of which had been detected on Dua.

But even though Una's supply of fresh water was sufficient to sustain life, it wasn't as plentiful as Earth's. Mayland Settlement was strategically located along one of the only large rivers on the main continent, and even that dried up to a trickle between rains.

Water was rationed carefully. Most of it was used for consumption and for growing crops. Very little was allowed for cleaning and bathing. Instead, the colonists took chemical baths similar to what they had on the colony ship that brought them here.

Except when it rained.

Once every few weeks, as Dua waxed toward full, clouds would gather and pour down a gentle rain for several hours. Every time the meteorologist announced that rain was coming, the whole settlement went out to meet it. Chemical baths were very effective and had minimal impact on the environment, but there was nothing quite like getting soaked to the skin for feeling clean.

Cara had been running all morning to get ahead of her schedule. She fell behind yesterday after her injury, and this morning had spent an extra hour locked in her father's office in deep discussion about the healing water. After a string of other meetings, she still had to do her follow up at the med center before she could grab lunch and hopefully spare time for a rain shower.

She glanced over at the timepiece on the wall. Maybe she could skip the lunch. A little hunger never hurt anyone.

Her stomach growled in protest.

As if on cue, a nurse came in with a tray of food. She set it down next to Cara, gave a nod to Bree, and hurried out again. No doubt she was waiting for the rain like everyone else.

"I should have known I could count on you," Cara said to her sister, leaning over the tray and breathing in the scent of her favorite spicy bunta nut sauce.

"I knew adding this into your schedule would make things tight, and when I heard about the rain…."

"You're the best," Cara said.

"I know. You can eat while I look at your knees," Bree said.

"They feel totally fine." Cara scooped up a mouthful of sauce-covered grain with a piece of flatbread.

"Good. That makes you like everyone else," Bree said. "We're just checking for long-term effects."

"How many people have you tested this on now?"

"There have been 13 subjects, including myself and Jak," Bree said. "Each represented a different potential complication, but each signed off on the experiment, and none have had any negative side-effects. All of them were completely healed."

"And they all know they aren't to talk about it yet?"

Bree rolled her eyes. "Yes, Father. They all received very explicit instructions. Still, the announcement is going to be tomorrow, right?"

"That's the plan, but the details still need to be worked out. That's what the meeting tonight is for. You got the invitation?"

"Yes, we'll be there."

"So, formal report aside, you actually used the water on nine more people?"

Bree grinned. "It's so amazing, Cara. It's hard not to want to cure everything, but there really were good reasons for each one. A broken bone, healed in three minutes. Contagious rash, gone in seconds. One of the patients has been suffering from arthritis for years, and the water took away the joint pain instantly. Another had a persistent cough and vocal chord damage. I had her drink a few drops, and her lungs are completely clear now. We even used it on a couple of kids…with their parents' full consent of course…who had severe food allergies. After two swallows, they could eat anything they wanted. This stuff is a miracle."

"How does it work?"

"We're still studying that," Bree said. "Jak has a couple of different theories, which he'll share at the meeting, but the short answer is that we honestly don't know. We can't see anything about the water that explains what it can do."

"I hope we aren't moving too quickly on this," Cara said. "I know the effects are wonderful, but using something we don't understand is a huge risk."

"Wonderful?" Bree said. "You know the effects are 'wonderful'? Cara, this stuff is healing people, making them whole, removing pain, getting them back to work and back to their loved ones. There's no moving too quickly on something like this. You have to see that. This is a gift. I don't ever have to look at someone in pain and tell them there's nothing I can do. I don't ever have to stay up all night wondering how to break the news to someone that their disease can't be cured."

"I know. And that's wonderful," Cara said. "It really is! But if this planet contains a substance that does things we can't explain, there's a whole new set of questions to face. We're going to have to redefine a lot of things."

"Good! Let's redefine it all. Just because a thing has always been that way doesn't mean it has to be. Isn't the belief in a better way of living the whole reason we came to Una?"

The knot in Cara's stomach refused to untie. She wished she had the words to explain the fear she felt. It was more than a fear of the unknown, more than a desire to keep things controllable. There was a danger here that she couldn't articulate.

"It's starting!" One of the interns, Nan, burst out of the triage room with a towel over one shoulder.

Cara looked out the glass doors and saw the rain painting dark spots on the walkways.

"Aren't you coming?" Nan asked the sisters as she skipped toward the door. The rest of the med center staff was pouring into the room now, too, most of them carrying towels and a few with their shoes already off.

"Absolutely," Bree said. "You, too, little sis. Let's go wash away some stress. We can have more serious talk at the meeting tonight."

"Not waiting for Jak?"

"He'll be along at some point, but you know Jak. Time doesn't mean the same thing to him that it does to other people."

Cara smiled and let her sister pull her to her feet. There was a still a sweet purple hurta fruit left on her tray, so she tucked it into her pocket for later. She reached for her tablet.

"Leave it," Bree said. "I know it's water proof, but you need a break from it for a while. No one will touch it if you leave it on my desk."

It felt strange to just walk away and leave her portable brain behind, but Cara allowed her sister to place the tablet in a drawer and hand her a towel.

"Remember that one time it only rained for half an hour and we missed all but one minute?"

Cara did remember. She was five when that happened, and she'd cried that night that her hair didn't even get all the way wet. Her father had sat her down and lectured her on what things were and were not appropriate causes for tears. Then Tom had snuck her out back and showed her his drinking water from dinner. He had saved it just for her, and he dumped the whole thing over her head while she squealed and laughed.

Outside, the sky was orange. The clouds looked like burning embers. It was Anha, the warmest month, though on Una that wasn't saying much. The water that fell from the glowing clouds was cool, and the residents of Mayland would all be huddling around heating units to dry off and warm up after their soaking.

Cara took a deep breath, smelling the particular scent of rain as Bree opened the door and led the way out.

"Hurry up, slowpoke," Bree called.

She stepped out into the rain, then wavered for a second and disappeared.

"Bree?" Cara said, her brain struggling to register what her eyes had seen.

She dropped her towel and darted forward, feeling the gentle pattering on her skin. It was cool and refreshing and then in an instant, it was bitterly, freezing cold.

The world went black.

Cara reeled.

Her eyes were closed.

No, they were open.

Why was it so dark?

Why was it so cold?

Where was everyone?

Where was...?

Her stomach churned.

She closed her eyes.

When she opened them again, she was standing in a field of tall grass dotted with white flowers.

Cara vomited.

Her stomach was completely empty before she finished retching. She tried to take a deep breath, but even though her lungs filled with air, she still felt like she was drowning. Gasping for more oxygen, she straightened up and tried to take in her surroundings.

The field was wide. Dark hills rose in the distance.

She wasn't alone. Though the grass was as tall as her shoulders, she could see other heads rising above it, but they were too far away for her to make out faces. Someone yelled something indistinct.

There was a strange wheezing noise down near her feet.

Cara turned toward it and saw a shape huddled on the ground.

"Bree!"

Cara dropped to her knees by her sister and pulled Bree's head onto her lap. Bree's eyes were closed, and she was gasping in small, shallow breaths.

"Bree? Can you hear me? It's Cara."

"Cara?!" Someone shouted her name from just behind her.

"I'm here!" she called.

Jak stumbled through the tall grass, panting.

"Where are we? What...?"

He saw Bree, and his questions cut off with a cry. He threw himself down next to her and took her hand.

"What happened?"

"I don't know." Cara tried to take a breath to steady herself, but there wasn't enough air. "We went outside and then...we were just...here. And she was there...."

It was hard to focus. The shouting in the distance was getting louder.

"It's her asthma," Jak was saying. "She's not getting enough oxygen. There's something wrong with the air."

A piercing scream interrupted his words. Cara lurched to her feet.

The figures which had been distant were now all racing toward her. Several of the faces looked familiar. Her addled brain couldn't put names to them, but these were her people, and their faces were etched with terror.

Two seconds later she saw what was chasing them.

# Chapter 6

# Loss

They were holding hands when they ran into the rain, so Tom felt the exact moment Lin was taken away.

His palm tingled. The pressure of her fingers disappeared.

He was standing alone.

"Tom? What…?"

His team poured out of the greenhouse, surrounding him with questions and confusion.

"She just…."

"What happened?"

Tom rubbed his right hand, panic competing with shock as the rain soaked his hair and ran down his face.

Someone yelled, "Hy!"

Tom whirled around.

"He was right there!" Sal gibbered. Her eyes were wide and full of confusion. "He was there, and then...he wasn't."

"I saw it, too," someone shouted.

"What's going on?" Pel demanded. "How do people vanish like that?"

"Settle down, everyone," said Grish. He was twice Tom's age, and he didn't speak up often. When he did, the team usually listened. "Whatever's happening, we won't figure it out by panicking."

His calm steadied Tom just enough.

*You're a Mayland,* Cara had told him before his last expedition. *That means something, even if you don't want it to.*

"Do a head count," he said to Pel. "Let's make sure everyone else is here."

She nodded, immediately beginning to run through their usual check-in procedure.

"Do you hear that?" Sal asked.

The sound of shouting came from the center of the settlement.

"Something's going on," Tom said.

Grish nodded.

"Everyone is here," Pel said. "Except Hy and Lin."

Tom refused to flinch at her name. "I know you're scared. It's going to be okay. Get everyone inside, and stay together. Get dry, and get on your tablets, so I can reach you when I need you. Grish and I will go see what else has happened."

Pel swallowed hard. "What if..."

But Tom couldn't do what-ifs right now. "Contact your families. Make sure everyone is okay. But please don't leave the greenhouses. I need to know where you all are."

"We'll be here," she said.

As soon as she turned away, Tom started running. He was vaguely aware of Grish running next to him, of the rain still streaming down his face.

*Where are you, Lin? What happened?*

From nowhere, a sudden surge of panic and confusion overcame him. His feet tangled, and he almost fell.

That was Cara.

Something was terribly wrong.

Cara's terror pounded at him as he sprinted the last dozen meters, rounding the corner of the med center and sliding on a patch of mud before crashing into a knot of people gathered by the front doors.

"Tom!" Nel was a nurse who had worked with his mother for years. She reached out both hands to steady him. "You heard? I'm so sorry. Your sister…."

"What happened to Cara? Did she disappear, too?"

"Cara? No…Bree."

"Yes!" Someone spoke up from the other side of the group. "I saw Cara vanish, too! They were together."

Nel recoiled from the look on Tom's face.

"Your father just went inside. You should go see him."

As Tom turned away, she put a hand on his arm. "It's going to be okay. He'll figure it out."

Lin. Cara. Bree. Hy. Tom had no intention of waiting for someone else to figure this out.

The doors to the med center slammed open, and a young apprentice ran toward them.

"The governor wants everyone to go inside. Go home or to your work. Get dry. Use tablets to check in with the governor's office, so we can get an accurate count."

The group immediately began to disperse. The apprentice darted off to spread the news.

Tom hurried inside, Grish at his heels.

"Tom! Thank the stars!" His mother threw herself on him, clutching him close as the dripping water pooled around their feet.

He let her hold him for a moment before pulling away. "I'm glad you're okay," he said. "Cara...Bree...."

"Everyone saw them disappear. They were there, and then just...gone." Her voice was choked with tears. "Jak, too. His apprentice witnessed it."

"And Lin."

"Oh, Tom."

His voice cracked. "She was right next to me."

"The count is up to ten, including two children," Cal said.

Tom looked over his mother's shoulder to where the governor was typing furiously.

"Make that eleven. Twelve."

"Who?"

"We're keeping a list, but right now we just need a final count to know what we're dealing with."

"These aren't numbers. They're people! It's our family!"

Jul squeezed Tom's shoulder, but he ignored the unspoken message.

"I'm aware of who they are, Son. Right now, it's not the individuals that matter. We need to know the loss to the colony."

Tom's explosion was fueled by all his own fear and the chaos of emotion he felt from Cara. "It DOES matter who they are! Who they are is the key to understanding what just happened! It's the key to finding them!"

Cal lowered his tablet and looked at his son with a patience that made Tom want to scream.

"Son, we have to assume that they're dead."

Jul flinched, her grip on Tom's shoulder becoming a claw.

"They're not dead," Tom said. "Mom, they're not dead."

"They're gone. It's the most likely possibility."

"They're alive. I know it."

"Wishful...."

"It's not wishful thinking." Cara's adrenalin was pulsing through him as he said it. "I can feel it. I can feel Cara. She's alive, and she's in trouble."

"Son..." The governor's tablet dinged, and when he looked at it, his shoulders slumped. "The final count is in. Fifteen. It's only fifteen. We can survive that."

Maybe the colony could. Maybe Cal could, too. But Tom couldn't.

He left the med center to find his team. They had work to do.

# Chapter 7

# Fight

Cara froze. This animal wasn't in any of the zoology texts.

It was four-legged and powerfully built like a panther, but its skin was scaled like a snake. Even from a distance, she could see that it was as big as a man.

The creature opened its mouth and screamed.

The woman nearest to Cara stumbled and fell. Cara leapt to help, sprinting toward the fallen woman as she grasped for some way to fight. She had no weapons and saw nothing but grass.

Skidding to a stop, she pulled the woman to her feet. Several of the others were almost to them. A teenage girl cried as she ran.

"Go!" Cara shouted. "That way!"

The woman ran, and the girl flew past Cara without a word. Behind her, a man with a beard pulled two children with him.

"It's coming!" he yelled without slowing.

Cara wanted to bolt. She saw the beast bound above the grass again, and this time a second one leapt up in the distance, and then a third. A pack.

Cara's heart pounded, and black spots danced in front of her eyes, but she forced herself to stay still and think.

Bree was unconscious, and those children were small. They couldn't outrun these animals.

They had to fight, or they were all going to die.

Someone burst out of the grass to her left, and before Cara could react, he grabbed her arm and pulled her back the way he had come.

"This way," he said without slowing down. His voice sounded familiar.

"The others…." She started.

"Not far."

He was right. In seconds he yanked Cara to a stop just before she stumbled over a pile of white stones.

"Find the biggest ones. As weapons."

Running had made the black spots grow. Cara blinked hard until the man's face swam into view. The mechanic from the med center. The one with the reattached fingers. Oz.

He was already picking through the pile.

"Here." He shoved something into her hands.

Numbly, Cara realized it was a long bone. She looked at the ground again. The white rocks weren't rocks. She filed this information away to be analyzed later and reached for a curved jawbone she saw lying nearby. It must have come from a good-sized animal because it was as long as her forearm. Some teeth were still attached.

"Let's go," Oz said, and urgency slammed back into Cara's reality.

She snatched one more jagged piece and ran after him, back toward her sister, back toward the monsters.

Every step she took was an effort. Lack of oxygen turned her vision black, but a scream echoed across the meadow. Cara pushed herself to go faster.

A sudden shadow appeared, and Cara was knocked to the ground. A heavy weight landed on her chest. Dimly, she saw long pointed teeth, and then the weight disappeared.

She tried to sit up. The grunting and growling around her was horrible, but her body wouldn't respond to her commands.

*One thing at a time*, her father's voice said in her head. *Do the first thing first.*

*Bend your arm. Now put it under you. Good. Now push against the ground. Bring in your other arm. There it is. Now your knees. Good. Now breathe.*

There was a horrible crunch right by her head and a howl.

*There's nothing you can do about that unless you breathe.* Cara breathed.

Something smacked the side of her face. She heard Oz yell.

*Push up with your legs.* Cara stood, swaying and dizzy.

The growling turned to an ugly gurgling noise.

*Keep breathing. Now, open your eyes.* Cara opened her eyes.

Oz was on the ground on his back, his arms around a monster's neck. There was green blood everywhere. With a grunt, Oz let go of the creature, and it fell to the side, dead.

Oz gasped air like a fish, and Cara wished she could breathe for him. *Don't waste time on the impossible. Do what you can do.* She reached down and pulled Oz to his feet.

Another scream rose up from the tall grass not far away. Oz gave Cara a small nod and began to stagger in that direction, still sucking in deep, rattling breaths. Cara forced herself to follow.

A few meters away they stumbled into a battle.

A knot of bodies huddled in the center of a ring of trampled grass. Two older women sheltered the others with their arms, while three huge beasts were being held off by a handful of people. Cara saw the flash of Lin's red hair as she darted around, swiping at one beast with a small pocket knife. A powerfully built man was wrestling barehanded with another, while Jak and another man pelted the third with small stones.

Cara yelled and sprinted toward Lin, raising the jagged jawbone in one hand. She had no plan, but Lin was already dripping blood from one shoulder, and the beast was fixated on its victim. Cara slammed into it from the side and brought the pointed teeth down on its head.

The creature screamed and twisted toward her, swiping with its claws. Cara heard her shirt rip but she felt no pain. The beast screamed again and jerked away. Lin was on the other side, lifting the knife dripping green blood. Cara swung both arms now, one with the long thin bone and the other with the jaw, pummeling the creature with a fury that had no precision.

It fell backward, still lashing out with its claws. One of them caught Cara's hand, and the sting made her drop her weapon. Then Lin threw herself onto the beast and swiped with the knife one more time.

The animal went limp. Lin fell onto her hands and knees next to it, retching and heaving.

Cara stood frozen for a moment, watching her friend struggle for breath, like it was on a video recording. Where were they? What was going on?

# TWIN

*There's a time for reflection and a time for action. A good leader knows the difference.*

Cara jerked into motion, stumbling toward Lin even while she looked around at the rest of the clearing. The men had taken down the other two beasts, and for a moment everyone was still. There was sobbing coming from the group in the middle, and moans of pain.

"Where are we?" someone asked.

"My watch is dead," someone else said.

"Does anyone have a comm device?"

No one answered.

Cara put a hand on Lin's back.

"I'm okay," Lin panted. "Hy...." She cut off with a choking noise and began to retch again.

"Don't talk. Just breathe," Cara rasped.

She tried to follow her own advice, taking deep breaths, hoping they would clear her brain. *In crisis, first take stock. You need a clear picture of both needs and resources.*

Cara pushed aside all the bigger questions that crowded her mind and forced herself to count.

Four men who had been fighting the beasts. Oz and Jak. The big man, who Cara now saw was barely more than a boy, maybe a year or two younger than her. She knew him from the files. His name would come to her later. The man she had seen before running with the children. She remembered him now. Jem. Agricultural engineer and father of two. Were those his children?

*Not important.* Cara squelched the question and continued her count.

Two older ladies. One with her back to Cara now, arms around a little girl, had white hair. The other was maybe fifty, hair still dark and straight. Cara didn't need to search for her name. Wyn Lee. When Cara was four, the woman had been the victim of attempted murder, the only case in Mayland's history and a big part of Cara's legal instruction.

The group the women were guarding consisted of five children and Bree, who was still unconscious. The little boy and girl looked about eight. Three teenaged girls sat next to them. Cara remembered the older two from the nursery, and when the younger teen lifted her head, she recognized Syl, one of the apprentice doctors.

Syl's eyes were red, but she looked at Cara steadily. Syl had only been an apprentice for a year, but she would still have some useful medical knowledge.

Cara made a note of that for later.

Lin. Herself. That was it.

Fourteen. Five were children. Two were old. One was unconscious. That left six who could fight, and at least four of them were bleeding from the attack.

*Deal with one problem at a time. Start with the most urgent.*

"Syl," Cara said, standing. "We need to take care of injuries. What can we use for bandages?"

Syl looked around as if hoping to see a med kit lying somewhere nearby.

"I have this," the white-haired woman said, shrugging out of a light jacket. Now that Cara saw her face, she recognized Ann, a former teacher and now master painter. Tom had one of her paintings on his bedroom wall. "Pol, dear, let us have your extra shirt, too."

The pale teenager sat numbly, while Ann tugged the light button-up off her shoulders and began to rip both garments into strips.

"Lin, we need to wrap your shoulder," Cara said. "Who else is bleeding?"

"Jak is the worst," Oz said, pointing at Cara's brother-in-law.

Jak's leg was ripped open from the ankle to the knee.

"It's not as bad as it looks," Jak said, though his pale face and shallow breaths contradicted him.

"Ann, you and Syl get him bandaged up. I'll see to Lin. Oz, can you help the other two?"

The big youth was holding one hand dripping with red blood and Jem, the ag engineer, had a gash on his forehead. Oz nodded and stepped toward them, but the kid pushed him away with his good hand.

"We don't have time," he said. "There are more of them out there hunting. We need to get somewhere safe before they come back."

Cara studied his face for a moment until she placed it. Zyk. Aged 18. Apprentice engineer.

"We don't know where we are, Zyk. We don't know if there is a safe place. If there are more, we need our strongest people able to fight them, and that means you. I need you bandaged up and ready to help defend us."

She saw the words take effect, heard her father's voice in her head again. *Some people like being important to the group. You can use that.*

"What weapons do we have?" Cara asked the others as she tore strips off the bottom of her own shirt to wrap Lin's shoulder. "Lin, you have a knife."

"Not much of one," Lin said through gritted teeth.

"We have the bones." Cara gestured at the pile. "How many stones?"

Jem spoke up for the first time. "Only a handful, and they're small. They didn't even slow that thing down. If Oz hadn't gotten here when he did, we'd be dead."

Cara saw the younger kids flinch. "With the bones as clubs, though, and Lin's knife, we took down four of them."

"The boy killed that one with his bare hands," Ann said.

"Which may not be repeatable," said Oz, attempting to tie up Zyk's mangled left hand.

A scream echoed across the field, and one of the kids began to whimper.

"We need fire," Jem said. "Animals fear fire."

"Torches?" Cara said.

"There's plenty of grass. Tied to the ends of the bones, that might work," Oz answered. "If we had a spark."

"We don't have much time," Ann said. A second scream, this time from a different direction, confirmed her.

"No fire," Jak wheezed.

"I'm sure we can find a way to make a spark," Cara said.

"Those rocks and the knife might be enough," Oz agreed.

"No fire," Jak repeated. He sucked in a breath. "Fire needs oxygen." He waved a hand. "So do we. Hard enough. To breathe. As is."

He was right. The air was thin. If they started a fire, it would make things worse.

A third roar sounded. Then a fourth, and a fifth. They were surrounded.

Cara looked at the pile of bones, the one small knife, the already wounded and terrified band of people. They weren't going to survive another attack like the last one.

"There's no choice. Fire is risky, but without it, we're dead anyway. Oz, how do we make torches?"

While the mechanic showed everyone how to knot the tall grass around the ends of the longer bones, Cara pulled Jak aside.

"This will buy us some time, but we need to get away from here," Cara said. "Anywhere is better than here." She thought of the piles of bones and suppressed a shudder. "How dangerous will it be to move Bree?"

"She can barely breathe," Jak said. "If you're going to start a fire, moving her is the least of her problems. I'd carry her out of here myself if my leg would hold up."

Cara ignored his anger. "We still have uninjured people to carry her. Have Ann and Wyn take charge of her, along with the two teenagers. I'll put Syl with the children. The rest of us will have our hands full."

"They're coming!" someone yelled.

"Get them lit!"

"Cara!" Oz said. "We need a circle."

Cara pushed to her feet and grabbed the makeshift torch he was holding out to her. Lin struck a spark and lit the end of the torch in Oz's other hand. The others turned to light more from the first.

A beast leapt out of the grass and hurtled toward Cara.

Instinctively, she ducked. She felt the heat of Oz's torch swing above her head and heard the awful shriek the beast made when the fire hit its face.

A hand grabbed Cara's arm and yanked her to her feet. Her torch was pulled to the side, and the next thing she knew it was on fire. Someone gave her a shove, and Cara saw Lin's bright head darting away.

Another beast appeared. Then another. They were coming from every direction.

Cara rushed forward, swinging her torch into the nearest monster. Its scales blackened instantly, though they didn't catch fire. It swerved away, revealing a second creature waiting behind. This one crouched, unmoving.

For one frozen second, Cara saw the light of her flame reflected in its dark eyes. Then the creature screamed, a horrible noise that was echoed by the others around the circle. The animals turned as one and disappeared into the darkness.

# Chapter 8

# *Hunt*

"What's the plan?" Grish asked. "A search?"

He didn't mention the governor. The third child from every family had been trained as an explorer and pioneer. Thirds didn't rely on their leaders to figure things out for them.

"Right away. Our team alone if necessary, but once they send out the full list of the disappeared, we should be able to recruit the families to help."

"Any idea where we start?"

"We start where we are. Fan out in groups of two. First inside the fence and then out. We'll go as far as we can before dark, then take a rest and go further tomorrow. Until we find them."

"You think they were transported?"

"It's the only explanation."

"Why them?"

That was what Tom wanted to know. Why everyone he loved and cared about but not him?

He could still feel the tingling in his right hand where Lin's had been. Cara's panic ran laps around his mind. The pull to be with them was unbearable.

Instead of obsessing, he forced himself to organize the search parties in his mind. Wishing wouldn't find them. Action would.

Back at the greenhouse, the team was waiting. Most already had jackets on and tablets covered for outside use.

"The governor just sent out the final list," Pel said. "I'm so sorry."

The rest of the team murmured agreement. The weight of their sympathy was more than Tom could bear.

"What matters is bringing them back," he said.

Only Pel spoke up. "The governor implied…."

"They're not dead," Tom said. "You're just going to have to trust me on that. They're somewhere dangerous, though, and they need help. We need to find them."

For a second, he thought they wouldn't believe him. Then Rik said, "Groups of two, then?"

Relief made Tom tremble. "Yes. We each get a vector, with this greenhouse as ground zero. Inside the fence or outside, we stick to our routes."

He handed out the assignments, and the team filed out with no further discussion. They already had protocols in place for search parties, something the governor had insisted on for travel outside the fence. Since the infrastructure of the colony was designed to be simple and localized, communication devices had a very limited range. In the field, training took the place of technology.

"Tom," Sal said, putting a hand on his arm. At forty, she was the one of the older Thirds who still qualified for exploration. "Bel needs to go home."

The girl standing next to Sal was their youngest team member, just turned 17. He often paired the two of them for balance.

"No!" Bel said. "I want to help find them."

"Her brother is on the list," Sal said. "Her family needs her."

"I checked in with them. They know I'm okay. Please let me stay and search." Bel's face reflected Tom's desperation.

"It's your decision," he said. "You're free to go, but if you want to search, you search."

"Tom," said Sal. "Her parents asked her to come home."

"It's her decision."

"I'm staying."

Before Sal could argue more, Tom pulled a coat over his wet clothes. "It's decided then. I'll see you both at check-in tonight." He left them, joining Grish in the mist that had followed the rain.

Grish had their vector set into his watch's compass, so he led the way south to the river, just a few meters outside the greenhouse walls. Even with today's rain the Vita River was shallow, and they waded across in minutes. Soon they were pushing through the tall grass of the plain that surrounded Mayland Settlement.

Cara's fear was mixed with pain now, and it beat at Tom, urging him forward, even as his own doubts began to creep in. What was he doing? How was this going to help find them? If they were anywhere near, wouldn't there be some kind of clue?

His tablet chimed, and Tom scrambled to check it, doubling over to protect the screen from the mist.

It wasn't a team member reporting a discovery. It was the governor. Ordering him home.

Tom slid the tablet back into its guard sleeve. At Grish's questioning look, he shook his head.

They continued on. Tom's tablet chimed again, but this time he ignored it.

Then Grish's watch beeped an incoming message.

The older man stopped. "He says it's an order."

"It's the wrong order."

"I know how you feel. But he has a lot more experience."

"You mean from the last time fifteen of our colonists disappeared without a trace?"

Grish just raised one brow and waited.

"Go back if you want. I'm going to keep looking."

"The order went out to everyone. No one is going to disobey the governor."

Tom heard what he didn't say. Without the whole team conducting an organized search, it was hopeless. There was nothing Tom could do on his own.

"Damn him to the stars! What good are we going to be sitting around at home?"

"The message says they are investigating the site of each disappearance. We're all first-hand witnesses."

Tom's palm tingled again. He looked south, where the empty countryside mocked him.

*Where are you, Cara?*

He felt nothing from her but the knot of terror. He turned and followed Grish back the way they had come.

# Chapter 9

# *Flight*

The silence left by the fading of the creature's screams was broken by ragged breathing.

Cara blinked away dark spots again and turned to see Jak holding Bree with a look of despair. Her heart stopped.

"Bree?" Cara hurried over and knelt down, reaching for her sister's hand.

"Get that thing out of here!" Jak snapped, pushing away the torch.

Cara reeled backward and looked up at the sky. It was getting dark, the sun fading behind a smudge on the horizon that looked like trees. *Where are we?*

"That's not going to hold them off forever," Zyk broke into her thoughts. "This burning grass only has a few more minutes." He stood over her, holding a torch in his bandaged hand and the jaw bone in the other. Cara thought of the illustrations of early cave people in her Earth history books.

"They'd never seen fire before," said Lin.

"They probably aren't used to prey fighting back at all," Jem said. "But Zyk is right. A pack that size needs food. Their fear won't keep them away for long."

"We need to move," Cara said, but it came out as a whisper.

"You need to put out those fires," Jak said. "We need air."

"We need to be able to defend ourselves," Zyk snarled.

"We need a plan, Cara," Lin said.

*Positive action keeps panic at bay.* Cara pushed to her feet. "We're going to move," she said louder. "Find someplace easier to defend before our torches are gone."

"How are we going to find someplace safer? We don't know where we are," Pol said.

Ann put an arm around the girl's shoulders, but she didn't have an answer. No one did.

*In times of crisis, being decisive is more important than being correct.* "We'll go that way," Cara said, pointing toward the distant trees. "Trees can be shelter. And more oxygen," she added pointedly for Jak.

He nodded blankly, then cringed as screeching broke out again in the distance.

"Lin, you and Zyk lead the way with torches. Jem, give yours to Syl so you can help Pol and Lil carry Bree. Ann, Wyn, escort the children. Jak, you'll need a torch, too. No arguing. Walk alongside those that don't have any. Oz and I will bring up the rear."

Everyone jumped into action, following her instructions. As soon as Jem and the girls had lifted Bree, Lin led the way through the grass toward the setting sun. She didn't run, but she set a fast pace. The screams began again, and they weren't far away.

They had only gone a few hundred meters when Cara glanced back and saw one of the creatures leap above the grass.

"There!" Lin shouted.

"Keep going!" Cara yelled, whirling around with her torch.

Oz stood his ground beside her as three of the monsters burst through the grass at the same time.

Cara didn't have time to see if the others had listened to her command. She ducked a swiping claw and thrust her torch straight into the face of the nearest monster. It screamed as its eyes took the full force of the blow.

Before she could pull back, a second monster crashed into her side, knocking her to the ground and sending her torch flying. Cara felt teeth close around her shoulder, but she struck as hard as she could with the rock clenched in her fist. She pulled her legs up under the creature and pushed it away with both feet. Oz immediately rushed at it with his torch.

Cara could see blood running down her arm, but for the moment there was no pain. She looked around for her torch, praying it hadn't gone out.

It hadn't.

It was half-buried in a clump of dead grass, and the fire was already starting to spread.

"Oz!" Cara yelled.

He was still grappling with one of the monsters, its side blackened from his torch, a splotch of green blood running from its leg.

"Oz, we have to go!"

Cara tried to grab the end of her torch, but the fire had already spread through the grass, and she would have had to reach into it to get to the long bone.

"OZ!"

He whirled around, and the creature he'd been fighting darted away. A quick widening of his eyes was his only reaction as he took in the rapidly spreading fire.

"Run!" Cara said.

It only took two minutes to catch up to the others as they stumbled along.

"Fire," Cara gasped. "The grass."

"Just…faster," Oz managed.

They tried. The entire group surged forward, but no one was getting enough air. They soon slowed again.

Cara glanced back and saw a bright glow. The whole field was going to go up in flames. Still, making her legs move forward took all her strength. There was nothing more she could do. At least for the moment, the screaming of the creatures had stopped.

Cara's vision wavered. She stumbled on.

Just as the sun disappeared completely behind the horizon, they burst out of the tall grass and onto uneven ground.

Oz stumbled and would have fallen, but Cara caught his arm. They were standing on rocky ground, and more flat rock stretched before them, swelling slightly up out of the grassland toward the line of trees in the distance.

It was a relief to be free of the tall grass, but the open terrain felt terribly exposed. They needed the shelter of the trees, and fast.

"Can't stop," Cara gasped, since everyone had done just that. "Trees."

She saw Lin nod and Jem hoisted Bree a little higher, but otherwise no one moved. They were all panting. Several of them were blinking dazedly. Zyk had dropped to his knees.

They were almost to their limit. Fear wasn't going to be enough to drive them. They needed hope.

"Trees…will have…shelter…oxygen," Cara said. "We can…rest there."

Oz staggered forward to where Zyk was kneeling. He reached down and pulled the larger man to his feet. "Lead," he said.

Zyk shook his head. One of the children whimpered.

"Oh," said Lin. She sounded angry, but she started walking. She was two meters away when Jem and the girls followed with Bree. Jak and Syl fell in automatically, Ann and Wyn and the children at their heels. Oz followed, leaving Cara alone with Zyk. She pried his torch from his hand and extinguished it on the rocky ground.

"Just a little more," Cara said. "You still have…a little more. Right?"

Zyk shook his head again, but he didn't resist when Cara took his good arm and pulled him forward.

It took over an hour of stumbling across the rocks to reach the shelter of the trees. Twice, Cara heard the cries of the beasts in the burning field behind them, but it was impossible to move any faster. Everyone was already spent.

The second they stepped off of hard stone and onto the springy undergrowth, they stopped.

Jem and the girls lowered Bree to the ground. The others collapsed on their own. Ragged breathing was the only sound.

Afraid that if she sat she would never get up, Cara leaned against a tree trunk and sucked in air. Each breath felt lacking, like drinking water when what you needed was food.

Slowly, though, the fog in her head began to clear. Her eyesight returned a little, too, and she could see her people's faces where they lay nearby.

Everyone looked numb. There was no sense of accomplishment or relief. Cara tried to summon words of encouragement, but none came.

Now that she had stopped moving, all the questions she had pushed away came crowding in. What had happened? Where were they? How had they gotten here?

And most important of all: how were they going to get home?

The thought of home threatened to overwhelm Cara's exhausted brain. Her mother. Her father. Tom.

*Cara?*

Thoughts of her brother brought his voice to mind.

*Cara, where are you?*

"Tom," she whispered.

*Cara. You're alive.*

Cara close her eyes. She'd been deprived of oxygen for a long time. Now she was hallucinating, giving in to her need for connection to home.

*Cara. I'm here. Where are you?*

*Tom.*

*Cara. We've been so worried. Where are you?*

*I don't know. Somewhere the air isn't right. Somewhere with monsters.*

*You're still alive. That's all that matters. Just stay that way. I'm going to find you.*

Of course he'd be looking. The whole colony would be looking.

*You're not alone now.*

*I know, Tom. I'm not alone. And somehow, I have to take care of them all.*

The Tom in her head didn't answer. That was okay. Even if he had been more than a voice she dreamed up, it wouldn't change anything.

Taking care of people was a job he'd always left to her.

# Chapter 10

# Investigation

The governor didn't waste time reprimanding his son. He had other ways to show his disapproval.

First, he interviewed each of Tom's teammates personally but assigned an admin to take Tom's statement.

The girl was fifteen and clearly terrified. When Tom described the sensation of Lin's fingers vanishing from between his own, her hands shook, and a tear splashed onto the screen where she was typing.

"They're still alive," he told her. "We'll find them."

She nodded wordlessly, but he knew she didn't believe him.

Outside the greenhouse, Tom pointed a group of scientists to the exact spot where Lin had been standing. They tested the area with a score of small instruments. Someone even swabbed Tom's palm.

When his father emerged from his last interview, Tom confronted him. "Have they found anything yet?"

Cal swept past without answering. Immediately three scientists converged on him, showing him readouts and gesturing toward the sky. Tom tried to edge closer to hear what they were saying, but Cal gave a few curt answers and strode away.

"They don't know anything yet," said a voice behind him.

Tom turned and saw his mother standing next to the path. Her eyes were red, but her dark hair was still in its immaculate pony tail, and her face was composed. She looked so much like Cara it hurt.

"None of the sites have had helpful data. Even the tests of the rainwater are coming back normal." Her voice was heavy with bitterness. "If it weren't for the list, we wouldn't know anything."

"The list?"

"Of those who disappeared. Didn't you look at it?"

"Of course I did. I recognized every name on it."

"And you didn't notice what they all had in common?"

Tom mentally ran through the names again in his mind. Young, old, men, women, from all jobs and all living situations.

"The water," Jul said. "Everyone who was healed by the water is on that list."

Tom's head began to throb in time with his heart.

"It's the only common factor."

"But… Not Lin," he said. "She was never healed. Or Hy."

"They were at the lake. They collected the sample. Can you guarantee they never touched it?"

"Yes. No. Well, Hy. He was always…but Lin was so careful."

Jul's dark eyes were full of resignation.

Tom's stomach roiled. The water. He had asked Lin to collect it. He had brought it here and given it to the doctors.

This was his fault.

"How…?"

"We don't know yet. We may never know. Somehow that water changed their chemical makeup, though, and it interacted with the rain. And...." Her voice cracked.

"They aren't dead, Mom."

She looked up at him.

"Occam's razor," said a middle-aged man in a lab coat. Tom should have known his name, but his brain was too overloaded to access it. "The simplest explanation is usually the correct one."

"The simplest explanation is death?"

"They vanished," the man said, gesturing around. "Not became invisible, but actually ceased to be in this place. In scientific terms, that means that the matter that made up their bodies disintegrated completely. Now, we could posit that the matter was reassembled in the same form in a different place, but that is a much more complex assumption. The most likely explanation is that the disintegration was final."

Jul stifled a sob, and Tom considered methods of disintegrating the man in front of him.

It must have showed on his face because the scientist took a step back. "Of course, I hope that isn't true," he stammered. "It's just...probability."

"Probability. Right. But unlikely isn't the same as impossible, so let me tell you this. If Lin and my sisters were dead, I would know it. Here." Tom tapped his heart. "And here." He tapped his temple. "But they are not dead. They are out there somewhere."

His mother put a hand on his shoulder and pulled him back a step or two. Tom realized he had closed the gap and was towering over the scientist. When he retreated, the man nodded thanks to Jul and hurried off to join the other scientists digging into the soft ground.

"They're not dead," Tom said again. "I can still feel Cara. I can feel her."

His mother closed her eyes. "I...I want to believe that." When she looked up, her eyes were clear and focused. "I haven't given up hope. I won't give up hope. But our feelings can lie to us, Tom. We can't count on them right now. Right now we have to do the work, and we have to rely on each other. If…if your sisters are alive, the data will eventually confirm it. For now, we have to let them do their jobs and we have to do ours."

"The governor just called me back from doing mine."

"No," she said. "You aren't just any explorer. You are the head of the exploration team that found this water. You saw the lake it came from and the animal that it healed. You were the last person to speak to Lin, and the only person touching one of the disappeared at the time they vanished. You need to make yourself available to the scientists as they work. They have a lot of questions."

Somehow his mother always knew how to point out when he was being childish without making him feel like a child.

"I'm sorry," he said. "Tell me where to go."

Jul took him to the medical building, where Cal had set up a crisis command center in an office near the labs. All afternoon, Tom met with doctors and scientists from every field. He answered questions. He sketched maps. He let them run tests on him.

He pretended that his father wasn't ignoring him.

It was dark outside when he saw his mother again. She had a tablet tucked under her arm and three packages of food in her hands.

"We're going home to eat," she announced.

Cal didn't look up from the screen he was studying. "That's good. Go ahead."

"We're going home to eat," she repeated. "All of us."

Tom took the food packs and avoided looking at Cal. To his surprise, the governor didn't argue with his wife. Instead, he stood and stretched a kink out of his neck.

"One hour?"

"One hour," she answered.

No one spoke as they made their way down the familiar paths to their family unit. The gashi that Jul had planted by the front door had no flowers at this time of year, but the rain had made them plump and green.

Tom stopped for a moment, staring at them. He didn't want to go inside. He didn't want to sit down at that table without Bree and Cara.

In his mind, he heard Cara's voice say his name.

*Cara.*

With all his heart he wished it were really her.

*Cara, where are you?*

*Tom.*

There was no mistaking it this time. Her voice in his head was clear, and it carried all the emotions that he already knew were hers. Relief flooded him.

*Cara. You're alive.*

He felt her mental confusion. She didn't think he was real. Which made him even more convinced that she was.

*Cara. I'm here. Where are you?*

*Tom.* She was in shock.

*Cara,* he said patiently. *We've been so worried. Where are you?*

*I don't know. Somewhere the air isn't right. Somewhere with monsters.*

A chill ran down his spine. *You're still alive. That's all that matters.* He tried to project a calm he didn't feel. *Just stay that way. I'm going to find you. You aren't alone now.*

*I know, Tom. I'm not alone. And somehow, I have to take care of them all.*

The word *all* unclenched something inside Tom. That meant the others were with her, right? Bree. Jak. Lin.

"Tom," his mother called. "Come and eat."

Tom strained after the presence of Cara in his mind, but it had slipped away. There was so much more he wanted to ask. So much he wanted to say.

For now, though, panic had turned to determination. She was alive. Which meant she could be found.

Tom went inside to tell his parents the good news.

# Chapter 11

## Regroup

Hallucinating had been remarkably helpful.

An imaginary Tom was better than no Tom at all. Even the memory of his voice made Cara stronger.

Slowly, she limped over to where Bree lay under a nearby tree.

Jak had his ear to his wife's chest and his eyes closed. Cara couldn't tell if he was listening or had passed out.

"How is she?" she whispered.

Jak's eyes opened. "Her breathing is a little better here." He gestured at the trees. "More oxygen. It's still not enough, though. Maybe if we...."

He trailed off as a scream echoed across the rocks. Several people sat up in alarm.

"We need to be ready for another attack," Cara said. The words grated against her raw throat.

Jak shook his head. "No more fire. Not here. These trees may be all that's keeping her alive."

Cara looked closer at the nearest tree, taking in its alien nature. It was the tallest growing thing she had ever seen, and several nearby trees were even taller. The trunk was slender, covered in knobby bark. The first branches, high out of reach, supported clusters of enormous leaves which curled in toward each other, forming bulbs twice the size of Cara's head. Its strangeness was mesmerizing. Staring up, it was hard to feel a sense of urgency and danger. It was hard to feel anything at all.

*You're in shock*, her father's voice said. *You need to keep moving, or it will paralyze you.*

Cara shook herself and tore her eyes away from the tree. She saw the others looking at her expectantly.

"We need to go further in." She gestured. "Find fallen branches. Other possible weapons. We can't risk fire here, but maybe out on the rocks. To keep them away. Zyk, Ann, help Jak move Bree and the children into the woods. Wyn, Jem, look for sticks and rocks that could be weapons. Oz, Lin, you can help me build some bonfires out there. It may be enough to ward them off."

Slowly the group came back to life, forcing exhausted limbs to move, creeping about their assigned tasks.

It wasn't hard to find fallen branches and twigs, and giant dead leaves carpeted the ground. Eventually Cara and the others had built three large pyres a dozen meters away from the tree line.

Cara's body dragged like a lead weight, but her head was clearer than it had been since arriving here. Jak was right about the trees providing more oxygen. She looked across the rocks at the fire in the distance, still lighting the night with its blaze.

"Maybe they can see that fire in Mayland," Jem said, coming up with two thick branches that would make excellent clubs. "Send someone to find us."

"Mayland is far way," Wyn said, dropping several large rocks by their feet. It was the first time she had spoken since they had arrived here. Something about her voice tugged at Cara's exhausted brain.

"How do you know? We have no idea where we are," Lin said.

"The stars," Wyn said, looking up at them. "They're all different."

A chill flooded Cara.

"How did we get here?" Jem whispered.

"Transported," Wyn said, "somehow."

Suddenly, Cara remembered. Wyn's vocal chords had been permanently damaged when her brother poisoned her all those years ago. She had barely been able to speak for fifteen years. Now she sounded perfectly normal.

A cry rang out.

"Did that seem closer?" Jem said.

"Light the fires," Cara answered. "Let's get back to the others. Bring the weapons with us."

"Someone needs to watch. Make sure the fire doesn't spread to the trees," Oz said. "I'll stay."

"I'll watch with you, but not out in the open," Cara said. Even if it weren't for the danger from the beasts, she didn't want to be under the gaze of those unfamiliar stars any longer. "We can watch from the trees."

Oz and Lin went to work lighting the fires while the others distributed weapons. When the flames were high, Cara felt more exposed than ever. She led the way back to the trees, and the relief she felt when they reached them was completely out of proportion to the safety they offered.

The others headed in to find the rest of the group. When they were gone, Cara leaned against a tree trunk, watching the flickering of the three fires.

"You should go with them," Oz said. "You need rest, too."

Cara shook her head. Officially or not, she was their leader. *A leader is the first to go hungry and the last to find rest. She never expects her people to do anything she isn't prepared to do first and longest.*

She couldn't see Oz's face clearly in the shadows, but she could feel his eyes watching her.

"You kept us together today," he said. "At least sit."

"You're the one who found the bones. And made the torches. You saved us."

There was a pause.

"I guess we'd both better sit then," he said.

Cara hesitated, afraid of the exhaustion that threatened to overwhelm her.

"I promise to help you up if you help me up," Oz said.

Yes. That could work.

Cara slid down the tree and sat at its roots. Oz did the same a few feet away.

For a long time, they watched the fires in silence. Cara even let her eyes close for a few moments, knowing Oz would keep his open.

She didn't know why she had so much trust in someone she had only really met two days ago. She thought back to their first interaction. The day her knees had been healed. The day his fingers had miraculously been regrown.

Her eyes flew open.

"The water," she said.

Oz straightened up, looking at her.

"You. Me. Bree. Jak. We all used the healing water. Maybe the others…. Maybe it has something to do with this."

Oz nodded. "The little twins. Hal and Em. They were there when I came for my checkup. Getting treated for allergies."

It made no difference. Knowing what they had in common, why it had been them sent here, didn't change anything. It didn't help them survive. It didn't help them get home. Still, Cara felt a little less lost than she had five minutes ago.

"The fires are lower now. They aren't spreading. We should go back to the others. Ask them."

Oz said nothing, but he held out a hand. Cara took it, and they pulled each other up.

For a moment they stood there, shoulder to shoulder, staring at the fire, listening to the night. There had been no more cries from the beasts in a while. Maybe they had given up, been scared away by the fire. Or maybe they were creeping silently across the rocks right now.

*Deal with facts, not possibilities*, her father's voice said.

"Let's go," said Cara.

About a kilometer in, they heard low voices and saw the knot of shadows that was their friends.

Zyk and Lin stood guard.

"No sign of the predators?" Lin asked.

"Nothing, and our fires are under control. How are the others?"

"Mostly asleep," said Lin. "There's been some crying. Bree's still struggling to breathe."

"Lin, did you ever touch any of that water from the lake?"

The question took Lin by surprise, and even in the darkness Cara could feel her tension.

"We have a theory…."

"My leg," Lin whispered. She took a deep breath. "I wore gloves to collect the sample, but some dripped onto my pants. Nothing happened, so I never mentioned it."

"The healing water?" Zyk said.

"Did you go to the clinic in the last few days?" Cara asked him.

"Yes," he said. "They used it on my eye."

"Oh stars," Lin said. She swayed, and Cara put a hand out to steady her. "Hy. He…he touched the yesela's tracks when they were still wet."

Her arm trembled.

"He…he came here, too. And the yesela. When I first arrived, I saw…I saw the animal, and then Hy looked over at me. He was in shock. And then the beast came out of nowhere. It ripped Hy open…I couldn't even…then I ran."

"Come here. Sit down," Cara said, easing Lin to the ground and putting an arm around her. She felt sick, but it was nothing to what Lin felt. Hy had been a part of her team. They'd been training together for years.

"So everyone who touched that water got sent here?" Zyk said. "They experimented on us without knowing what they were doing? And now we're…stars know where!"

"Quiet," Oz said. "Don't wake the others."

"A little sleep isn't going to help them when we get ripped apart by beasts! Or when we starve to death. Have you seen any water here? Have you noticed that it's hard to breathe?"

Lin pulled away from Cara and began to retch again.

Cara stood, stepping toward Zyk and looking up into his face. "Sleep is going to help them be ready to fight off those beasts. It's going to give them strength to find water and food until we can get home. You know what I've seen here? I've seen you fight off a monster with only your own hands. I've seen children making bandages out of their clothes. I've seen us survive."

Zyk closed his mouth.

More gently, Cara said, "You've done a lot today. You're wounded and tired. Now that Oz and I are here, you should sleep for a while."

"I don't need...."

Oz put a hand on Zyk's arm, and the younger man stopped. Cara turned back to Lin. Oz could take it from there.

Lin was wiping her mouth on a corner of her shirt. "Sorry," she said.

"Don't be."

"Wish I had some water."

"We're all going to wish that soon."

It wasn't a cheerful thought.

"We should have been more careful," Lin said.

"'The past is done. We live now,'" Cara quoted dully.

"Your father?"

Cara nodded.

"He always manages to be right, doesn't he?"

"You should get some sleep," Cara said.

Lin didn't argue, but she didn't move either.

"Tom," she said finally. "He'll be frantic."

Cara remembered her imaginary conversation. "I'm sure he's looking for us right now."

It was like the words opened a floodgate inside of Cara. All of the fear and adrenaline and shock of her own situation had taken center stage, but now a new rush of emotion flooded in. Desperation. Determination. Worry. Anger.

Tom.

A hand on her shoulder made Cara jump. She pushed Tom's emotions down and turned to find Jak crouched next to her.

"Bree needs air," he said. "I want to get some of those leaves." He gestured up at the bulbs hanging high over their heads.

"For what?"

"To see what they're protecting. Why they grow like that."

"We can't...."

"I think I can climb up," he said.

Cara eyed the tall, slim tree trunks doubtfully.

"I want to try."

She pushed to her feet. "I'll do it."

"You don't..."

Cara pointed at his injured leg. "You'd never make it."

"I'll go," Lin said. "Your shoulder needs bandaging, and climbing was part of our team training."

Before Cara could mention Lin's own injured shoulder, Lin was under the nearest tree, wrapping the ends of her long sleeves around her palms.

Cara thought of a thousand warnings, but none of them would be helpful. Being careful wasn't really an option at this point.

Lin began to shimmy up the trunk, using her feet to grip in a way that showed she knew what she was doing. Oz came up next to Cara, raising his eyebrows in question.

Too tired to explain, Cara shrugged.

It took ten long, painful minutes for Lin to inch up to one of the lowest branches. When she got there, she hooked one elbow around it, pulled her knife out of a pocket, and began to saw at the base of the nearest bulb of leaves.

When the black spots began to dance in front of Cara's eyes again, she realized she was holding her breath. She forced herself to exhale.

There was a light crack and the leaf bulb, still attached to a bit of branch, dropped out of the tree. Lin immediately began attacking another as Jak limped over to investigate her work.

Cara looked over Jak's shoulder. The leaves were each bigger than a dining plate and slightly arrow-shaped. They overlapped all around the base, and their pointed ends came together perfectly at the top. Jak began to pull back one leaf, but Oz stopped him.

"Move it," he said, gesturing upward to where Lin was about to drop another bulb on their heads.

Cara helped pull Jak to his feet as Oz grabbed the branch and dragged it away from the tree. Two seconds later another bulb fell, but Jak ignored it as he peeled open the first.

Cara briefly imagined toxic pollen spraying them, but arguing caution seemed ridiculous when anything they touched could be deadly. That didn't stop her from unconsciously holding her breath again as the bulb opened.

"Oh," Jak said. "Thank the stars."

Cara breathed in. It was the first satisfying breath she'd had since arriving here, no rush of energy or elation, just a sense of finally getting enough air in her lungs.

Two breaths later, it was gone.

"These trees are producing oxygen at a much higher rate than photosynthesis explains," Jak said. "Even trapping the air inside this bulb shouldn't have made it noticeably different. I wonder how...."

"Does it matter?" Cara asked.

Jak shook his head. "Probably not. There may be some kind of microscopic plant...like phytoplankton that...."

"Jak, do we need to know how it works? Bree needs the air."

"It's...well, yes...we're fine. It's only if the organisms are toxic, but yes...beggars can't...."

A third bulb fell right next to the sleepers, and two people jerked awake. Pol gave a little yell, and Ann looked around frantically.

Cara hurried over to reassure them, noticing as she went that Oz was helping Jak drag one of the bulbs over to where Bree lay.

After a hurried explanation to Ann, Cara left the older woman to comfort the now sobbing Pol and went back to the tree.

"Lin, that's enough," she whispered as loudly as she could. "Come down."

For a second she wasn't sure if Lin had heard, but then her friend unhooked her arm from the branch, swaying alarmingly as she did.

Lin clutched at the trunk, slid down about halfway and then pitched away from the tree, dropping like a stone. Out of instinct, Cara leapt to catch her, which resulted in the two of them crashing to the ground together. Lin's weight landed on Cara's chest, knocking the air from her lungs.

The world went black as Cara struggled to breathe.

Someone pulled her upright, and she sucked in air. Not enough. Not nearly enough. But she was breathing. *Breathe, Cara. Just breathe.* The pounding in her head slowly subsided, and she was aware of arms holding her up.

"Lin?" she gasped.

"I'm okay," Lin panted. "That was really stupid."

"You're exhausted."

"Not me. You. Trying to catch me." Lin shook her head.

A bubble of hysterical laughter rose up in Cara's chest. She didn't have enough air to really laugh, so it came out as short gasps instead.

Oz had been holding her up, but now she doubled over, and he pulled back, trying to see her face.

Cara held up a hand. "I'm…I…It's…okay."

She tried to get herself under control, to pull the emotion in, contain it in her core, breathe calmly.

She looked up at Oz's worried face. "I'm fine," she said. "Just…need to see Bree."

She tried to get up but didn't succeed until Lin pulled her to her feet. Together they crept around the circle to where Jak was huddled over his wife. Cara put a hand on his shoulder.

He looked up with tears in his eyes, and Cara's heart constricted.

"It worked," he whispered. "I put it to her face. She breathed, and…her eyes opened for just a second. She saw me."

Cara's legs gave out as all the relief she hadn't felt until now washed away the last of her strength. She was vaguely aware of Lin's words of encouragement, of Oz bringing over the third bulb, of Ann's hands settling her onto a pile of brush.

Then sleep took over.

# Chapter 12

## Plans

Tom didn't touch his food, and his mother stopped after a few bites. Cal continued to eat with the same slow, steady rhythm.

Tom watched him lift a fork full of grain to his mouth. It was all he could do not to scream.

"I know it sounds crazy, but we've always been like this. Knowing where the other one is. Feeling what they're feeling. This is the first time I heard her voice so clearly, but it's not really new."

"Can you hear her right now?" Cal's tone indicated danger ahead.

"No, it's like we lost connection when Mom called me, but I can still feel her there, just a little. She's exhausted and scared. But she's alive, and she said she's not alone. The others must be with her. You have to believe me. This is good news."

Jul looked at Cal before speaking up. "Tom, we're all exhausted and scared right now. Don't you think...?"

"That this is my mind playing tricks on me? No, I don't. Cara's feelings are…Cara. They aren't the same as my own. Do you think I can't tell the difference?"

"I don't know…."

"Well, I do. It was her. And if I talked to her once, I can talk to her again. Find out where they are. What they need. This is the breakthrough we've been looking for."

"No," Cal said. "The breakthrough we were looking for happened an hour ago when the science team made an ipit altered by healing water disappear by dripping rainwater onto it."

"How does that…?"

"Now we know for sure that it was the healing water that was responsible. We know exactly how it happened and, therefore, how to prevent it happening again. There's no longer any need for panic."

"What about the people who are already missing? That doesn't help us find them!"

Cal took one more bite, then neatly set his fork on the table. "What do you want me to do, Son?"

"I want you to believe me. I want you to believe that Cara is alive and that I can communicate with her. And I want you to use that to find a way to get her back, along with all the others."

"I heard three requests," Cal said. "Let me answer them in order. One, I do believe you. I believe that you have a special connection with your sister and she with you. Your mother and I have always known that, and Cara has said things over the years. That kind of bond between twins is common. I believe that you have uncanny empathy toward each other's feelings. And I believe that you heard a voice in your head that you thought was Cara."

"I—"

Cal held up a hand. "Two. As much as I wish with all my heart for my daughters to be alive, I cannot believe it with the confidence you are asking. I have not given up hope, but I cannot disregard probability, either. More importantly, it does not matter what I believe. Belief will not help us in this situation. Only facts will help us."

Tom didn't even try to interrupt this time. "Three. It is my responsibility to look after the well-being of this colony. That means making a plan for navigating this crisis that is based on reality. Attempting to make a plan based on voices you hear in your head, or even asking others to entertain such a possibility, would be a grave lapse of my duty. It would cause confusion in a time that we need clarity and expend resources that we can ill afford after all that we have already lost."

"You aren't listening to me. I'm telling you we haven't already lost them. I'm telling you we could expend resources to get back what we lost. How is that not in the best interest of this colony?"

"You don't have a plan, Son. You have a wish. We can't lead others forward on a path of wishes. We have to lead them forward on the solid ground of facts."

"But you're ignoring the most important facts! You're overlooking the truth because it's difficult to explain, because it doesn't fit into the plans you've already made."

That was finally enough to spark Cal's temper. He pushed back from the table, his voice cold but not as controlled as before. "You never did like plans. You never liked living in reality. I knew you were undisciplined, but I thought you had matured enough to set aside your own selfish wishes."

"I have no problem with plans," Tom said. "Only with who gets to make them."

Father and son glared at each other, neither blinking.

"How is this helping Bree and Cara?" Jul said. "How is it helping the colony?"

"It isn't," Cal said, all business again. "I'm going back to my office. There will be a gathering in the morning. I will explain the connection between the healing water and the disappearances. I will explain the security protocols we've placed around the sample of water. Everyone needs to know that they and their children are safe."

"And the families of the disappeared?" Jul asked.

"Anyone who needs a period of mourning will be allowed one." He spoke over Tom's objection. "I am not officially declaring them dead. We will continue to explore all theories and to study every angle of the disappearances. But if we do not discover any further proof that they are alive, we will need some sort of memorial service by the end of the week."

"Not *every* angle," Tom said.

"Every *possible* angle," said Cal. "This is not a good time for the colony to be worried about my son's sanity."

Tom ignored the jab. This was too important. "Who are you to say what is possible? What already happened should have been impossible, but we saw it with our own eyes."

"I don't have time for this," Cal said. He gathered up the plates, including the food his wife and son never ate. "I'll drop these at the kitchens on my way."

Jul stood. "I'll be in the office in a little bit."

Cal stopped, put a hand on her shoulder. His voice softened. "You don't need to come back tonight. You should get some rest while you can."

Tom shook his head in disbelief. It was like his father had pushed a button and transformed into a caring version of himself.

"I can't sleep. I can't even sit for more than a few minutes," Jul said.

"We'll work, then."

"We'll work."

A second later, Cal snapped out of their private moment and was out the door without another word for his son.

"This is killing him," Jul said.

"Why won't he listen to me?"

"Why won't you listen to him?"

"Mom, I talked to Cara."

She closed her eyes. "This is too much, Tom. It's too much."

She swayed, and Tom put out a hand to steady her, but she straightened her spine and stepped away before he could.

"We're all in over our heads right now. And without.... We need time. It's all happening too fast."

"The end of the week. That's when he said he'd declare them dead."

"Maybe. Probably. A lot could happen between now and then."

It could, and Tom would make sure it did.

His mother disappeared into her room for a few minutes, and Tom sat down with his tablet to do some research. He was so engrossed in reading about twin connections and extrasensory perception that he scarcely noticed when she left for the office.

None of this was useful. Most writers dismissed the possibility of mind to mind communication, and even those who were open to it described it as something totally different than what he had experienced. He dropped the tablet in frustration.

Tom knew that his family thought he let his emotions sway him too much, but he wasn't crazy, and he wasn't making this up. He was never more sure of anything than he was of this. He could feel Cara's presence. He always had. It wasn't even difficult to imagine using that to talk to her.

Forget the research. Forget convincing his parents. He needed to focus on Cara.

For a long time he sat, examining the place where his sister lived in his mind. He felt the qualitative difference between her emotion and his. Cara's fear was entangled with responsibility. She didn't want to let everyone down. His own was wrapped up in a sense of helplessness. He was powerless to stop what had happened. What else was outside his control?

Though he could still feel Cara's terror and confusion, her emotions were muted at the moment, like he was hearing them through a closed door. Slowly, he reached out in his mind toward that door. He eased it open.

He said her name.

# Chapter 13

## Water

*Cara.*

His voice jolted her from a deep sleep. Black spots swam before her eyes and then cleared, showing a dim light among the trees. Everyone was asleep except Zyk, who stood guard on the other side of the circle.

Cara's mouth was dry. Her head throbbed, and every muscle in her body ached, but adrenalin made her mind clear and sharp.

Tom's voice. Had she been dreaming?

*Cara.*

The word came with a rush of emotion: fear, worry, anger. Cara's gut churned with it.

*Tom?*

Was it the real Tom? A few times over the years, she had almost felt that he was reading her thoughts, but it had been nothing like this.

*Yes, Cara, it's me. I can hear you.*

It almost didn't matter if she was going insane. It felt so good to hear his voice.

*We have a count of the missing. 15 people. Where are you?*

*They're with me, Tom. We're together. All of us.*

Except one. Cara thought of Lin's story last night. Hy.

*Hy? What happened?*

Right. Real or not, he was in her head.

*Tom? I want this to be you, but I'm afraid I'm just losing my mind.*

A rush of warmth and humor came through. *Well, at least I know it's really you.*

Cara almost smiled.

*Lin. Is she with you?*

*Yes.*

Relief. *Tell her I said a wedding by the river is fine. She didn't need to run away to convince me. She'll know what I mean, and then you'll know you didn't make this up.*

A bubble of hope rose up in Cara. She looked around for Lin, saw her sleeping a meter away, red hair stark against her unnaturally pale face. The thin bandage on her shoulder was matted with blood.

*She's sleeping. I can't wake her yet.* She tried not to think about Lin's injury, but a spike of alarm from her brother told her that she didn't do it well. *I thought you guys weren't talking about getting married yet*, she said to cover.

He ignored her attempt at distraction. *I need to find you.*

*It's far, Tom. The stars...the stars are different here.*

Other than a churn of emotion, she received no answer.

*Tom?*

*Can you tell me what you've seen? I need details.*

She did her best to describe the meadow, the rocks, the forest. She started to tell him about the creatures, then shuddered and pushed the images out of her mind.

*Thank you,* he said. His voice was gentle. *I'm so sorry this happened. I'm going to make it right. Be safe, Six. Keep the others safe. We'll talk soon.*

For a long time, Cara sat and let the conversation play over in her mind. If she really could communicate with Tom, if she wasn't just losing her mind, they would have access to the whole colony. They could figure out a way home together. All they had to do was survive that long.

*Prioritize needs*, her father's voice instructed.

Safety. The fact that the monsters hadn't attacked again in the night seemed like a good sign. Maybe they had a very specific hunting ground and wouldn't come into the trees. Maybe the fire had scared them away. They couldn't count on it, of course, but there was reason to hope. If there were other predators, they had yet to see them. They would work on refining their weapons just in case.

Air. They had a way to get oxygen for Bree, and the rest of them were breathing better now that they were among the trees.

Their next priority was water. They'd be dead in another two days without it. There must be water somewhere if all these trees were growing. They just had to find it.

In her mind, she organized the group. Most would stay here to rest, work on weapons, treat wounds, and gather more oxygen bulbs. She would leave Oz in charge of all of that with Jem to help him. Ann, Wyn, and Syl could help keep the younger kids busy. Jak would take care of Bree. She would take Lin and Zyk along with her to search for water. Lin had the wilderness skills she needed, and Zyk was a fighter if they ran into trouble. With any luck, they wouldn't need to go far.

There had to be water nearby. There had to be.

"But what if it's far?" Jak asked an hour later when she had woken everyone and explained the plan. "Maybe we should all go together."

"If it's far, that's all the more reason to send a small group. We'll move faster," Lin said. "Then we'll bring water back."

"What are you going to carry it in?" Jem asked.

Cara's inadequacy washed over her. She hadn't even considered that.

"The leaves," Lin said, holding up a huge one. "They're sturdy. We can fold them into bowls."

Cara felt a rush of affection for her friend.

"What about food?" Zyk asked.

They had shared out the last bits of food that they had accidentally brought in their pockets, three protein bars and Cara's hurta fruit. It didn't go far, and without water, it had been hard to swallow the few bites they each got.

"One thing at a time," Cara said.

"We can survive a while without food," Jem added.

"What about home?" Lil asked.

"One thing at a time," Lin snapped.

Cara threw her friend a warning glance and put a hand on Lil's shoulder. She hadn't said anything about her possible contact with Tom, not even to Lin. She needed to get everyone moving first.

"We're going to get home," she said. "But like any long journey, it takes careful preparation. That's what we're doing now. Working together on the preparation. That's how we get home."

Lil nodded, and even Pol, who had begun crying again the moment she woke up, straightened her shoulders a bit.

"You each have a job to do. Focus on the job, and make sure you stick together at all times. The three of us will be back before you know it."

No one offered any more objections, so Cara handed Lin's knife to Zyk. "Mark the trees as we go. We don't want to get lost."

They headed out in the direction Cara thought of as north, though it was hard to judge the sun's position from under the trees. She let Lin lead the way. Her friend was trained for this sort of thing.

"Keep your eyes open for animal tracks," Lin said. "They often lead to water."

"Or to being mauled," Zyk muttered. He had been glowering since the moment he saw the three bites of food that were his portion, and now he was slashing the tree trunks with his good arm as he walked. Cara made sure to give him plenty of space.

Two hours later, Cara started to see the black spots again. Her breath was coming in shallow gasps, and her tongue was dry and swollen.

Lin stopped them. "We need to rest."

"No," Cara said, the word sticking in her dry throat. "Not until we find water."

"Cara," Lin was having trouble getting the words out. "The air is wrong. Conserve our strength."

Cara wanted to argue, to vent the desperate urgency she felt inside, but she didn't have the energy. "Five minutes," she said.

Zyk buried the knife in a tree and slumped to the ground.

Staring at the hilt, trying to make her mind focus on it and not on her own pain, Cara let herself think about what would happen if they didn't find water. In one more day, they would be too weak to move. She wondered if they would feel their organs shut down or if it would just be like falling asleep.

That wouldn't be too bad. Sleep sounded welcoming.

*Cara.*

Tom's voice was urgent, but he didn't say any more. It was enough.

"Let's go," she whispered.

Lin nodded and tapped Zyk on the shoulder. At first Cara thought he wouldn't get up, but, luckily, he did. If he hadn't, she would have had to leave him there.

Lin started moving again, swaying as she walked. Zyk followed, and Cara took a few steps before remembering the hilt of the knife. She stumbled back and pulled it out of the tree. If they got lost, they were all dead.

It was harder to score the trees than she had thought. Even injured, Zyk was a lot stronger than she. Still, Cara stumbled on, chipping off bark and cutting down undergrowth where she could find it.

The black spots had turned into black patches now, and twice Cara tripped over tree roots or rocks that she never saw. Her head was a block of pain, her tongue filled her whole mouth, her chest ached with each breath.

She lost track of time, walking in a half-dream, until she heard Lin's cry of surprise. A second later, she stumbled into something warm and solid. When it rumbled, she realized that it was Zyk.

They were all beyond talking, but Lin grunted as she gestured ahead. A mound of rock rose up from the forest floor in front of them. Under normal circumstances, it would have been easy to climb. At the moment, it seemed impassible.

Cara stared at this new obstacle for a long time, trying to make her fuzzy brain think of a new plan. Then she heard something. It was a sound she knew she ought to recognize, a happy memory. She wanted to find that sound, though she couldn't remember why.

Pushing past Zyk and Lin, she skirted the rocks for a while until she found an easier slope. Then she started to climb.

The effort made the muscles in her legs cramp and her wounded shoulder burn. She doubled over in pain, started to turn back, but...that noise teased her, called to her, dared her to remember.

She climbed some more.

Once she was up the first incline, she didn't need to use her hands. It was more like walking uphill than climbing. The rocks rose to the height of the treetops, and then leveled off for a few meters before sloping down again and getting lost under the branches.

And there, in a rift between two slopes of rock, was the source of the sound.

Water, bubbling up from underground and running away down the far side of the rocks.

A cry behind her announced that Zyk had followed her up. Before she could stop him, he had thrown himself down by the stream and was scooping water into his mouth.

She tried to say his name, but it came out as a squawk. It was too late to warn him anyway. He was drinking as quickly as he could.

Cara closed her eyes and prayed that the water was safe. When she opened them, Lin was standing next to her, looking on in horror, but Zyk was grinning widely.

"So good," he mumbled, scooping more water into his mouth and then sighing. "So good."

Cara and Lin exchanged a look. They both knew that the safe thing to do would be to wait and see if it had any ill-effect on Zyk before drinking, but the temptation was overpowering. They came to a decision at the same time.

It didn't really matter, Cara thought as the blessed water hit her swollen tongue. They were going to die of dehydration if this didn't work. If the water killed them, at least they would die more quickly. She hoped.

The water had a strong mineral taste that Cara would have called bitter if she had drunk it at home. Here, it was perfection.

She was three handfuls in when Lin pulled her away.

"Slow. Make you sick."

Cara knew her friend was right. She helped her pull Zyk back, too. He already looked dangerously uncomfortable.

"Slow," she repeated, though it was a bit late to give that advice now.

They all sat, then lay back on the rocks and let the sun beat down on their faces.

Cara could feel her brain slowly clearing. Her head still throbbed, her tongue still felt too big for her mouth, and her stomach and legs cramped and twitched, but she could think again.

They needed to get the water back to the others. Several of them had lost blood. They would be feeling worse than she did by now.

With heroic effort, she pushed up on her elbows. Zyk lay next to her with his eyes shut, but his breathing seemed even and strong. Lin didn't move, though her eyes were open, watching Cara's face.

"The others," Cara rasped.

Lin's eyes drifted shut, and she nodded.

"Leaves," she whispered. "I lost them."

Cara looked around. The outcropping of rocks was completely surrounded by the same strange trees they had walked through all day. Luckily, its height was even with their tops, and it looked like some grew close enough that she could reach the leaf clusters without having to do anything dangerous.

That was good because pushing onto her hands and knees was as strenuous an activity as she could manage. Slowly, Cara crawled to the edge and reached for the nearest leaves.

"The knife," Lin mumbled. Somehow, she had dragged herself closer, and she gestured at Cara's belt, where the now-dull knife was tucked.

It took longer than Cara liked to saw off a leaf cluster and pull back the five huge leaves that curled together. She and Lin leaned over the top, breathing in the oxygen-rich air inside, their heads clearing even more as they did.

Gratitude was the first feeling Cara was aware of. Water and oxygen. They had all they needed. Suddenly she remembered the voice that had spurred her on.

"Lin," she said. "Were you and Tom talking about where you would have your wedding?"

Lin flinched. "Did he tell you that?"

"I think so." *Better to look foolish than to be foolish.* "I think Tom spoke to me today." Cara swallowed. "In my head."

Lin's face was impassive.

"I...for a long time...forever really...I can feel his feelings sometimes, and he can feel mine. I know it sounds crazy, but I think it's...being twins...sometimes there's this emotional rush, and I know it's not my own."

"I know," Lin said. "Tom told me."

"He did?" Why was she surprised that Tom broke the promise they'd made to always keep it a secret? And why was she upset? It made this easier. "Okay. Well, yesterday I felt that. And then…then it wasn't just the feelings. It was his voice in my head. Talking to me just like he was there. I thought I was imagining it, but it came back this morning, and he said…."

Lin waited.

Cara took a deep breath. "He said to tell you that if you wanted to get married down by the river, he'd go along. You didn't need to disappear to convince him."

A bark of laughter escaped Lin's lips before she pressed them together. The tightness around her mouth and eyes betrayed her pain.

"It was real, wasn't it? He said you would know what he was talking about, and then I'd know I wasn't crazy."

Lin jerked her head in a nod.

A lightning bolt of joy shot through Cara before she realized Lin was crying. She was too dehydrated for tears, but her shoulders shook.

Cara put a hand on her leg. "Is there anything you want me to tell him?"

It took Lin a long time to answer. "Just what he already knows."

"So it's the river or nowhere?"

Lin didn't quite smile, but she did finally meet Cara's eye. "It's the river or anywhere at all." Before Cara could answer, she grabbed a dangling leaf pod. "Let's get this water back to the others."

By the time Lin had shown Cara how to fold the leaves into a cup shape, both girls were panting with thirst again. They took several long drinks, then splashed water on Zyk's face.

"Wake time," Lin said when he groaned and cracked one eye open.

"No," he mumbled.

"Sit up and you can have another drink," Cara said.

He didn't answer, but after a minute, his eyes opened fully and he slowly sat up.

"Drink," Cara said.

He didn't have to be told twice.

Carefully, they filled the leaf containers with water. It took a few tries to figure out how to get the maximum amount inside and still be able to carry them. Cara and Lin would each carry two, and Zyk would carry one in his good hand.

"It's not enough," Lin said.

"It's all we can do," Cara answered. Their only hope was that it would give the group enough strength to travel here for more.

They took turns balancing the full cups while they each drank their fill one last time. Then, they pushed to their feet and headed back to their friends.

# Chapter 14

# *Research*

"Okay, out with it," Grish said. "Whatever you're brooding about, just say it."

They were six kilometers south of Mayland, following Tom's original search plan. The governor had approved the search this morning in spite of the fact that Tom now knew it was pointless. Tom didn't even have the energy to be angry. Instead, he had spent the morning's walk putting together his own plan of action and trying to find a way to keep his friends out of it.

They had stopped for lunch under a lone naki tree. Its hair-like leaves hung low enough to tickle Tom's ear. He twitched the branch away.

"I think I need to ask you for a favor, but you can't ask any questions or tell anyone what I'm doing."

"You know something about the disappeared?"

"I… I'm sorry. I can't say what this is. Not yet."

"Okay. I like a mystery."

"I won't lie. It might get you into trouble."

"But it would help you. And it would help them."

"I hope so."

"Then I'm in. What do we have to steal?"

Tom laughed. "No stealing. I need you to draw some field sketches."

Grish's eyebrows disappeared into his hairline. "Field sketches? That's your big dangerous ask?"

"The danger is mostly that people will think you're as crazy as I am."

"Oh. Well that's okay, then. People already think that. What am I drawing? You have samples?"

"No, these are new species. I only have descriptions."

Grish narrowed his eyes. "And I'm not supposed to ask where those descriptions came from." He sighed and waved a hand at the empty countryside. "We aren't finding them out here, are we?"

Tom didn't answer.

"Okay. Sketches from a description won't have the same accuracy. Unless you can give me good details, they may not be accurate at all. Would you have a way to verify them when we're done?"

"I don't think so."

"So this is a long shot."

"Probably. But it's the only one I have right now."

"That's all I need to know. When do we start?"

Six hours later, Tom entered the biology department with his tablet clutched tightly in his hands. He had come straight here on their return. At this hour, most of the colony would be at dinner in the main hall. Hopefully that included the governor.

Hopefully it didn't include the entire biology team.

Cara's description of the tall grass where she had arrived was too vague to be useful, but the trees were a different matter. They were unlike naki or any other tree that grew near Mayland, and Cara had given enough detail that Grish's sketches were distinctive. Hopefully they were close enough to the real thing for an expert to identify.

Outside a door marked "Botany," Tom took a deep breath. He knocked.

Tom had his story in place, so when a young woman looked up at him from the corner desk, he smiled, every bit the confident but grieving son of the governor.

"I hope I'm not interrupting anything urgent," he said. "I need some help identifying a species of flora. I believe it's a tree, but our sketches may not be accurate. Our team only saw it from a distance, and there's some dispute about whether we've discovered a new species or are just displaying our ignorance." He let his smile turn sheepish. "I know this isn't important with everything else going on, but I'm trying to keep my team's spirits up, and this debate has been a distraction."

Her face was full of sympathy, and she immediately dropped whatever she had been working on. "Let me see."

As she flipped back and forth between Grish's two best efforts, her forehead wrinkled, and her mouth turned into a frown.

"This doesn't look like anything I've seen before. Certainly not any of the catalogued trees here on Una. The leaf pattern is distinctive, of course, but the height is the puzzling part. Are you sure you are correct about how tall they are?"

"Not sure, no. This is our best guess."

She pursed her lips. "Una's climate doesn't grow things as tall as you've estimated. Maybe the ground was higher than you could see from that distance?"

Tom's heart sank, but he didn't let it show on his face. "Maybe. That would explain it. I sure would like to know what those bulbs on top are, though. If it does turn out we've discovered a new species, the team will be so proud. They could use the lift right now."

"Well, it's definitely possible. This doesn't look like anything I know of, but I'm still only an apprentice. If you wait until tomorrow, Nel will be here. She knows every species of flora ever known to mankind, and she could tell you where this fits."

Tom didn't have to exaggerate his disappointment. "Okay. I was hoping to have news for everyone tonight. It was a hard day of searching. But we'll just have to wait, I guess."

Suddenly the girl's face brightened. "Wait! I have an idea. The database has a species recognition function that was designed for the first colonists. We never use it anymore, but I think they still keep it updated."

She quickly sent the images from Tom's tablet to her own. "Let me try this…."

Tom watched over her shoulder as the program scanned the sketches and began to run a comparison with all the trees in its database. Species after species flicked by, most of which must have been from Earth because they were nothing short of weird. The people of Mayland had no contact with Earth, and even though they still taught Earth history and biology in school, Tom could barely remember most of it. It had never seemed relevant.

The tablet buzzed when the search was complete. It displayed two species of tree, both tall and slender and with branches that sprouted large leaves. Neither had leaves curled into bulbs, and neither had the knobby bark that Cara had described.

"These are the closest match, but they certainly aren't the same. They're also both from Earth, more particularly from tropical Earth climates that don't exist on Una. I think you may have found something new."

She thought she was giving him good news, so Tom tried to look happy. "Wow. Thank you. But you're sure we got the height wrong? Can you explain that to me?"

"Sure. Basically, everything on Una is adapted to its cold, dry environment. It's not just that plants tend to huddle closer to the earth for reflected warmth, the geological makeup of Una wouldn't be able to sustain trees of the height you indicated. Una doesn't have the permafrost of Earth tundra, but the ground is frozen for most of the year, which means plants have shallower roots. These are usually spread wide to gather water from infrequent rains. In the forests, the trees have interlaced roots allowing them the stability and protection to grow taller, but still the tallest we've measured are three or three-and-a-half meters. The five or six meters you estimated just wouldn't be possible."

"So it would take a warmer climate to grow a tree that tall?"

"Yes, and preferably one with more groundwater reserves than Una. Your tree is really exciting, though, if it's anything close to what those sketches show. I hope we can get closer to take more accurate measurements."

"Thanks for your help."

"No problem. You want me to send you the descriptions of those Earth trees? Just for comparison?"

"Um…sure. Thanks. And then I'll let you get back to your work. Please don't tell Nel I kept you from it for something so personal."

"Oh, she wouldn't mind. We're all so sorry about your sisters. And your teammates, too."

The girl was starting to tear up, so Tom ducked his head and backed toward the door. "Thank you."

"If they're still out there, the governor will find them," she said.

He was already out the door, so he closed it quickly and pretended he hadn't heard.

If Cara's trees were an unknown species, then she really was far away. There must be a microclimate somewhere on the planet that the Mayland colonists hadn't discovered, maybe near the salt lake or in a sheltered area of the mountains. Knowing the conditions they were looking for should make it easier to locate. Tom clung to that hope as he jogged toward the earth sciences building.

It would be harder to explain his reasons for these questions, so he weighed the risks of telling whomever he found that the governor had sent him. He could cite security reasons for not explaining himself, but the chances were high that his request would get back to his father.

It was a pointless debate. No one was there.

Frustrated, Tom headed to the dining hall. There was still time to grab food without his lateness being too conspicuous.

When he slipped inside, he automatically glanced toward his parents' table. His mother wasn't there, but Cal was eating at his usual steady pace, eyes glued to a report on his tablet. Tom grabbed food from the kitchens and joined his team before the governor looked up again.

Now that the small worry of being discovered by Cal was gone, the larger worry took over. If Cara was right about those trees, she was somewhere with a completely different climate. The salt lake was thousands of kilometers away, and while Mayland Settlement maintained the technological knowledge that had brought their grandparents to another galaxy, all their resources were invested in

**118**

survival in isolation. Medical science, agriculture, and basic manufacturing had been priorities. Advanced facilities had been constructed for each of those areas by dismantling the ship that brought them here. The colony had no vehicles beyond basic carts and no long-distance communications system.

They could probably put together a mechanized rover that would run on solar power, but manufacturing something on that level would take a long time with their current facilities. And even then, the vehicle wouldn't be much use if there were mountains to cross, or a sizeable body of water.

Of course, he could get to Cara and Lin faster if he traveled the same way they had. If he were prepared for his own transport, he could take maps along and help lead them home.

"It was only the first day," Sal said, jolting Tom out of his thoughts. "We're going to keep going until we find them."

"I know," he said.

"You didn't look like it just then," she said.

Tom smoothed his face. "No," he said, "I do know we'll find them. I was just thinking about something someone asked me."

She raised her brows in question.

"It's a planetology thing. Have you ever heard anyone theorize that there could be microclimates somewhere on Una?"

She hadn't been expecting such an obscure question, but she answered it thoughtfully anyway. "I've never heard that, but my uncle is a geologist, and my cousin is his apprentice. I could ask them about it."

"It's not…it's just a question that came up. It's kind of nice to distract myself."

He tried to suppress his guilt at the sympathy in her nod.

"It won't be a bother to them. They love it when someone actually cares about their work." Sal craned her neck, looking around the dining hall. "I don't see either of them, but I'll send them a message."

"Thanks."

She was already typing. "I'm telling them to send their answer directly to you, okay? In case it takes a while."

"Perfect. Thank you."

"Anything, anytime," she said.

Tom picked at his dinner, delaying the inevitable moment when he had to go home. One by one, his teammates said good-night and headed out. Cal had left a long time ago. The dining hall was all but empty when Tom's tablet chimed.

The message from Sal's uncle was short. *Because of the potential agricultural benefits, the possibility of microclimates was thoroughly explored in collaboration with multiple teams. The results were considered conclusive. Though the climate transitions to true tundra closer to the poles, no areas of significant climatic differences exist on Una. I can explain the reasons for that if you want, but there really isn't any debate about our findings.*

Tom's stomach clenched. Dead end. The trees had been his only substantial clue, and apparently their existence wasn't possible.

For a long time, he sat in the empty hall, battling despair.

He thought of Cara, searching for water and food and a way to survive in a strange place. There was no giving up.

Quickly, he composed a reply thanking Sal's uncle for his help. It was only after he sent it that he realized that both messages had been copied to the governor.

Tom's heart sank, but at least now he had a reason to go home. Better to get the inevitable over.

*120*

# TWIN

When he walked in the door, both of his parents were reading in chairs by the heating unit.

His mother greeted him with a sad smile. Cal just gave a nod and returned to his tablet.

Tom kissed his mother on the head.

"How was it today?" she asked.

"We knew we weren't going to find them. They are too far away."

Jul sighed. Cal said nothing.

Tom wasn't waiting. "Aren't you going to reprimand me for making inquiries? Don't you want to know what I found and whether I told anyone why I was asking?"

Finally, Cal put his tablet aside. "I don't need to ask. I've been monitoring you and your team all day. If you told Grish why you wanted the sketches, he hasn't said anything to anyone else. And your communication with the scientists seems to have been discreet."

"Thanks for the compliment. Your spying was equally discreet. Why didn't you just stop me if you were so worried?"

"My only concern was for the anxiety you might cause others if you explained too much. I wanted you to investigate your information. I hoped it would help you."

"It didn't. I'm no closer to finding them than I was this morning. Which, of course, you already know."

"You discovered that the descriptions you heard in your head are for places and objects that do not exist."

"You let me do this so I would find out on my own that I'm crazy?"

"Not crazy. Overwhelmed with grief and stress. And yes, I hoped you would see it for yourself."

Tom felt like a fool. Running around all day like a puppet on a string, deceiving himself into thinking he was taking control of the situation.

Without a word, he turned and left the house.

# Chapter 15

## Disaster

Water was the difference between despair and hope. Cara passed around the cups and watched life come back into the eyes of each person who drank it. The tight knot in her stomach eased just a little.

She let Lin give the good news that more water was just a few hours march away.

When she saw their exhausted stares, Cara stepped in. "We'll have all the water we need there, and the rocks will provide some defense. We should be able to camp there and rest up while we heal. This is one last push."

Oz and Ann nodded, and Jem began to gather up the weapons he'd been working on. The others stood listlessly.

The silence was filled only by wind rustling the tree branches.

And something else, faint but audible.

"Did you hear that?" Syl asked.

The distant scream came again.

"It's them," Zyk said.

Immediately, the group sprang into action, gathering up weapons and laying Bree out on the stretcher Oz and Jem had made. Everyone was armed now, even the children, though some had only sharpened sticks. Jak gave Zyk a huge spear made from a branch and a piece of sharpened bone.

"Drink up all the water," Lin said. "We'll have more when we arrive. Cara, you'll lead?"

"No, you. I'll help with Bree."

"I've—"

"Got the best tracking skills," Cara snapped. "Take the lead."

Another scream split the air, closer than before.

"Now," Cara said, but it wasn't necessary. They were already moving.

She bent down and got a firm grip on the branches that served as handles. Then, she and Oz lifted together. Everyone had already followed Lin, except Jak, who hovered by Bree, leaning on a makeshift crutch, and Zyk and Jem, who would act as a rear guard.

They didn't run—that wouldn't have been possible with the undergrowth and the low oxygen level—but they walked at a pace not far short of it. After only a few minutes, Cara was panting. Her arms, especially her wounded shoulder, ached from the effort of carrying the stretcher. She gritted her teeth and kept on.

Something crashed in the trees to her right, and Cara's already painful heartbeats nearly burst through her chest.

"Keep on!" Jem said. "We'll guard you."

Cara put her head down and focused on moving faster.

Another crash and another blood-freezing cry from the creature, and then Zyk yelled, and something burst through the undergrowth.

Cara stumbled and would have dropped the stretcher if her hands hadn't already cramped into claws around the handles.

Oz had the other side, and he didn't slow down, so Cara was yanked forward. Her feet somehow kept up, but it took all her concentration not to fall. The chaos of noise and motion behind her was a distant echo in her mind.

Another creature screamed from the right, this time slightly ahead of the group. She could no longer see those who had gone first.

"It's coming," she gasped.

Oz just grunted, but Jak said, "They're armed." He was leaning on his stick with his right hand. The left gripped a club.

A human shout from ahead brought horrible visions into Cara's mind. More yelling echoed through the air, followed by another bestial cry from the left.

They were surrounded. They were injured and exhausted. They were still hours from the rocks and any chance for a defensible position.

The brief hope that came with the water had fled. They were all going to die here, and no one back home would ever know what had happened to them.

Cara shivered. She should have moved them all this morning. She shouldn't have waited so long.

Somehow her feet were still moving, but she couldn't feel them anymore. Her hands were numb, too.

"What's happening?" Jak asked.

They were dying.

"Wind," Oz yelled back.

Until he said it, Cara hadn't even noticed the breeze making loose strands of hair dance around her face.

She shivered again and realized that it wasn't just fear. The temperature had dropped as the sun faded. She didn't remember it getting this cold the night before, but there had been no wind then.

The frigid air cleared Cara's head, even as it numbed the pain in her limbs. She was suddenly aware that the yelling had stopped.

"The others?"

"I see them," Oz said. He slowed, and Cara almost fell again. Jak gripped the edge of the stretcher and steadied her.

They moved on.

There was no noise from behind them now, and Cara tried not to think that Jem and Zyk were both dead. Time passed with nothing more than a slight increase in the wind and the return of the black spots along with a sharp pain in her side.

One hour. Cara couldn't feel her legs at all. Two hours. Someone up front was crying, the sound brought to Cara's ears by the now icy wind.

"There!" an excited voice cried.

"We made it," Ann said.

Oz stopped, and Cara stumbled to a halt, knees buckling. Jak dropped his stick and helped her set the stretcher gently down. Then he knelt by Bree, checking her vital signs.

"We can't go up the rocks now," Oz said. He was looking at the treetops, which swayed wildly in the wind.

"Water," Cara said.

"A few can go. Bring some down."

She nodded, turned around to look back the way they came. Was there motion under the trees?

At first she thought it was just the wind, but then a weirdly-shaped figure emerged from the shadows. Jem and Zyk stumbled toward them, leaning on each other like toddlers in a three-legged race.

She ran toward them, saw the blood that stained both of their shirts.

"He's bad off," Jem said. "Took claws to the chest."

Cara slid under Zyk's other shoulder, helped support his weight as they tottered the last few meters to the others.

"Bandages!" she yelled when they got to the stretcher. Slowly they lowered Zyk's huge frame to the ground under a tree as Wyn hurried over with a pile of leaves and a few strips of someone's clothes.

"They just disappeared," Jem said. He was swaying on his feet, covered in blood. A long scratch ran down one cheek.

"You need help," she said.

"Not my blood. Zyk's. The animals. There were three. We couldn't...we were dead. Then suddenly they all pulled back, ran away."

"Why?"

"Don't know."

"The same happened to us," Ann said, handing Jem a tiny scrap of cloth to wipe blood from his face.

"It can't be good," Jem said.

He was right. The creatures had been determined to catch their prey. What could have scared them away? A bigger predator?

"The wind," Jem said. "It started right after they left."

"You think they fear storms?" Ann said.

He shrugged. "Animals know when to find shelter."

Which meant they were going to need shelter, too.

As if on cue, a gust of wind whipped Cara's hair into her face. She tasted grit in the air. Zyk moaned in pain.

"We need cover," Cara said.

Jem cupped a hand to his ear.

"Shelter!" she shouted over the wind.

He nodded grimly.

A fallen branch tumbled past, smacking the side of Cara's leg. The trees were bending and swaying wildly. Their slender trunks weren't going to provide much protection.

"Up against the rocks!" Cara yelled.

Ann flashed her a thumbs up and tugged Wyn's arm. The two women began herding the children toward the rocks.

Cara and Jem struggled to get Zyk to his feet again. He yelled in pain, and his thrashing arms hit Jem twice before they succeeded in moving him. By the time they had stumbled the last few meters to where the rest of the group huddled, the dirt and debris whipping through the air were a constant assault.

Pushing Zyk against the rocks, Cara saw Pol, wide-eyed, get hit in the shoulder with a slender branch that sliced open her shirt. Pol screamed, and Wyn pulled her toward the ground, protecting the girl with her own body.

Desperately, Cara tried to do a head count. She could see the twins huddled up next to Jak and Bree. Ann and Lil were crouched over them.

Where was Lin? And Oz?

Syl separated from the group and staggered toward her, leaning on the rock. Her eyes were red, her dark hair danced madly behind her, but she pushed past Cara. "Wound?" she shouted. The wind carried her voice away.

Cara tried to block her path, but the girl bent over Zyk. When she sat up, her eyes were haunted. She shook her head.

"I know," Cara said, knowing that Syl couldn't hear her. She reached out to wrap her arms around the younger girl, to shelter her from the wind and the helplessness. As she did, a small rock tumbled through the air and bounced off the young medic's skull. Syl looked dazed as a trickle of blood ran down her face.

Cara pulled her to the ground against the rocks, lifting Syl's arm to press her own sleeve against the wound. "Stay down!" she said into her ear.

The two girls huddled there, Zyk's legs half under them, the rocks behind Syl's back. Cara felt Jem crouching behind her, trying to provide even more protection. His body warmed her for a moment, but the wind grew colder and colder, and its grit bit into every exposed part.

It was completely dark, but in a world gone mad, the lack of light barely counted as interesting. As the minutes dragged by into hours, Cara was thankful that she couldn't see her friends' suffering.

Jem's body protected her head, but Cara's arms and legs felt like their skin was being peeled off. Syl trembled under her, and Zyk's legs twitched. Then they stopped, which was worse. Cara tried not to think about his wounds.

She tried not to think at all.

At one point a tiny spark of alarm went off in her head. Vaguely, she thought it must be Tom, and she tried to focus on his voice, but her own pain filled everything.

She gave herself up to the misery.

# Chapter 16

## Weakness

Tom kept his head down, following the well-ordered paths at random.

He could feel Cara's pain like a weight in the back of his mind. For the first time, he hoped that this wasn't real, that she didn't really feel like that.

Darkness was falling, and the cold came with it. At this hour, most of the colonists were cozy at home. They would be reading or practicing their hobbies or tucking their children into bed.

For most of them, life continued as if the events of the last few days hadn't happened.

The thought filled him with bitterness so strong he could taste it. He didn't blame those innocent families. It wasn't their fault they had what he couldn't have. He blamed himself for bringing home the healing water so thoughtlessly. He blamed everyone who had signed off on those experiments. He blamed his father for refusing to open his mind so they could make this right. He blamed the universe for creating a trap for them all.

He was so caught up in his thoughts that he didn't see Bel until he bumped into her.

"Hey!" she said. "You're going the wrong way. It's in Classroom 7."

Tom looked around. His feet had carried him to the front of the school wing. A door was propped open, and people filtered inside.

Bel took his arm. "You by yourself?" Before he could answer, she nodded knowingly. "I'm not surprised. You can sit with us."

Tom saw that Bel's parents were waiting for her by the door. He waved hello, but Bel's father frowned and turned away.

"Don't mind him," Bel said, not bothering to lower her voice. "He blames us for bringing back the water that made Zyk disappear. Not that blame is going to help get him home."

She led Tom into the building and through the door marked 7. Tom had studied history and social sciences in this room every year from ten to thirteen. Now it was half-full of people of all ages.

"Let's sit here," Bel said, choosing seats not far from the door. Her parents sat a few rows back, and Bel rolled her eyes.

"They're right," Tom said. "We should have been more careful."

"We didn't know," said Bel. "I'm glad you came anyway. I promise that most people don't blame you."

Tom looked around the room, registering the faces. Fer Rayson. Ming Vance, with her two children. Harm and Bea Demar. Xi Lee-Herrera. These were the families of the disappeared.

He didn't see Lin's parents, but her older sisters were on the other side of the room. Val caught his eye, and he was relieved to see no accusation there. She nudged Moll, who gave Tom a small wave.

"What is this?" he asked.

"The message wasn't very clear, was it?" Bel said. "Just called it a gathering. I heard Jof Harson and Bea Demar organized it, but I'm not sure if there's a plan beyond getting everyone together."

More people were arriving. Hy's parents took a seat on the other side of the room, and Tom had to swallow hard as he looked away. A tall man with dark skin came in and hurried to Ming's side. Jem's brother.

Jak's mother, Kay, came alone. Her husband had passed away two years before, and Mel, Jak's younger sister, was probably working a night shift. Tom stood up, and Kay immediately pulled him into a long hug. He didn't pull away until she did. Her eyes were wet with tears as he helped her into a seat next to Val.

An old man with an angular face and piercing blue eyes stood at the front of the room and raised a hand for quiet. Tom recognized Jof Harson, retired engineer and husband of Ann Harson. Ann had been Tom's teacher when he was seven, but she retired the year after.

"Thank you all for coming," Jof said. He had the strong, clear voice of a younger man. "We have no agenda tonight, and I know many of you are exhausted by the last few days. But as the investigation continues and an official memorial is being planned, we thought it was important for us to see each other face to face. If you have something to say, you are free to do so. It doesn't matter what it is. If you only want to listen, you are equally free to be silent. We just wanted the chance to see each other, to look into the eyes of others who know what we are experiencing. To be together. So. Thank you for the gift of your presence."

His eyes fell on Tom, and Tom was suddenly very aware that he had not received a message inviting him here. Maybe he wasn't welcome. Maybe more people blamed him than Bel thought.

Jof nodded. "If you wish to express anger along with your grief, this is a safe place to do that. We would only ask that you remember that every person in this circle brought pain with them. Yours is not the only hurt that matters."

With that, he stepped back, and Bea Demar rose to her feet. "I'm Bea," she said, "and my son Oz disappeared in front of the machine shop right before my eyes. I haven't slept much since then, so it may be that I don't make much sense tonight. I hope you'll forgive me. I still can't wrap my mind around what happened or how it could be real. I've worked with machines all my life. Machines make sense, and they do what they're designed to do. I've always thought of the universe as just a much bigger machine, but this? This isn't how anything is supposed to work. What happened to my boy isn't supposed to even be possible. Still, it happened, so that shows what we know. And Oz. He was my apprentice, and now he's a better mechanic than I ever was, but he's not like me. He always loved questions that don't have answers. So wherever he is, however he is, I think some part of him must be happy. He's inside the biggest question yet, and it must be giving him a lot to think about."

She sat down, and her husband took her hand. Tom saw that the old man's hands were twisted with disease.

"I'm Fer," a voice said. Tom hadn't even seen the man stand. "My children are...were...only 8. They're gone. Just...gone, and no one can tell me if they're alive or dead. My wife is...She can't leave her bed. I don't know what I'm supposed to do."

Tom's insides were lead. He told himself to stand, to tell this man that his children were alive, that they were with Cara and Lin, who would take care of them. But could he guarantee that? Was he sure enough to break his word to his father? Would these people believe him, and if they did, would it help their pain?

"No one is doing anything," Bel's father said angrily. "That's the problem. They used a new substance on our families and didn't tell us about the risks. They didn't tell us anything at all. And now our families…my son…are just gone. What else don't we know? What else is the governor hiding?"

He turned his rage on Tom, jabbing the air with one finger. "What were you really trying to do with that water? Did you know this would happen? Do you know where they are?"

Tom opened his mouth to answer, but Bel cut her father off. "Of course Tom and his father didn't know this would happen! Do you think they would have used it on Cara and Bree if they did? And Lin? We thought it was healing people! We thought it was going to help us all. No one knew this would happen."

Several voices murmured agreement. A lump rose in Tom's throat.

"It's just so hard not knowing," Ming Vance said. "I think we could handle whatever we have to handle if we just knew what happened to them."

"I know my Lil is still alive somewhere," a woman said. He knew she must be Cher Savari, but he couldn't ever remember seeing her before. "I can feel it. She is lost and she is scared, but she is still alive."

"I would know if Syl had died," said a young man sitting with Syl Harambe's family. Ken was almost eighteen, had a long earnest face, and had been Syl's boyfriend for less than a year. "My heart would tell me if she were gone. But even though I miss her, I know I will see her again."

No one greeted this pronouncement with mockery. In fact, several people nodded.

"I cannot imagine that water with healing properties like this would evolve just to end life." Xi's voice was louder than her small frame indicated, maybe because she had always been her mother's voice as well. "There must be some other evolutionary purpose. It makes more sense for it to function as a method of transference. Though what dangers might await on the other end, I couldn't say."

"Pol was at work when she disappeared, but I felt it the moment it happened," Pol's grandmother said. "I knew as soon as the rain started that something had happened to her. And when I heard the news, I wasn't alarmed because I knew whatever it was, it wasn't death."

"I can't say I've felt anything that clear, but I do believe Jem is alive," said his brother. "I have to for his kids' sake, and for Ming. And I'm certainly not giving up hope this soon."

"Neither are we," said Moll. "Our sister is as tough as they come. There's no way some water was the end of her."

"Yes," said Val. "I can practically hear Lin's voice in my head telling me not to give up on her."

Tom's mind raced. He wasn't the only one who was certain. Maybe these people really could sense their loved ones, even without the twin connection.

"Me, too," said Hy's father. Bert was the shortest man Tom had ever met, and one of the most intense. He waved his hands as he talked. "I can feel my son Hy right here in my heart. He was always such a lively boy, and I can still feel that life. Even as I walked here today, I heard him whisper to me, 'Da, don't give up. I'm still here.'"

Tom's heart plummeted. What was he thinking? These people weren't receiving messages from the disappeared. They were grief-stricken and desperate and believing what they wanted to believe.

No wonder that's what his father thought of him. That's what anyone would think. And how could Tom convince them otherwise?

What could he tell the hurting families? That he heard from his sister in a way that was more real than theirs? That Hy was already dead, and the others didn't have food or water and were being attacked by wild animals? That even now he could feel his sister in excruciating pain, and he didn't know what was happening to her?

The meeting continued, but Tom slipped out the door into the night air. No, he couldn't tell these people anything. Not until there was good news to give. Not until he had more solid proof. And he couldn't get proof until he heard from Cara.

Once again, it was up to her.

# Chapter 17

## Shelter

The first thing Cara heard was sobbing.

It went on for a long time before she realized that it wasn't the wind. It was Syl.

Slowly, Cara lifted her head. Her neck and back were clenched so tight that each millimeter of motion was excruciating.

The wind had died down to gentle puffs of breeze, cool against her raw skin. It was painful to open her dry eyes, and they didn't focus properly when she did.

There was light now--the fading light of early evening, but still enough to see the destruction.

The trees had been stripped of most of their leaves. Those leaf pods that remained had drawn into tight balls, half their original size. A few trunks bent all the way to the ground, including one that was less than two meters from where her friends still huddled.

A moan behind her made her turn.

Jem was on his knees, face contorted with pain, eyes unfocused. Even as she reached toward him, he toppled forward. The clothes on his back were shredded, showing the flayed and bruised skin beneath.

Cara stared, frozen in horror.

"Water," Syl whispered. She had pushed onto hands and knees and was studying Jem's wounds. "Get water."

Still, Cara didn't move.

He had protected her with his own body, and this was the price he had paid.

"Cara!"

She was aware of Lin's voice, but she didn't turn even when her friend touched her shoulder.

"Oh, stars," Lin said. She had seen Jem. "Oz! Here!"

Two seconds later, Oz was kneeling next to Jem, dripping water onto his back.

"Here," Lin said gently. "Drink."

Cara turned her face away.

"Cara. Take a drink. Then give some to the others."

Cara blinked. The others. Jem wasn't the only one who had been sheltering people.

Lin pressed a leaf cup against her lips, and reflexively, Cara drank. It was hard to swallow, but the water helped clear her head. She took a second drink, then passed the cup to Syl.

Cara turned questioning eyes to Lin.

"We made it up to the water last night," Lin said, "but the wind on top was incredible. It knocked me back, and I slid down the far side. Oz followed. In the end it saved us. The rocks curve around over there where the water trickles down, and it's more sheltered from the wind. There was no climbing out during the storm, so we hunkered down and waited. I'm so sorry we left you...."

"You did...good."

Oz looked up. "We're going to need more water, and maybe we can use the leaves to bandage his back."

Syl pushed to her feet, swaying a bit. "I can find leaves."

"I'll go for the water," Lin said. "Here." She pushed another cup into Cara's hands. "Give this to the others. If anyone is strong enough to go up to the source, show them where."

Cara followed her orders, thankful that someone was still clear-headed enough to give them.

The rest of the group were slowly moving. Bree had been under everyone and was unharmed by the storm. The children had cuts and bruises on their arms and legs, but Jak and the older women had taken the brunt of the wind and flying debris. None of them was as bad off as Jem—their position had been a little more sheltered—but even so, their clothes were torn, their skin red and lacerated.

After everyone had drunk, Cara used the last drops of water to start washing their wounds. Soon, Lin and Syl brought more water and some of the giant leaves. Cara insisted that they treat everyone else before dealing with her arms.

Zyk was barely breathing. Syl spent a long time dripping water into his mouth, but Cara couldn't tell if he swallowed any.

After all that had happened, she knew they were lucky that any of them were still alive, but it didn't feel lucky. It felt senseless that someone as young and strong as Zyk would be on death's door. And Hy. Gone before he even knew where he was.

Cara felt a surge of anger. She couldn't save Hy, but Zyk was still alive. She was going to see to it that he stayed that way.

"Lin!"

The redhead straightened up from where she was working on Lil's foot.

"We need to get everyone into that shelter you found. Can you get them to the top of the rocks? Take them one at a time if you have to. The children can help. Once they're up by the water, everyone drinks their fill and washes their wounds thoroughly. Have Jak gather some of the fallen leaf pods for Bree. He can stay with her...and Jem and Zyk...until we figure out how to move them."

Lin's eyes widened at her tone, but she nodded. Eight-year-old Hal tugged on her hand and said something quietly that made her smile.

Cara left them to it.

"Oz," she said, gingerly kneeling next to him as he added layers to Zyk's leaf bandages. "I need you to help me find a way around the rocks to the sheltered spot you found. We'll never get them up there in their condition, so we need to go around, but we need to move. I want them protected and near the water before dark if possible."

"He's lost a lot of blood," Oz said. "Moving him will cause him to lose more."

Cara clenched her jaw. He was right, but staying here was not an option. Now that the storm was gone, the beasts could come back. Or another storm. *When the best option is a bad one, you choose it anyway. Regretting the impossible helps no one.*

Zyk would have to survive one last effort.

Even with storm debris everywhere, it didn't take long to circle around the rock outcropping. The undergrowth on the far side was less damaged. Cara heard the sound of running water, and a little further, the rocks opened into a shallow grotto with water cascading down the inner wall.

As shelter went, it wasn't much. Two-and-a-half walls and no roof. But after everything they'd been through, it was a haven of safety.

"There are fallen trees in the forest," Oz said. "In time, we can drag them over to build an outside wall."

"If the beasts wait that long."

"If not, the rocks give us a safe place to make a fire again."

"It's the best we've found so far."

He nodded.

"Let's get everyone here, then."

They worked as quickly as possible to get each person over or around the rocks. Even so, darkness had fallen by the time Oz and Lin staggered the last few feet with Zyk on the stretcher. Cara had been steadying them as they went, but now she slumped to the ground, allowing Syl and the twins to take over Zyk's care.

Someone touched Cara's arm. She looked down and saw Wyn lying nearby. She had bandages all along her side and back.

"How are you?" Cara asked gently. "Have you had enough water?"

Wyn shook her head, but when Cara looked around for Syl, Wyn tapped her arm again.

"No...." Her voice was weak but still clear. "Not water. I...."

"It's okay," Cara said when she trailed off. "We have shelter and water here. We can heal."

"No!" Wyn said, then closed her eyes, swallowed hard. "I...yes, good, but...."

This time Cara waited for her to go on.

"I know where we are," Wyn whispered.

Cara's heart thumped. That was good news, so why did her mouth feel suddenly dry?

"Good," she said finally. "That will help."

"No," Wyn said again.

"Cara!" Syl said. "I…I think he's…."

Cara leapt to her feet.

Zyk was completely still on his stretcher. A leaf bandage covered half of his wounds. Cara tried to ignore the gaping hole that was still visible.

"I don't think he's breathing," Syl whispered.

Cara knelt down, black dread pressing in from every side. She put her fingers on Zyk's neck, holding her own breath as she listened. There. A faint pulse beneath the surface.

"He's alive," she said. Her vision faded, and she knew there was something she was supposed to do. What was it?

*Breathe,* a voice in her head said.

*Okay,* she answered.

Then the darkness pulled her under.

# Chapter 18

## Dream

In Tom's dream, Cara was home.

She was sitting under a tree in the courtyard where they had played as children. In the way of dreams, it felt natural that she was there. Tom sat down beside her, tilting his face up to catch the dappled sunlight coming through the branches.

Movement caught his eye. His mother and father stood in the doorway of the house, looking out anxiously. Tom knew they were looking for Cara.

Cara had noticed them, too. She waved and smiled.

Tom waited for their shout of joy, but instead of waving back, his father said something Tom couldn't hear, and Jul started to cry.

"Mom! Dad! It's okay! I'm here!" Cara called.

They both turned away.

"They can't hear you," Tom said.

Cara turned to look at him. She didn't seem surprised that he was there.

"Can't you tell them I'm here?" she asked.

"I already did. They don't believe me." Tom pulled up a blade of kudo grass and nibbled one bitter end. "I think Mom wants to, but she's too afraid."

"Is this a dream?"

"I think so."

"But you're really here, aren't you?"

"I am if you are." Tom put the blade of grass between his lips and blew, making a piercing whistle. "Weird. That feels so real."

"How are we doing this?" She asked it without anxiety. This whole place was wrapped in dream-calm.

Tom shrugged. "Does it matter?"

"I guess not." But now she seemed uneasy. "We can't be too far away, though, right? Or how would we meet up here?"

He sighed. "I think it's far."

"Yes, but there has to be some kind of limit to how far we can reach each other."

Tom laughed. "We don't know what we're doing, or how, and already you want to make rules for it?"

"Not make rules. Understand the rules."

"What if there aren't any?"

*Then we're lost*, Cara thought.

*We already know you're lost,* Tom said.

"So you really can hear my thoughts. That's one question answered."

"You're unstoppable," Tom said, poking her in the ribs. He could feel the soft fibers of her shirt.

"We don't have to call it figuring out the rules, if that makes you uncomfortable. We can call it…making a map of new territory."

She was teasing, but her words made him sit up. "I thought of a map already, but we couldn't do it. I need more information."

"I meant a metaphorical map," she said, but he ignored her.

"Just tell me again what happened to you. Don't leave anything out this time," he said.

She did. She told him all about the rain and the suffocating darkness and suddenly finding herself standing in an unknown field. She told him about Hy and about Bree and the others. About the beasts and the fire. About the forest and finding water. About the storm.

"You've been so amazing," Tom said.

"I've been bumbling and terrified."

"You kept them all together."

"Not all of them."

Tom looked straight into her eyes. "Most people think…thought…you were all dead. This is a miracle."

"But…this place is dangerous. We don't know what's coming next."

"You're going to get home. I'll make sure of it." *I just need to figure out how to convince everyone to keep looking.*

"They're giving up?" Her voice was small, and Tom cursed himself for forgetting that she could read his thoughts.

*You always forget the rules.*

*Because you always remember them for me.*

*But now I'm not there.*

"You are. You're right here." He took her hand. It felt warm and solid in his.

"Tell me what's happening," she said.

"The investigation is still going on, and there are search parties. But we're not finding anything, Cara. And…they're planning a memorial service for you all. Cal is working on a speech about how we all need to pull together and find a way to move on. He doesn't believe that I can talk to you."

"I don't blame him. We never told him about our connection. He can't afford to believe it. He has to think about the colony."

"I do blame him. His daughters are missing, and his son is telling him that they are alive. He should *want* to believe me. He should move heaven and earth to find you."

"Even I didn't believe it at first. I thought the stress was making me crazy. Trust me, he wants to believe. He just thinks he shouldn't. We have to find a message he can't explain away." He could practically hear her brain sorting through possibilities. "Tell him…tell him that he was right about the heating units. I checked the shed the morning I disappeared. They aren't locking the door properly, and there are signs that ipits have gotten inside."

Tom couldn't suppress a snort. "That's your secret message? Ipits in a mechanical shed?"

"No one else knew he sent me to check on it."

It felt good to laugh.

She raised a brow and waited for him to finish. "If he believes you," she said when Tom was calm again, "he'll know how to convince everyone else."

"And then we can all work together to find your way home."

She nodded, but he could feel her doubt.

*148*

"We're going to find you," he said.

She stiffened for a moment as a thought came to her. "Wyn says she knows where we are."

"What?! Why didn't you say so?"

"I...it's all hazy."

"Where are you?"

She shook her head. "I don't know. We got interrupted. Zyk...he's badly hurt. We thought...."

"Cara, if we can find you, we can help him! Wake up and find out what she knows!"

Tears pricked the corners of her eyes, and he saw that she was shaking. Tom cursed himself. He sounded like his father.

"I'm sorry, Six. I'm so sorry. You're exhausted." She closed her eyes as he took her hand again. "It can wait a few hours. Stay asleep. Stay here in this dream with me."

"Just a little while. So much to do."

"Just a little while," he agreed.

She was still for so long that he thought she had fallen asleep even here in the dream.

*What Wyn knows...Tom, I don't think it's good news.*

*That's okay. Whatever it is, it's better to know.*

*Is it? I'm not sure. I...yes. It would be nice to know something. I'm so tired of not knowing. I'm so tired....*

He had never seen her like this, lost and unsure. Without her unshakeable calm, she was a different Cara.

For the first time, he realized that meant he had to be a different Tom. She needed him.

"Not all different," she whispered. "I like…the old…."

"Don't worry," he said. "I'll always be me, here to sing you that song you love. 'Double the trouble, double the fun, two is so obviously better than one….'"

A tiny smile curved her lips.

*Just rest, Six. I'm here. I'll watch over you.*

# Chapter 19

# Food

Cara woke to the sun on her face and the sound of running water. She had no idea where she was, but she was content for a moment not to remember.

The sound of voices brought her back to reality.

"He's not going to make it."

"We don't know that yet."

"There's no way to stop infection. He's so weak."

"We have water now. We'll keep the wounds clean and hope for the best."

Cara sat up, counted the figures stretched out on the ground around her.

Fourteen. All but two fast asleep. Or unconscious.

They were starving, exhausted, and wounded, but her people had all survived the night.

Standing was difficult, but Cara used the rock wall to steady herself. When the first rush of dizziness passed, she made her way over to where Lin and Syl crouched next to Zyk.

"How is he?"

"The same," Lin said.

Syl swallowed hard.

"Did you two sleep?"

"Yes, Oz kept watch until an hour ago."

In the morning light, Cara saw the slight rise and fall of Zyk's chest. The wounds were completely covered in leaf bandages now. "You've done well with him," she said.

Tears stood out in Syl's eyes, but she blinked them back. "Your arms," she said. "They need cleaning."

Cara wanted to brush off her concern, but her father's voice echoed in her head. *Know when to let others serve you. Accepting help shows that you trust them.*

"Could you take care of them for me?" she asked.

Cara sipped a cup of water as Syl worked on her left arm. It wasn't pretty. The skin was chapped and red from the wind's assault, and several nasty scrapes and bruises showed where debris had hit her during the storm. The cold water stung and then soothed and then dried, leaving the skin clean but brittle. Syl pressed cool leaves against it.

As the girl went to work on Cara's right arm, Cara thought about her dream. Tom said they had done experiments and were sure about the connection. If they altered a living organism with the healing water, a few drops of rainwater made it disappear.

So now they knew why they were here. The next step was figuring out where here was.

Her stomach growled painfully. Strike that. The next step was finding something to eat, so they wouldn't starve to death while they figured out where they were.

The hunger drew her attention to all the other aches and pains of her body. She hurt everywhere. Her throbbing head felt like it would swim off her shoulders. Even after Syl's careful work, her arms burned.

"This will heal in a few days if we can keep infection away," Syl said. She bit her lip. "Infection is the biggest danger for everyone now."

"Slightly less scary than vicious monsters," Lin said.

"Just as deadly, though."

Cara put a hand on the girl's shoulder. "We're going to figure this out. One thing at a time."

"One thing at a time," Syl repeated.

"Jem is our best resource for finding food and potential medicines. Ag engineers have a strong base in botany."

"Should I wake him?"

"I'll do it in a minute. First give me the medical updates. Who needs special attention? Who is still strong enough to work?"

Syl squared her shoulders and talked through the group. Oz and Lin were the strongest, having been protected during the storm. Lin's shoulder was injured from the first attack, but it wasn't deep enough to stop her. The children were unharmed but the exhaustion and lack of food affected them the most. They were very weak. Syl, Pol, and Lil all had minor injuries but were more or less fully functional. Jem, Ann, and Wyn were torn up from the storm. Their backs and limbs would heal if infection didn't set in, and they were all conscious, but they wouldn't be able to move much for a few days.

Bree was still struggling to breathe. Her airway was swollen to only a tiny opening, and the air here was just not enough for her. Oz had gathered more leaf pods, and Jak gave her oxygen from them every hour or so. She was holding steady, but still hadn't come awake for more than a few eye-fluttering moments at a time. Jak's leg wound was serious. Walking on it had made it worse. Syl was worried that it was already infected, though Jak didn't show signs of fever yet, so maybe she was wrong.

No one mentioned Zyk.

"You've done well," Cara said. "Today, everyone with significant injuries rests. Plenty of water, plenty of sleep. You are in charge of medical care, and Lil and Pol can help you keep wounds clean and everyone hydrated. When no one has any particular needs, you three should also rest as much as possible."

That left Cara, Oz, and Lin to secure the shelter and find some kind of food. Jem could advise them on the latter. Hopefully.

Cara pushed to her feet. "Food is our priority, and then improving our shelter. Any ideas?"

"I haven't seen any animals since we arrived," Lin said, "other than the ones that attacked us, and I'm not going to hunt down one of those. Some of these plants might be edible, but I don't recognize anything. I couldn't tell you what's safe."

"We'll search the area around the grotto. Maybe we'll notice something familiar when we're not running for our lives or dying of thirst."

"I appreciate the assumption that we won't be doing either of those things today."

"'Always focus on the most optimistic outcome that lies within the realm of realism.'"

"Your father is a fountain of wisdom."

*154*

"That was my grandmother."

"In that case, I stand by the words and retract the sarcasm."

"He's a good man, you know. A good leader." Cara wasn't sure why she felt the need to defend him. It hardly seemed relevant standing in an unfamiliar forest far from home. But his voice in her head had kept her alive so far.

"I know," Lin said. She didn't add the "but" out loud. "Want to scout for a bit while the others sleep?"

Oz looked up as they passed. Cara nodded, and he joined them.

They headed into the woods, gathering plants, branches, and fungi as they went. None of them were species Cara recognized, but there was still a chance that Jem would.

When they were far enough from the grotto that they wouldn't be overheard, she told Oz and Lin about her dream. It was Oz's first time hearing of Cara's connection to Tom, but he accepted it without question. Lin, on the other hand, questioned everything and made her repeat Tom's words several times.

When she was satisfied, she gave a tight nod. "I don't know how you're doing this, but it's definitely Tom."

"So our families know we're alive." Oz said.

"They will soon."

"Which means we need to stay alive," Lin said. "Let's get these plants back to Jem and find out what we can eat."

Their friends were awake, though most still sat with blank, exhausted faces. Syl and Lil moved through the group, offering leaf cups of water to each person in turn.

Jem was at the back of the grotto, lying on his side.

Cara knelt next to him. "How are you?"

"I'll survive," he answered. "That boy make it through?"

"He's in bad shape, but he's alive."

"Gonna need antibiotics."

Cara held out the plants. "We gathered as many as we could find. Recognize anything?"

"Help me sit up."

She and Lin made a neat pile of the samples before each taking one of Jem's arms and lifting him into an upright position. Syl hurried over, but Jem waved her back.

"I'm fine. Doesn't hurt any worse like this."

Syl nodded, her face tight as she watched him pick through the plants.

"I can't identify any of the species," Jem said. Cara's heart sank. "But we have knowledge of the flora of two planets, which has taught us something about naturally occurring universal patterns. This and this." He held up a knot of red berries and a spiral shaped fungus. "Could be food, but more likely toxic. Keep them away from the children."

Cara set them aside as he continued to sort.

He found a feathery leaf, sniffed it, then rubbed the ends between two fingers.

"Where is this from? A shrub? A vine?"

"Under the trees, growing out of the ground."

"Next one of these you find, dig up the roots. It looks like the top of a root vegetable that might be edible."

Cara felt stupid for not thinking of roots.

"This one here." Now he was holding up a cluster of tiny leaves that had come off a short bush. "Smell it."

It had a tangy odor. Cara breathed it in and then sneezed violently.

Jem laughed. "That's a good sign, actually. It's some kind of herb, but there's no way to know what effect it has except by trying it out."

In just a few minutes, he had three piles. One, with the berries and a few fungi, which he said should be avoided. The largest pile, mostly different kinds of leaves, which he said were harmless but also useless. The final pile had two herbs and the feathery root top. He said he'd experiment carefully with the herbs while they went back to work.

"Don't do anything dangerous," Cara said.

Jem just raised one brow at her.

"Well...don't be reckless," she amended.

"I never am. Except this one time I let a doctor heal me with miracle water."

Cara glanced over at her sister, still stretched out on the ground. Jak sat sleeping against the stone wall next to her.

Wyn was on the other side, watching Cara with dark eyes.

It was as good a time for answers as any.

"How is your back?" Cara asked as she approached the older woman.

Wyn shrugged like her injuries were unimportant, though the motion caused her to wince.

Cara took a deep breath. "Yesterday. You said you knew...."

"Where we are," Wyn finished for her. "It was the windstorm. The stars were...but I still thought...and then the wind. It was an eclipse. Exactly like our model."

"I don't understand."

"I told you we're far from home. But I didn't know then...Still, it makes sense...the flora and fauna...."

"Wyn," Cara said. "You aren't answering the question. Where are we?"

"Dua," Wyn whispered. "We're on Dua."

For a second the words made no impact on Cara's brain at all. Then she leaned back. "That's…not possible."

Dua was Una's sister planet, separated by hundreds of thousands of kilometers and the vacuum of space.

"No," Wyn said. "It's not possible."

"So why did you say it?"

"Because it's true."

"It can't be."

Wyn didn't argue. She just looked at Cara with the eyes of someone who has seen their world remade before. Cara thought of Wyn's earlier rambling. The plants. The animals. They were in an entirely different ecosystem. Wyn was a respected astronomer. If she didn't recognize the stars….

"What was that about the windstorm?"

"We've been observing them for decades. They sweep across Dua's continent. We think…we believe they are caused by the solar eclipse…when Una blocks the sun…the temperature drops."

Exactly what had happened yesterday. The darkness. The cold.

"It can't be."

Wyn shook her head.

"Don't tell anyone," Cara said softly. When Wyn didn't respond, she added, "We don't know for sure."

"It doesn't mean there's no hope," Wyn said.

Cara couldn't think about hope. She was still trying to wrap her mind around the impossible.

She looked up, saw Jak watching her across Bree's sleeping form.

He had heard, and his haunted eyes showed that he believed it.

The extra weight of his look was too much to bear. Cara put the whole problem in a back corner of her mind and closed the door on it. Survival was their first priority. Everything else could wait.

"You'll keep quiet?" she asked Jak.

He nodded wearily as a hand on her shoulder made Cara jump.

"We're ready to go," Oz said.

Good. Work was what she needed.

It wasn't long before they discovered more of the feathery greens among some tree roots. Oz dug under them with a stick and found, as Jem predicted, a pair of thick, starchy tubers. They gathered a handful and hunted for more, but the farther they went from the grotto, the more storm damage they encountered. It was hard to see the low-growing plants under the mess of fallen greenery.

Eventually, they carried what they had back to the grotto, where Jem examined them. He was fairly certain that they were safe, and everyone agreed without hesitation that it was worth the risk. They were weak with hunger.

Oz built a fire, and Syl roasted the handful of roots they had found. When they were ready, Cara insisted on being the first to test them.

The pale yellow flesh was soft now and mealy. She took an experimental bite, ready to make herself spit it back up if necessary. It had a slightly smoky flavor from the fire but was otherwise bland. Her stomach growled as the food hit it, then churned a little as if it had forgotten what to do. Otherwise, she felt no ill-effects.

On Jak's advice, she ate a few more bites, and then they all waited half an hour to make sure she hadn't been poisoned.

It was painful to see the eager hunger on each face as they eyed the small pile of roots. At last, Jem said it was safe, and everyone quickly divvied up the food.

There were sighs of relief and even a few laughs as everyone ate, but it was done all too soon. Cara hadn't eaten any more than those first few bites, and she knew the others were as unsatisfied as she was.

Still, no one complained. Instead, their faces looked hopeful for the first time since they had arrived here. Even if it wasn't much, they had a source of food. They had water and a shelter, however incomplete. Somehow, they had survived two full days in this foreign place.

It felt like a promise that they could survive more.

Cara looked around at the little group. Lin and Pol were passing out water in rough bark cups. Several people murmured their gratitude. Syl was changing Jem's bandages, and she laughed at something he said. Ann lifted up a mat she had woven from long plant fibers, and Lil gave a quiet exclamation of wonder.

These people deserved to live. They deserved to go home to their families.

*Tom*, Cara thought. *You have to convince them. We need their help to find a way home.*

There was no answer but the twinkling of unknown stars above.

# Chapter 20

# Proof

In the grey light before sunrise, Tom found his father standing at the back door. He had a cup of tea held in both hands, and he stared out into the courtyard just as he had in Tom's dream. For a minute, Tom believed that if he looked over Cal's shoulder, he would see Cara sitting under the maki tree.

"I talked to her again last night," he said.

Cal didn't turn around, but his shoulder slumped.

Still thinking of the dream, Tom forced himself to imagine what his father must feel. Cal believed his daughters were dead and his son was having grief-stricken hallucinations. Bree was her father's heart, and Cara was his life. Now Tom was all he had left, and he was damaged.

"I understand why you don't believe me," Tom said. "Cara...she said if she were you, she wouldn't believe either. So she gave me a message for you."

Tom hesitated, but Cal still didn't turn. "She said to tell you that you were right about the heating units. She checked the shed the morning she disappeared. They aren't locking the door properly and there are signs that ipits have gotten inside. She said only you would understand, that you and she were the only ones who knew she went there."

When Cal didn't respond, Tom went to stand next to him. The empty courtyard was too hard to face, so Tom turned toward his father.

A tear made a trail down Cal's cheek.

"It's really her, Dad," Tom said. "She's alive, and she wants to get back to you."

There was a long pause. Then Cal nodded, and turned away. He set his tea on the table and picked up his tablet instead, typing away for a few minutes.

Tom waited, unsure of his next move.

"There's no record of her visit to the shed. It's not on her schedule or checklist, either."

There was no holding back the anger. "Seriously? That's your problem? You can't believe she might have done something without documenting it?"

Cal looked up. "No. I'm sure she did. The lack of documentation means there is no other way you could have known."

The abrupt change of direction made Tom's head spin. "So you do believe me now?"

Cal took a deep breath, released it explosively. "I don't know. Now I believe…that it may be possible."

Tom's laugh didn't carry much humor. "It *may* be possible. I just gave you proof. What would it take for you to actually believe?"

"My belief isn't what matters, Son. That is what you never seem to understand. You want me to believe in my heart that my daughter is alive? Okay. For the first time, I might be able to allow myself to do that. I can have hope that she is out there, that both of them are out there. All of them even. But my personal trust is not what you really want, is it? It isn't what you need, or what anyone needs. The proof you gave is only proof to me. It won't give me the complete confidence to act because it won't give me the ability to convince others. I can't act without the agreement of the colony. And without action, my personal belief means nothing."

"What's going on?" Jul asked, emerging from her bedroom wearing rumpled work clothes from the day before. There were dark circles under her eyes.

Cal gestured at his son, so Tom explained.

When he finished, Jul looked a question at her husband. He nodded, and she started to cry. Cal wrapped his arms around her.

"I knew it," she said into his chest. "I knew it. I knew my girls couldn't just be gone."

Cal closed his eyes, and Tom saw how much Jul's hope pained him.

"It's a long way from knowing they're alive to finding them and bringing them home."

She pulled back, wiping her eyes. "No," she said. "We all know what we're up against, and no one is suggesting the danger is past, but you aren't going to take away the joy of this moment. They are alive. Now we know it and we have contact with them. That's more than I dared hope for yesterday."

It hurt a little that she believed Cal so implicitly when she hadn't believed Tom, but when she turned those red-rimmed eyes on him, Tom couldn't be angry.

"I'm sorry I didn't trust you. I hope you understand why I didn't think I could."

He nodded.

"Now tell me everything Cara said."

As Tom told the story, Jul poured tea for everyone and took out a packet of protein bars. By the time he was describing the storm they survived, though, she had forgotten all about breakfast and was pacing around their living area.

"Infection is going to be a real problem," she said when he fell silent. "Especially for the animal wounds. They might be able to create a crude antibiotic from molds, which they can grow themselves. I'll give you detailed instructions to pass on to Cara. And I'm concerned that Bree's asthma attack is lasting so long. If they are at high altitude, which the lack of oxygen suggests, then it isn't surprising that she would have a more severe problem than normal, but with regular applications of oxygen as you described, she ought to be recovering by now. I wonder if there is some other environmental allergen that's causing her body to shut down. Jak should explore that possibility, see if there's a way to isolate her from whatever it is."

"Mom," Tom said. "I'll pass on any messages you want, but wherever they are, everything is different. All the plants, the animals, even the air. The trees Cara described...they can't grow in any place we know of. Isolating allergens isn't an option. We just need to focus on bringing them home."

"We will," she said. "But we also have to keep them alive in the meantime. Field medicine is not my specialty, but there are a few of the staff who have studied it more. They'll be able to provide better ideas than I can."

"We can't include those people until we've brought the heads of the key science teams on board," Cal said. "It won't be any easier for them to trust me than it was for us to trust Tom without proof. We have to approach this cautiously."

"I could get more personal messages from the others with Cara. Convince some of the families and co-workers. The more people who get messages that have to be from the disappeared, the more proof we have that we're actually talking to them."

"Maybe," Cal said. "But that kind of personal testimony from people who are emotionally connected is only going to get us so far. We need the team heads to listen, to question, and to be satisfied that this is real. Once they are convinced, their teams will have an easier time believing."

"We'll start there if you want," Tom said, "but we have to tell the families of the disappeared, too. They deserve to know their loved ones are alive."

"No. It's too many people. It would be the same as telling everyone. Word would spread, and if people have doubts or find it impossible to believe, it could divide the whole colony."

"You didn't hear the families talking. They had this gathering last night."

"I was informed about it," Cal said.

Informed, Tom noted, not invited.

"You weren't there, though. They are all hurting. They talked about the pain of not knowing. They are clinging to belief, but it's killing them. And a lot of them are blaming you. Blaming me. Blaming the doctors. That's got to be more dangerous than them knowing."

"I do know their pain. My own daughters are missing. I have talked to each of the families personally. Knowing those they have lost are still alive may ease the pain for now, but it won't stop the blame. Their sons and daughters, sisters and brothers, are still lost, and we don't have any plan to recover them. We are still on very shaky ground."

"Your father is right," Jul said. "Meet with the team heads today, and bring them around. The two of you together are very convincing. It may be that we can have a plan for telling everyone by tonight."

Tom bit his lip. It went against everything in him to keep secrets. But they weren't really keeping secrets, were they? They were just telling a few people at a time.

Finally, he nodded. "Soon, though."

Cal was already typing. "I'm setting up the meeting right now."

# Chapter 21

# *Sustenance*

Gnawing hunger dragged Cara out of sleep. The ravenous feeling was worse than yesterday, as if those few bites of root had reminded her body of its need.

She pushed to her feet, thankful that the ache in her shoulder and stinging of her arms and legs felt better today. Her muscles were stiff and sore, but that seemed like nothing compared to the gaping emptiness inside.

Oz and Lin were already awake, leaning against the rocks nearby.

"Today we find more food," she said as she joined them.

"I hope that's a promise," Lin said.

"Me, too," Cara answered.

"Any more dreams?" Oz asked.

Cara shook her head. "Not the kind you mean. I can still feel Tom, but he hasn't said anything since yesterday morning."

"Do you think your father believed him?"

"I…yes, I do."

Lin raised a brow. "But…."

"But I'm afraid it won't matter what anyone believes."

Oz's dark eyes watched her. "You know something?"

"I don't know anything. That's the problem. But Wyn…Wyn thinks she knows where we are."

She told them.

When she finished, Oz said nothing, drumming his fingers on his leg as he digested the idea.

The nervous action made Cara twitchy. "I told her not to tell anyone because I don't see how she can be right."

"But if she is?" Lin asked.

"Then getting home isn't going to be as simple as we hoped."

"Which means finding a way to survive here is even more important," Oz said.

Lin nodded grimly. "So we're back where we started. Today we look for more food."

"Yes," said Cara. "We don't need to worry about where we are yet. Today, we just send out everyone who can walk in groups to search for roots. Last night wasn't even a full meal. We need as many as we can find."

It was a good plan, but it turned out to be useless.

Even though they split into four pairs and scoured the forest floor within a two-kilometer radius of their new camp, they only found enough roots for one small meal by midday.

Cara let Ann take charge of cooking what they'd found, while she, Oz, and Lin huddled near Jem.

"There aren't enough roots nearby. We're going to keep searching, but if they grow this sparsely, we need to find another source of food."

"We can send a smaller group out further to search," Oz said. "Even if they have to travel a couple of days, we can survive on what we have."

"Ideally we need to find animal life. The protein would serve us better, and fauna is less likely to be poisonous," said Jem.

"It's dangerous for a small group to range far from the shelter overnight," said Cara. "Possibly more dangerous than attempting to eat strange leaves."

"But the reward is higher," Jem said. "Even if some of these leaves are edible, they won't provide enough calories to sustain us."

No one spoke for a few minutes.

"How is Zyk?" Oz asked. Since he couldn't walk without pain, Jem had been watching over the sick.

"No better. Probably worse. We've been giving him as much water as we can and keeping the wounds clean, but he's feverish. We can't see the infection yet, but it's there."

"And none of these plants can help?" Cara asked.

"I don't think so."

"Okay. We'll try again this afternoon to search nearby. Even if we don't find more roots, we may find other plants that could help."

"Look for animal signs, too," Jem added.

Cara nodded. "And unless we find more than expected, tomorrow we'll send the smaller group at first light. Those who stay can continue to search locally and to fortify the shelter."

"No sign of the beasts since the storm," Jem said.

"It might be better if they came," Lin answered. "Once we killed them, we could eat them."

Cara looked pointedly at Zyk, and Lin shrugged. "I know. I didn't say it would be good. Just better than starving. Unless we get magically transported back home, there's no good at this point."

Her words stuck with Cara all afternoon. She led Pol and little Em through the forest, digging under fallen leaves for roots and overturning logs in search of mold or useful fungi. It wasn't the knowledge that all their options were bad that haunted her. She had accepted that two days ago. It was the idea of being magically transported back home.

How had they gotten here? No scientific principle that Cara had ever been taught could explain what had happened. Did that mean there really was magic in the universe? And if so, who controlled it? Did anyone? Did it follow laws or was it random?

The more questions Cara asked, the less answers she had. As the afternoon wore on, the calm she had created by ceaseless action was battered by a whirlwind of confusion.

When darkness fell, she led the way back to the shelter with only a handful of edible roots and two moldering sticks that were probably worthless. Outside the grotto, she paused and looked up. Dua was a sliver on the horizon, most of her light still hidden behind the trees.

Or was that Una?

The thought made Cara feel dizzy.

*Tom. Are you here somewhere? Or is that you up there?*

*Cara?* A flood of relief came through the connection, followed by concern. *What happened? Where have you been? I've been trying to reach you, but you didn't answer.*

*I tried to reach you, too.*

# TWIN

*Our connection comes and goes. I can't tell why.*

Cara looked up at the planet rising in the distance and shivered.

*Your message convinced Cal. He believes me now, and he and Mom send their love. He's still being himself, though. He's worried that no one else will believe and that they'll lose confidence in him. He wants to control the message. He spent all day yesterday gathering evidence and dropping hints to people while making me promise to say nothing without his permission. He finally set up a meeting this morning with a few scientists he wants to convince first.*

*He's right.* She didn't bother to hide that it was a reprimand. *This will be hard for people to believe, and we need them fully on our side. I need their help. I'm wandering around like a blind person here. Dad knows what he's doing.*

*He's just as lost as the rest of us. You have to know that.*

*He may not have the map we need, but he has the field guide. That's better than nothing.*

*There's no field guide for this, Cara.*

She felt a surge of anger. Did he think she didn't know that this was light-years away from anyone's experience? Did he think it helped to dwell on that? Was she not terrified enough for him? Was his resentment toward their father more important than her tenuous grasp on her sanity?

Cara's self-control cracked.

She retreated a few meters into the forest as all of the shock and fear, horror and homesickness of the last few days came flooding out of the boxes where she had carefully locked them. She knew she needed to stay focused on their survival, that she couldn't afford the luxury of emotion right now, but in the dark under the trees, she let down her guard for just a moment. She let Tom feel it all.

It was a mistake.

Her body was too depleted for tears, but it had other ways of falling apart. She began to tremble all over, waves of hot and cold sweeping through her. She slid to the ground under a tree and curled over her knees, pulling herself in tight as her whole body shook. Her thoughts flew in a million directions. She broke into pieces.

*Six! I'm sorry. I should have...I'm so, so sorry.*

She couldn't bring herself to respond, and after a while Tom's voice faded, leaving only her shattered thoughts.

In the end, the thin air saved her. All other sensations were pushed away by the desperate feeling that she couldn't breathe. Every instinct screamed, and Cara sucked in air as if it were the only thing in the world. Maybe it was.

The breathing slowly steadied her heart and cleared her head. She still shivered but not as violently as before.

She had no idea how long she sat there pulling herself together before she heard footsteps. When she looked up, Oz was watching her quietly.

She wanted to say something, make a light excuse, assure him that she was fine, but her voice wouldn't work.

He didn't speak either, just stepped in and sat down beside her, close enough that his arm brushed hers. He must have felt her trembling, but he didn't ask questions.

A long time passed. His silent presence was an anchor in a strange sea. The point where their arms touched felt like the only solid thing in her world. Slowly, her trembling stopped.

Just as she was beginning to search for words, he said, "There was enough for everyone to eat a little."

Cara tried to answer, cleared her throat, tried again. "Good."

"Ann saved some for you."

The thought of food was repulsive, but Cara needed strength. She nodded.

When he didn't speak again for a while, she knew he was waiting for her. It was time to go back, to reassure everyone and make plans for tomorrow. She should tell him she was ready.

"Nothing makes sense here," she said instead.

He didn't answer, and she felt like a fool. This was no time to share her doubts. She opened her mouth to apologize.

"Not yet," he said, "but it will."

It was an empty promise.

"I don't think I believe that."

"That's because you're trying to believe it on your own. You want to be strong for the others, but you should tell them what you fear. They could help."

"I have no hope to give them. We don't even know where we are. Only that it's impossibly far from home."

"Except it wasn't impossible. We're here."

"Magically transported."

"I think magic is an interesting idea," he said. "We use the word 'magical' as if it were the opposite of scientific, but we also use it to describe something wonderful. The last one makes more sense to me. Just because something is unpredictable and beyond our understanding doesn't mean it doesn't follow rules or couldn't be understood scientifically someday. If we were transported in a wonderful way once, couldn't we be again? And in the meantime, the chance to discover new patterns and learn new rules could be a wonderful adventure."

Cara stared at Oz in the darkness. She had never heard him say so many words at once. A sudden urge to kiss him seized her, but she pushed it away.

"It's only a wonderful adventure if we live to see home again," she said.

His smile disagreed, but his only answer was to stand and hold out a hand. "So let's live."

Back in the grotto, Cara gathered everyone together.

"There isn't enough food nearby to keep everyone fed, so tomorrow a couple of us are going to make a longer trek to search for more. I will go with Lin, and Jem, too, if he's up for it."

Jem nodded.

"You can help us identify what we find. We'll walk until we find something, or until night. Then we'll come back the next day. The rest of you will stay here and work on building up an outer wall. Oz will be in charge." Cara bit her lip. "I hate splitting up with no way to communicate, but...."

"When the only other option is waiting around to starve, splitting up doesn't seem so bad."

"It's good you're here, Lin," Cara said. "We need someone cheerful to keep our spirits up."

"Happy to help."

Cara took a deep breath. "There are a couple of other things I need to tell you about, and they might be hard to believe, so bear with me."

"Just say it," said Lin. "Without you, we'd all be dead already. We'd believe you if you said unicorns were coming to rescue us."

It wasn't true, of course. Oz and Lin and Jem and Jak were the ones who knew what they were doing. Still, Cara's throat swelled with emotion.

When she could talk again, she told them about communicating with Tom.

Incredibly, Lin was right. Not only did everyone believe her, no one even questioned what she told them. But the hope that now lit their faces was more terrifying than doubt could ever be.

"So now they know we're alive? And they can come and find us?" Lil asked.

"Tom knows. He'll find a way to explain it to the others."

"But they have to believe him, right? I mean, you gave them a secret password or something?" Pol's face was shining.

"Yes, my father is convinced. But it might take time to help everyone understand."

"People think it's just pretend," Em said.

"They might at first, but Tom will help them believe."

"Mommy didn't believe us."

Cara's spine tingled. "What do you mean?"

Em looked down.

Hal took her hand. "We told her that Em could hear me even when I wasn't there. She said it was our imagination."

Cara gaped at the children. "You two can talk to each other in your heads?"

Hal nodded. "Em is better at listening, and I'm better at talking, but sometimes we can do both."

No one spoke for a long time.

"That can't be a coincidence," Lin said finally.

"They're twins," said Jak.

"It's a twin thing?" Lil asked.

Out of the corner of her eye, Cara saw Wyn sway.

"Wyn!" she said.

Syl rushed over just as Wyn slumped to the ground. Her eyes were open, but her breathing was shallow.

"Is she okay?"

"Wyn? Can you hear me? What happened?"

For several heartbeats, the woman didn't move, then she blinked and gasped in a breath.

"Wyn?"

Wyn sat up, looking around in confusion.

"Are you all right?" Syl asked.

"I…yes,I…sorry." Wyn was pale, but slowly she composed herself. "I'm…fine."

"Sit over here. Rest for a while," Syl said, leading her to a spot next to the wall.

"We're all tired and weak," Cara said. "That's why we're focusing on the search for food."

"But now that we can talk to home, they'll be coming to find us soon, right?" Pol asked.

Cara looked at Lin and Oz. Oz gave her a nod, but Lin's face was tense.

She couldn't tell them they might not even be on Una. Not yet. Not when they still didn't have enough food to last past tomorrow.

"We don't know how long it will be," Cara said, "so for now, we'll have to work hard to survive. That part is still up to us."

The determined nods around the circle told her she had made the right decision. Most of them were just kids. They weren't ready for the burden of knowing everything.

Lin looked relieved as Cara began handing out assignments for the next day.

If Oz was disappointed, he didn't say anything.

# Chapter 22

# *Truth*

"I asked Tom to make his report to you first because I'd like your insight before we share this with the rest of the colony."

Cal's voice carried all its usual calming authority, but Tom recognized his stiff posture and precise gestures for what they were. The governor was nervous.

The guilt Tom had felt since causing Cara's breakdown threatened to choke him. He was an idiot to think that the careful control his father and sister displayed meant they didn't feel things as much as he did. He knew better now. The faint presence of Cara's fear and anger was a constant reminder. *I'm sorry, Six,* he said for the hundredth time, but he knew she couldn't hear him. The connection had faded again.

"A revelation of this magnitude coming on the heels of the disappearance of our people will cause panic if we don't handle it correctly. I'd like to understand the phenomenon as much as possible in order to communicate it in a way that allays fears. I've asked you here because I believe you are the best people to help achieve that understanding."

"You certainly have us intrigued now," said Gal. She was the head of the biology department and was known for a tongue as sharp as her mind.

Nev, the head psychologist, just steepled his hands together and put on his professional listening face.

How many times had Tom seen that face during his psych evaluations before and after missions? How many times had he made fun of it to Lin or to Cara? Now he'd give anything to know what the man was thinking behind that mask.

The only other person in the room was the head of communications, Vern Trumble. He shifted in his seat and looked profoundly uncomfortable. Tom was grateful that he wasn't the only one.

Cal gestured at his son to begin, and Tom tried to imitate his father's calm.

"I'll tell you everything just as it's happened from the moment of the disappearances, but I do want to make one thing clear first. This is something new, but I won't say that it was completely unexpected. All our lives, Cara and I been able to…sense each other. I could tell what she was feeling and more or less where she was at any time. Mostly, we ignored that, choosing to block it rather than think too much about what it meant, but we both knew it was real, and we accepted it, though Cara, especially, was never comfortable with the idea. I think it's important that you understand the connection that's always been there, because it helps to make sense of the rest."

Gal's thoughtful nod was encouraging, and Vern's look of confusion was no more than what Tom had expected. It was Nev's guarded hostility that sent a cold shiver down his spine.

He reached out to the distant presence of Cara's exhaustion and steeled himself to the task. For her sake, for Lin and Bree and Jak, he had to make these people understand.

*Okay, Six. How would you do this?*

Focusing on Cara helped him lay out the story calmly and logically, even the parts that defied belief. He did his best to keep the passionate urging out of his voice and to choose words that made him sound sane and reasonable.

He wished he could tell if it was working.

At the very least, it accomplished the purpose of getting them to listen. No one interrupted his story to scoff or question. In fact, they didn't react at all. Each person sat in the same attitude they had when he began. The longer he talked, the more he had the panicked feeling that they couldn't hear him.

"The rain transported them somewhere far away, but as long as they are alive, we can still find them. My direct communication with Cara gives us a way to work on the problem together. We may not fully understand how all this is possible, but we can get our people back, which is the most important thing."

There really was nothing more to say, but he wanted to go on, to fill the silence with convincing words. Instead, he bit his cheek and waited for a reaction.

Vern shook his head, looking more bewildered than ever. Gal studied Tom like he was an alien specimen under her microscope.

"Thank you for sharing, Tom," said Nev in his smooth, clinical voice. "Could you perhaps give us the room for a few moments, so we can discuss this with the governor?"

Cal answered for him. "I don't think that's necessary, Nev. If you have concerns or questions, there is no reason that Tom shouldn't hear them himself."

"Respectfully, Governor, I disagree with that assessment, and you will hopefully admit that this is my area of expertise," the psychologist said.

"It is, and that is why your thoughts have due weight in this situation, but I hope you will admit that this is not only an issue of vital importance to the entire colony but is also intensely personal to my family, and my wishes as to how we conduct the conversation should be respected."

Tom had never seen his father clash so openly with one of his peers. The two older men stared at each other with polite expressions and eyes of unbending steel. Nev looked away first.

"Of course," he said. "I was only hoping to spare Tom further pain."

Cal ignored the sentiment. "I assure you, Tom will listen to you as respectfully as you have listened to him."

"Of course." The psychologist paused for a moment as if choosing his words carefully. Tom felt a sudden storm of dread sweep in.

"This is not the first time I have heard a patient describe the phenomenon of being able to 'hear' another person in their head." He held up a hand when Tom started to speak. "Not just a voice, but a specific person as you have described. As a matter of fact, it was also a sibling, a twin." Nev's look was one of pure pity. "I'm speaking, of course, of Ny Lee."

Everyone in the room recoiled at the name.

Tom's heart sank. He might not have memorized the entire history of Mayland like Cara had, but every kid knew the story of Ny Lee, the only would-be murderer since the founding.

It was his twin sister Wyn he attacked, and he claimed she had stolen his ideas right out of his head and passed them off as her own work.

*She probably did*, Tom thought. *She probably read his mind, and no one believed him*. He was smart enough not to say that out loud.

"I also noted the similarities in their stories," Cal said carefully. "The key difference here is that Tom received information that could only have come from Cara. Specific instructions that I gave her which a delusion could not have reproduced."

"That's exactly how rumors of mental telepathy are always propagated, but science has proven over and over that even when intentional fraud is not the case, the knowledge of supposedly secret information is invariably the brain's informed deduction based on context clues that often even the person in question is unaware of having perceived. Combine this with a small dose of coincidence, and apparent prescience is the result."

"I didn't see any clues that Cara was checking a storage shed for rodents," Tom said.

"Not that you remember. But the brain is a complicated place."

"I'm not imagining Cara's voice. It's her. As different from my own thoughts as she is from me."

"Multiple personalities are always distinct, and often modeled closely on individuals that have greatly impacted the patient."

"Patient?" Tom knew that getting angry wouldn't help his case. He clenched his jaw as his father leaned back in his chair, studying the psychologist.

"I certainly understand your theory, Nev, and I appreciate your professional skepticism. We need that kind of objectivity if we're to proceed appropriately. I would like to point out that we can only call it objectivity, however, if we are also holding open the possibility that Tom's interpretation of events is the accurate one. After all, we have seen equally impossible events occur in the last weeks, beginning with the healing water and through the disappearance of 15 of our citizens, with dozens of witnesses on hand."

Nev's eyes were narrowed, his hands now folded tensely on the table in front of him. The others looked frozen.

After a long moment, Nev nodded slightly. "I'm willing to grant the point, for the sake of objectivity. I will repeat, though, that I spent weeks speaking with Ny Lee and studying his mind. The fact that his delusions led to violence was, in my professional opinion, an inevitable progression. It would be foolish not to proceed with caution here."

"You think I'm going to become violent?" Tom said. Maybe Nev wasn't wrong about everything.

"Honestly, yes. And I think you would find it completely reasonable and justified when it happened."

The man had a point.

"What do you propose?" Cal asked, putting one hand on his son's shoulder. To an outside observer, it might have seemed like a show of solidarity, but Tom knew his father was trying to restrain him.

"Give me a few days with Tom. Let me conduct the same interviews and tests I did with Mr. Lee. There is a medication we synthesized for Ny near the end which helped him a great deal. Let's see what effect it would have on Tom. If I am wrong, and this is no delusion, careful study of his reaction to the medication should reveal that."

"No way." Tom shook off his father's hand. "You are not drugging me. You want to interview me, fine. Interview me. We're wasting time that could and should be spent rescuing my sisters and the others who disappeared, but I understand that this is a lot to take in. So we can keep talking if that's what you need, but I am not taking any drugs. I need my head clear. It's the only connection we have to those we lost."

Nev turned a look of sad understanding to Cal. "You see? The delusions are always precious and to be protected at all cost."

"I see that his reaction would also be reasonable if he really was able to communicate with his sister."

"Perhaps. And I know how much you want his delusions to be real."

There was a dangerous edge to these last words, and Tom felt his father stiffen.

"You may conduct whatever studies you deem necessary. Including the medication." He squeezed Tom's shoulder tightly. "But five days is all I am granting. The disappeared have already been gone too long."

Nev's smug smile made Tom want to hit him. "Five days may not be enough for conclusive results," he cautioned. "But I'll certainly do my best."

"I'm sure you will," Cal said.

"Father…."

Cal's hand was now a vise that shot pain down Tom's arm. "Thank you all for your time. We'll meet again each evening to discuss Nev's findings from the day. If any of you have other tests you'd like to run or if you'd like to meet with Tom for more questions, you are free to do so. We'll work out the schedule. For right now, could you give me a few minutes alone with my son?"

Gal nodded professionally and was the first one out of the room. Vern scuttled after her like a mouse escaping a cat. Nev took his time gathering his things together before stepping to the door.

"I'll wait outside to take him to my office?" It wasn't really a question.

"Yes. A few minutes is all we need."

When the door shut behind the psychologist, Tom tore himself from his father's grip. "This is insane," he said. "You have to see what a waste of time this is. And giving me medication? Do you even know what it is? What it might do to me? If he finds a way to destroy this connection, we'll never see Cara and Bree again."

"This is necessary," his father answered. "I told you this revelation might make people lose confidence in us, and I was right. Nev is personally invested in disbelieving you. The work he did with Ny Lee led directly to his becoming head of his team. He doesn't want to reconsider his conclusions, and he is a well-respected scientist who can sway many people. The colony is already in crisis. We can't afford infighting. We need to win the scientists over by using science and not emotional appeals. Of course I will demand all the data on this medication and will monitor everything closely, but you WILL cooperate. We can only help your sisters if we have these people on our side. Do you understand me?"

"He's not going to believe me. It doesn't matter what I say or do."

"It's not about him. It's about all the others. Did you watch Gal and Vern? They still don't know what to think. They must see that we believe with enough confidence to put it to the test."

"Do you? Believe me that confidently?"

Cal hesitated, and Tom threw up his hands with a noise of disgust.

"I believe you, but I won't deny that I have some doubts, son. And you should be glad I do. Because if I can be convinced, so can others. So convince me."

Tom faced his father eye to eye and realized for the first time that he was slightly taller now. "Your daughters are lost and starving. There isn't enough oxygen, and Bree has been unconscious for days. I will do anything to help them. Even this. But if it doesn't work, if you decide to do nothing at all, I will find them on my own. And once I know they are safe, I will leave here, and I will never come back."

Cal didn't so much as twitch. Reaching behind him, he opened the door and turned to face the psychologist waiting outside.

"He's ready for you," he said. Then he walked away without a backward glance.

# Chapter 23

# *Healing*

The food gathering team left at first light the next day, and they took little Hal with them. His connection with Em meant that they would be able to communicate with the main group. Cara hated using the children as communication devices, but they weren't in a position to overlook any of their resources.

Having the boy along changed everything. They moved slowly for Jem's sake, and Hal darted back and forth under the trees as they walked, hunting for more root vegetables and occasionally bringing back new plant varieties to show the adults. His enthusiasm was more helpful than his discoveries.

Lin led, marking their trail and hunting unsuccessfully for signs of animal life. Every hour, Cara stopped them so that Jem could rest and everyone could drink. They used the time to sort through any new plant samples Hal had found while Lin cut the tops off the roots they'd collected.

There weren't many. The tubers grew in clumps of three or four plants, but the clumps were few and far between. The bag they had brought (made of Jem's shredded shirt reinforced and folded together with woven-grass ropes) was only a quarter full by midday.

"Maybe when we get out of this forest, there will be more growing in the open sun," Jem said.

"And what if we never do?" muttered Lin.

So far, there was no sign of the trees coming to an end.

At their midday stop, Hal checked in with Em, giving her the full report to pass on to Oz. She sent back word that they had found a few more roots nearby, so there would be a meal to celebrate their success in building the wall two logs high.

When Cara asked about Zyk, Hal's face scrunched up. "He's breathing," he said after a while, "but she's scared. I don't know."

They moved on. There was nothing else to do.

By midafternoon, Cara had started the debate in her head. Should they return to the group? They would be safer in the shelter tonight, and they could start in a new direction tomorrow. But that would mean today had been wasted. They couldn't afford wasted days.

She had almost decided to turn back anyway when the trees abruptly ended.

The tree line extended as far as the eye could see to their left and ended in the far distance to their right at the feet of the biggest mountains Cara had ever seen.

Straight ahead, wide open plains stretched out before them, dotted here and there with scraggly bushes and clumps of short trees. Something huge and dark, like a spiky hill, rose out of the flatness in the north.

"What is that?" Hal asked.

"A rock formation, I think," Jem said.

"It looks like it's about ten kilometers or so. We could get there before dark if we pushed it," said Lin.

"If there are predators, we won't have any place to hide," Jem pointed out.

"It's a risk, but everything is now," Lin said.

Cara weighed the options. They were here now. The variety of plants ahead might represent the food they needed, even without discovering animal life. Turning back empty-handed could be the end of them.

"Eyes open, weapons out," she said. "Hal, you can keep gathering plants, but you stay close now."

The boy squared his shoulders.

Lin pointed at a large clump of trees about a kilometer out onto the plain. "We can go there and take a water break. It's far enough to see if there's any wildlife but not so far that we can't still turn back if needed."

"Okay," Cara said. "Hal, you can let Em know what we decide when we get there."

The ground sloped gently down out of the trees and leveled off a few meters later. It felt hard and dry after the springy undergrowth of the forest. The air also felt thinner. After ten minutes, Cara was breathing hard. It was a relief to arrive at their stop.

"Still no sign of animal life," Lin said, scanning the ground. "Even insects. It's weird."

"Em says that Oz is getting worried about us. What should I tell her?" Hal asked.

Cara looked at the other adults. Lin shrugged, but Jem nodded toward the hill in the distance.

"Tell her that we found the end of the forest. We're going to get to that hill, see what there is to see. Then we'll turn back and be with them by tomorrow night."

Hal nodded and closed his eyes.

It took an hour to make the fire, cook roots, and eat, but it gave Jem a much-needed rest. Cara inspected his bandages while Lin cooked. Jem's back was still red and raw, but she was relieved that it didn't look inflamed.

After eating, they hiked on. The sun was warm and the earth dry beneath their feet. Several times they had to stop for a sip of water in the shade of another clump of trees.

The day seemed to stretch out. Walk for an hour. Stop in a shadow. One swallow of water each. Walk on.

On their seventh stop, the rocks finally loomed close. They were taller than they had seemed from a distance, but Cara could make out a crack that ran down the middle of the outcropping.

The sun had sunk nearly to the horizon now, but at least some form of shelter was in sight.

No one wanted to wait. After a quick drink, they set off, moving faster than before.

The world was quiet here. No living creature stirred in the increasing gloom. No breeze rustled the tough trees or the stubby grass. Only the sounds of four pairs of feet interrupted the wide silence.

*I can't keep denying it, Tom. This place is nothing like home.*

A flood of love and confidence washed over Cara. He was listening. He had hope. In a solution. In her. The feeling buoyed her as she forced herself to keep pace with the others.

When they reached the rocks, they paused to catch their breath. Jagged black cliffs rose straight up out of the earth to a height of fifty meters

*192*

or so. A black crevice split the sheer wall, and Hal darted toward it. Lin held him back with a quick hand on his shoulder.

"Careful," she said. "We don't know what might be in there."

Lin took some vines she had tied around her waist and knotted them at the end of her spear, lighting it with her makeshift flint to make a torch.

Cara walked forward and pressed one hand against the rock wall. It was rough and jagged, and up close she could see that the black was shot through with some kind of crystal that glittered darkly in the last rays of the sun.

"Torch won't last long," Lin said. "We should hurry."

She led the way into the crevice. Cara followed close behind, her own spear at the ready.

Though the crack was barely as wide as Cara's shoulders, it soon opened up into a wider passageway. At first, she could see sky above, but after a while, the rocks closed in. They were in a cave.

"It slopes down," Lin said. "Watch your step."

"What's that smell?" Hal asked.

Cara had noticed it, too, very faintly. A sweet, earthy odor.

"Can you see anything?" she asked Lin.

"The tunnel curves up there."

The back of Cara's neck prickled. "Stop for a minute," she said.

When everyone was still, Cara strained her ears, listening for any sound of motion or breath, any sign of something alive.

There was nothing.

Lin raised one brow. Cara shrugged.

They went on.

Around the corner the ground angled downward even more sharply. Cara put a hand to the wall to steady herself.

Suddenly there was a splash, and Lin jerked to a halt.

"Oh," she said and stepped back.

Stretched out in front of them was an underground lake so large it disappeared into the darkness.

The light from Lin's torch reflected off of a thousand crystals in the arched ceiling and the nearby walls.

"Water," Hal said.

Cara struggled to take in the sight.

"And food," said Jem.

He pointed down to where the ripples from Lin's feet were disappearing into the distance. A sleek form darted by, its silvery back glinting briefly.

"Fish," Lin whispered.

Then her torch guttered out, and they were left in darkness.

The next morning, they went fishing with no bait. Jem had made two makeshift nets out of grass, and Cara and Lin each had a spear but no experience using one.

They should have failed completely, but Lin's torch changed the equation.

Perhaps from living so long in darkness, the fish were fascinated by the flickering light. When Lin held the flame close to the surface, whole schools swirled around her feet. Jem and Hal scooped them out with ease. Each fish was the length of Cara's forearm and their silver scales glittered.

When they had caught a handful, they carried them to the surface and built a small cooking fire. Jem assured them cooked fish was unlikely to be poisonous, but to be safe, Cara would once again test it on herself before letting the others touch it.

The skin was blackened from the flames, but the flesh underneath was silvery white. It had a rich, oily taste, which combined with the smokiness from cooking to make it very pleasant to eat. Cara chewed slowly.

She felt the eyes of her friends on her throat as she swallowed.

The second the fish hit her stomach, the hollowness of hunger subsided. She felt a sense of well-being blossom out from her core and slowly spread to the rest of her body.

"Are you okay?" Lin asked. "Your face…"

Cara realized she had closed her eyes. "I'm…Is there any chance this fish could be like…? I don't know. I feel…good. Better than I should."

"Anything is possible," Jem said. "Take deep breaths. You only ate one bite. The effects should be limited."

They all waited. Exultation filled Cara as her body relaxed for the first time in days, her sore muscles easing and the pain in her shoulder slowly fading. The others watched anxiously, and she wanted to reassure them, but a small part of her mind knew that this could be the beginning of her body shutting down completely. In her current state of mind, the idea didn't even seem frightening.

Jem was right. After fifteen minutes, the euphoria began to fade. A short while after that, her hunger returned, not sharp and ravenous but empty and craving, like the hunger at the end of a long day's work.

"I think I'm okay," she said. She was more than okay. Though the hunger had returned, the aches in her body had not. She felt energized, and her shoulder felt....

Cara unwrapped her bandage and rolled her shoulder back.

"It healed," Hal whispered. His eyes were wide.

Though blood still stuck to her skin in places, the wound had completely closed, leaving only smooth new skin. Cara extended her arms and saw that all the scratches from the storm had disappeared.

"It's like the water," Lin said, her voice trembling.

"*Was* it the water?" Cara asked. They had all drunk from the pool down below. Maybe she had healed then and not noticed.

Lin gestured at her own shoulder. "Not likely. This hurts like fire."

"Time to eat, then," said Cara. The euphoria was returning, but this time it wasn't brought on by the fish. This was what it felt like to know that she could take care of her people. That she could make sure they all survived.

"Wait," Jem said. He was looking at Hal with a pained expression. "The last time we used something we didn't understand, we ended up here."

"Maybe this will take us back home then," Lin muttered.

"No, Jem's right," Cara said. She tried to ignore the bliss of being pain-free for the first time in days. She tried to think clearly, logically, like her father would. "We need to be careful. We can't afford any more mistakes."

What would her father say about this?

There was no way to know. Her father had never faced a situation like this.

# TWIN

*Tom? Please tell me you're listening. I could use some advice right now.*

The connection was silent.

Then she heard the echo of a voice that was neither her father nor her brother. *The chance to discover new patterns and learn new rules could be a wonderful adventure.*

There was no precedent for this, which meant there was no right and wrong choice already mapped out. Oz was right. There was freedom in that.

Cara tilted her head and looked up, her mind as empty as the cloudless sky overhead. She felt the answer already. She only needed to put words to it.

"We don't know what will happen if we eat the fish," she said after a minute. "But we do know what will happen if we don't."

She glanced at Hal, hesitated, then decided that he deserved the unvarnished truth. He had proven himself as capable as anyone.

"Zyk is days or maybe hours away from dying from his injuries. Bree has been unconscious since we arrived. Everyone is in danger from infection, and even if we miraculously avoid that, we're all slowly starving to death. These fish are the protein we need. And if they can also heal us...whatever happens after that, at least we'll be strong again to face it."

Lin looked relieved and Hal eager.

Jem nodded slowly. "I know that's true. I just...."

"You want to get home to your family," Cara said.

"I have to."

"So we'll take the risks we have to take to make that happen."

In answer he pinched off a piece of the fish and studied it for a moment. Then he swallowed it whole.

Without waiting, Lin took a bite for herself.

"I know you're hungry," Cara said to Hal, "but wait just a few minutes to make sure they're okay. You're our best hope if something goes wrong."

Hal swallowed hard but didn't complain. Instead he watched as Jem closed his eyes and Lin jumped to her feet and started to pace back and forth.

"This is…the weirdest…it's like…oh, thank the stars." Lin ripped the bandage off her shoulder. The jagged wound was just a pink mark on her light skin now, and even that disappeared as she began to move her arm in circles.

Jem was taking the deep, steady breaths of someone who is trying to stay calm. His eyes were still closed, and Cara noticed that his hands were trembling.

"Are you okay?" she asked him, reaching out to touch his arm. His skin radiated heat.

A tear slid down one cheek, but he managed a quick nod, mouth pressed in a tight line.

Lin was too caught up in her own bliss to notice what was happening, but Cara traded a worried look with Hal.

"If this goes wrong for us, you tell Em all about it, okay? Tell the others to follow the trail Lin marked and come to you. You don't try to walk back alone. All right?"

Hal's eyes widened, and Cara took his hand. "You understand? You'll be okay if you wait for them here."

"Cara, you're scaring the boy," Jem said.

She whipped back around to see him smiling at her. His face was wet with tears, but the trembling had stopped.

"Are you…?"

"Pain's all gone. Turns out the pain was helping to hold back the sadness."

"Screw sadness. I haven't felt this good in…ever," Lin said. At Cara's look, she smiled. "Don't worry. All this positivity won't last. It's just the fish talking."

"That's what I'm worried about."

"Understandable. Talking fish would be terrifying."

Cara stared. "Did you just make a joke?"

Lin shrugged, but she was grinning. After a few minutes, she sat back down. "Okay," she said, taking a deep breath. "The high is wearing off. I'm not even sure if it was the fish. It just felt so good to have the pain gone." She gestured at Hal. "You have to let him have some, Cara."

Cara saw the eagerness in Hal's eyes. She handed him a piece of fish.

He gobbled it down, then shivered. His face smoothed and the tension in his small shoulders relaxed. It wasn't until she saw him look like a child again that Cara realized how much the last few days had aged him.

"So we take this back to the others," Jem said. "Feed them."

"Heal them," Lin said.

"And then we bring them here," Cara finished. "These caves are better shelter, plus the water and food."

"And healing," Lin said.

"Yes. That."

"We're going to make it." Lin laughed wonderingly. "Stars above, we actually may not die here."

*You hear that, Tom?* Cara thought as they wrapped the fish in leaves and set out for the grotto as quickly as they could. *We're not going to die here. Now it's up to you to make sure we don't have to live here.*

*Tom?*

She didn't feel her brother anywhere.

# Chapter 24

## Tests

Cara's turbulent emotions had given way to determination, and Tom tried to focus on that as a way of dampening his own anger.

It almost worked.

Yesterday, Nev's team had spent the entire afternoon and evening putting Tom through tests and evaluations. They had even hooked him up to brain monitors while he tossed and turned on a bed in their lab last night. Tom's frustration and impatience weren't improved by lack of sleep.

*If you can survive monsters and storms and starvation, I can survive a team of scientists.*

Seated now on the plush chair in Nev's office, he managed to put on a neutral face and wait for the older man to speak first.

Nev took his time, pouring a glass of water, seating himself next to a small table, pulling up a file on his tablet. Finally, he looked up at Tom with his most condescending smile.

"I usually offer complete confidentiality, but I think in this case it's necessary to record our sessions. Do you agree?"

Tom nodded. He didn't trust himself to speak yet.

*Hang in there, Six. I'm doing my best for you.*

"I would like to begin by going back as far as you can remember. What is the first time that you noticed your sister's voice in your head?"

"I told you, she didn't really speak to me until after the disappearance. It was her emotions that I could feel. And she could feel mine."

"She told you this?"

"She didn't like to talk about it, but yes."

Nev took a moment to add a note to his file. "We'll get back to that later. For now, tell me about the first time you felt an emotion that you believed came from your sister."

Tom tried to ignore the way the question was worded. The point was to prove that he wasn't a dangerous psychopath. Punching the psychologist in the face wouldn't accomplish that.

"I think her feelings have always been a part of me, but I didn't know they weren't just me until one day when we were about five. We were playing football in the courtyard, just the two of us, and the score was tied. I managed to get past Cara, sped down, and scored the winning goal. I was so happy. Cara was always better than me at football, and I had never won before that day. So. I was next to the goal, doing my celebration dance when all of a sudden I felt this surge of frustration and a pain in my ankle."

Tom looked away from Nev studiously typing notes and focused on how that day had felt.

"It was enough to make me stop my dance and look down at my foot. I felt fine. I felt victorious. Then I turned around. Cara was on the ground, crying. Not only had she lost her first football match, but she had twisted her ankle. Her foot was already swelling. Suddenly, I knew that what I had felt was what she was feeling."

Nev continued typing for several minutes after Tom stopped speaking.

"Didn't you say you were recording this?" Tom asked.

"Yes. These are my own notes on our conversation."

"And what do they say? 'Delusions began at the age of 5'?"

Nev put the tablet down. "Tom, I'm not your enemy. I'm not trying to discredit you or cause you harm. I'm trying to understand you. I hope in time you will come to trust that."

"It would help me trust you if I knew what you were writing about me."

Nev studied him for a moment. "Okay. In this case, I merely noted that your first experience of empathy made a strong impression on you. Five years old is a typical age for empathy to begin to develop."

"Empathy," Tom said. "You could call it that, I guess. If by empathy, you mean the ability to know that someone is in pain without even seeing them."

"Yes, the strongest forms of empathy often require no direct data, as one can extrapolate the feelings of another through knowledge of the context alone."

"What about when I had no idea where she was and what was happening to her?"

"Why don't you tell me about that?"

For two hours, Tom kept his temper in check and told story after story of times that he and Cara had sensed each other when it shouldn't have been possible. He could have gone longer, but he didn't have the patience.

"By the time we were teenagers and started our apprenticeships, we were both used to having two people's emotions in our head. It got harder when we weren't together as much. We needed to be able to focus on our jobs, so we started working on suppressing the other person's feelings. Sort of learning to push them away so that we didn't feel them, or at least not as strongly. Cara was a lot better at it than I was, but she also needed to be. The governor doesn't exactly give his apprentice time to be distracted."

"Was that how your sister felt? That the governor was stifling her?"

"Of course not. She worships him. But I could see it happening."

"Because you felt what she was feeling?"

"No. She felt worried about distractions. She felt exhausted by her duties. She didn't call that being stifled. I did."

"It was your interpretation of her emotion."

Tom felt himself being backed into a corner. "Yes, but I always understood that as something different than her actual feelings."

"Because she felt very differently about your father than you did."

Tom stiffened. "I know you're a psychologist, but we aren't going there. None of this has anything to do with my father."

Nev lifted a shoulder in acquiescence, but his face said he didn't agree.

"So. Your sister asked you to work on suppressing these distracting emotions."

"She told me she was working on it. She asked that we stop talking about it."

"Why do think she was reluctant to discuss your…connection?"

The urge to punch Nev's smug face was back, stronger than ever. It didn't help that Cara's excitement and anxiety had suddenly spiked. What was she doing?

"Let's be clear. Cara never denied in any way that what we felt was real. She just didn't want other people to find out. She worried they would think we were crazy. Which I have to congratulate her for, since I now know she was right. Being Cara, she also worried that even if people believed us, it would become too big of a deal, would take away from our more useful functions in the colony. We finally had a team of Thirds large enough to begin a new settlement when we were fully trained. She didn't want anything to take away from the Plan."

"So she insisted you tell no one."

Tom tried to shrug, but it was hard to remember those conversations casually. He had always understood Cara's point of view, but he hadn't been able to push away her feelings as easily as she had pushed away his. She never totally understood that.

"I didn't really want to tell people about it either. It was kind of fun to have a secret. But Cara didn't want to talk about it even with me. In case someone overheard. And, also, because it made too big of a deal out of it even between us."

"What makes you so certain she really felt what you felt? That she hadn't just pretended when you were children?"

The question didn't surprise Tom. He had asked himself that same thing. He had doubted those memories, wondered if it was just his own problem. But all that was before she disappeared. He didn't have doubts any more.

"Obviously she didn't feel exactly what I felt. We're different people. But I told you the stories. I told you how often we talked about it. And what has happened in the last few days confirms that it was all real."

"You told me your perspective on the stories. You told me she agreed with your theories. You told me she wasn't as comfortable talking about it as you were."

"She just…." Tom cut off as a flood of adrenalin rushed through him. *Cara.* Something was happening to her. He doubled over as his head pulsed with sensations he couldn't name.

"Tom?" Nev's voice sounded far away.

It was like every cell in Tom's body came alive at once. It was more than he could take. Tom crossed his arms, holding them tight to his chest to still the shaking.

Somewhere a door opened. Voices were speaking. Something sharp pricked his arm.

The electricity began to fade. The psychologist's face swam back into view, now just inches from his own. Two women were standing behind him.

A very different kind of feeling was spreading out from his right arm. His muscles relaxed. The intense emotions faded. Then all emotion faded.

*Cara?*

He couldn't feel her in his head any more. His own panic and fear were still there, but even those were dampened, like voices heard through a thick wall.

He saw a needle in the doctor's hand. Saw the worried look on the faces of the women. They had given him something. A drug. What was it?

His curiosity was vague and unreal.

*Cara?* He tried to make his foggy mind focus. *Are you okay?*

*Cara?*

But she was gone.

# Chapter 25

# Loss

When Cara saw Oz through the trees, she wanted to run to him but settled for giving him the first real smile she had mustered since they came here.

His return nod was tight and strained.

"Zyk?" she asked. Her main worry for the last several kilometers had been arriving too late.

Oz's face was grave. "I'm sorry."

"He's…?"

"Barely holding on, Cara. He won't last the night."

Relief flooded her. "Yes, he will," she said, fumbling in her makeshift pack for the fish they had wrapped in leaves.

Hal had passed on the news about their miraculous healing, but Cara didn't blame them for not believing it until they saw it. They would see it now.

She hurried into the grotto and past everyone's welcome until she was kneeling next to Zyk. Syl crouched beside to her and took Zyk's hand.

"He can't even swallow water," she said. "He's…"

"…going to get better now," said Cara, though doubt crept in. If he couldn't eat the fish, how could it heal him?

She pinched off a small bite of pale silver flesh. Opening Zyk's lips, she pressed the fish under his tongue, praying that this would be enough. She stared at his face, waiting for a response, avoiding Syl's questioning eyes.

A minute passed. Then two.

Zyk stopped breathing.

For one thrilling moment, Cara thought it had worked.

Then Syl choked on a sob. She had two fingers on his neck, where his pulse should have been.

"Just wait," Cara whispered.

No one moved. No one breathed.

Finally, Syl pulled her hand back. "He's gone," she said.

Ann wrapped her arms around the girl as she broke down.

Cara couldn't believe it. She wouldn't.

They had found healing fish. Had brought it all the way here. He had been alive just moments before. How could they have missed saving him by so little? It wasn't possible.

All around her people were crying. They didn't understand. This fish could heal anything. Everything would be okay soon.

A strong hand touched her shoulder, but she shrugged it off. She stared intently at Zyk's bandaged chest, waiting for the tell-tale rise and fall that would show that the fish had done its work.

It would just take a little more time.

A smaller hand rested on the back of her neck, and this time it wouldn't move. Lin knelt down by Cara, gently turning her face away.

"You did everything you could," she said. "But he was too far gone."

Hot anger shot through Cara, and she pushed Lin away. How could she be so cold?

Cara pushed to her feet, furious at every crying person in the crowded grotto. Someone said her name, but she ignored them and stalked out into the forest. Undergrowth tangled around her feet and tried to slow her progress. She kicked it aside.

Her fury carried her a few hundred meters into the trees before abruptly abandoning her. Without it, her vision wavered, and she sank to her knees, then curled into a ball on the forest floor.

All she could think about was Zyk's face, flushed from fever, his mouth dry, his breathing shallow. Over and over, she watched her hands putting the fish into his mouth. Each time, she willed it to work. Each time, his breathing stopped.

Why didn't she give him water with the fish? Why didn't she force him to swallow? Why didn't they walk faster on the way home? Leave earlier? Go looking for food a day sooner? She had known he had infection. She had known he needed medicine urgently. Why hadn't she done more?

This grief was self-indulgent. Not being strong enough was how she had lost Zyk.

*Get up,* she told herself. *You need to make sure everyone eats that fish. There are others with wounds. Bree is sick. Go back and do your job.*

With effort, Cara pushed up onto her hands and knees. Her body ached, but she deserved the pain. She straightened up.

Oz was standing by a nearby tree, a rough wood cup in one hand, something wrapped in leaves in the other. It was the second time he had found her like this, and Cara knew she should be ashamed, but she was too numb to care.

"Water," he said. "And a few bites of fish. Lin sent it for you."

"The others…."

"The others know you need some time alone."

"They need to eat it, not me. I already…."

"We've all had some. Everyone's injuries are healed. Jak was giving it to Bree when I left."

"Oh." Without the urgency of a task, Cara's energy left her. She tried to summon a thought. "I should go see her."

Instead of answering, he handed her the cup of water.

Reflexively, Cara took a drink. The cold stung her raw throat.

He gave her a piece of fish.

Cara looked at the silvery flesh in the palm of her hand, hating it. It had failed her, had offered healing and then fallen short just when it was most needed. It was dangerous. It would make her feel good. But only for a while.

"It can just be a bite of food," Oz said.

It couldn't. It was more than just protein for her body to burn into the energy needed for the next step. It was an offer of hope that turned out to be empty.

Her hand trembled. Her eyesight wavered. Stars curse it all. She didn't need hope right now. She needed a bite of food.

She ate the fish.

The roughness in her throat was smoothed away. The aching of her muscles disappeared. The knot of hunger in her core untangled. The heavy stone in her chest stayed, but now she felt that she could bear it.

"The others already ate?" she asked.

"Everyone," he said.

She shuddered at the word.

"He hadn't been able to swallow water since yesterday," Oz said. "There was no way you could have gotten back in time."

Cara didn't answer.

"You did everything you could. This was not your fault."

That was a thing people said when things went wrong, her father had told her. As soon as grief enters the picture, they want to get rid of guilt. The two emotions are too heavy together. But her father had also taught her that a leader takes responsibility for those that follow her. She doesn't shrink from the weight.

For five days, she had kept them all alive. Then she had let one of them die. That was her failure, and she had to bear it.

"It's not about you," Oz said.

"No," Cara snapped. "It's about Zyk. I told him we were going to make it."

"Yes, it is about Zyk. About the day he found himself flung across to an unknown world, where he immediately killed a monster with his bare hands. About the moment he didn't think he had the strength to go on, but he found it in his friends. About his courage in facing down monsters with one hand, because he was willing to defend those who couldn't defend themselves. He met a challenge beyond anything he could have imagined, and he lived up to it. He paid the price for his own brave actions. You do not get to take that away from him."

Something inside Cara broke. Tears streamed down her face, and she didn't try to stop them.

When they finally ran dry, Oz reached out and wiped one away. "We need you," he said. "You keep us moving forward. But our lives are our own to save or to lose."

She nodded. Looking into Oz's eyes this close, she saw how eating the fish had changed him. He had always seemed steady and solid, but now the lines around his eyes were smoother, his jaw less tight. How much pain had he been hiding?

"We should go back," she whispered.

"When you're ready," he said. "Ann and Jem are taking care of everyone."

"We need to...bury him."

"They are taking care of that, too."

"When it's time, you should speak, say what you just said."

"I will."

"Thank you," she said. "My father..."

"...was right about a lot of things. But he never conceived of a situation like this."

Unable to resist, she leaned in and rested her head against his chest for just a minute. He wrapped both arms around her shoulders. It felt just as good as she had imagined.

It was more than a minute before he spoke, his voice rumbling against her ear.

"What do you miss the most?"

"Tom," she said without thinking. "And my parents. And...at home everything made sense."

He chuckled at that. "Did it?"

The question jabbed. Cara pulled back to look at him. "Of course it did. I may not have understood every bit of science that made our lives run, but I knew what I needed to know. I knew where I fit. I knew what to expect next and what was expected of me. I knew the rules."

"And here?"

She threw up her hands. "Here there are no rules."

"Sure there are. We just don't know them yet."

He had made that argument before, and she knew the answer to it now.

"Rules we don't know don't help us. They get us killed."

"So we learn them," he said, and his voice carried an intensity she had never heard before. "Instead of being afraid, we continue what we've started. And the more we learn, the closer we are to home."

"That's what I'm saying. Somehow I have to figure this out. I have to find us a way home."

"It's not on you, Cara. We're alive. But just because you pulled off that miracle doesn't mean you have to perform another."

"'There are no miracles. Just hard work,'" she said, hearing the emptiness of her father's words after everything that had happened.

Oz looked at her.

"Okay, so maybe there are miracles," she admitted. "The problem is that we need too many of them. It's not a workable system."

For the first time since she'd known him, he laughed loudly. She liked the way it creased his face, even if he was laughing at her.

"I know," she said, throwing up her hands. "If Tom heard me talking about a system of miracles, he'd drop me in the river mud after a rain."

"No," Oz said. "I like it. A system of miracles. It's the best description of the universe I've heard yet. But you're wrong about one thing. It does work."

"So we just sit around and wait for the next miracle?"

"No," he said. "We work hard, like your father said. We also rest. And play. We live."

"With no plan for the future, no hope for getting home, which means no provision for long-term survival."

"No plan is not the same as no hope. Only one of them is necessary to live."

There were too many answers to that, and none at all. So Cara did what she always did. She did the next thing, slowly unbraiding her tangle of hair and rebraiding it neatly. When she was done, she nodded that she was ready, and Oz led the way back toward their friends.

In the grotto, everyone was busy with something. A few people were crying as they worked, and a few others looked up at her and smiled encouragingly. Cara saw the children making up packs. She pointedly ignored the hole being dug next to the rock wall.

Jak was kneeling next to Bree, all trace of his injuries gone. When Cara came close, she met her sister's eyes over Jak's shoulder.

"Thank the stars," Bree said, pushing her husband aside and pulling her sister close.

Cara didn't know where she found more tears, but they came readily.

When she finally pulled back, Bree was smiling and crying at the same time. "I thought I was having the weirdest dream," she said.

Cara shook her head. "Trust me. Waking up is going to be even weirder."

"Jak told me. I can't even…. It's a miracle we're all alive." She shook her head when Cara flinched. "I'm sorry. Zyk. I know. I just…when I first woke up, I was so…But Jak says the baby is okay."

Cara's heart stopped.

"Baby?" she said.

Bree nodded. "I didn't have a chance to tell anyone yet, not even Jak." Her hands went to her belly. "But he says there's been no bleeding. And the way the air affected me is a good sign. It means my body was giving oxygen to the baby first."

The hand squeezing Cara's heart loosened but only a little.

"That's…that's good," she said. "And…congratulations."

Bree smiled brilliantly at Jak, and the smile he gave back was so tender that Cara couldn't bear to look. With one last squeeze of her sister's hands, she slipped away and left them to their joy.

# Chapter 26

# Release

Tom wasn't sure how long he had been in the bed. Days, certainly. A week?

Somewhere in his brain, he knew that he should be worried about the passing time, but he couldn't summon enough emotion to care.

Yes, Cara was out there. No, he couldn't feel her at all. He knew there was something important about that, but when he tried to focus on it, it slipped away.

The pattern of the days had been the same. The moment he woke up, someone came in with breakfast and an injection. Then he was taken to a courtyard for an hour or so. After a while, Nev came and spoke to him, asked questions. Sometimes other doctors were with him. Usually in the afternoon Tom's father came, but he said very little to Tom, choosing to spend most of his visit huddled with Nev and talking in a low voice.

That should have meaning. Shouldn't it?

Tom lay as still as he could. If they were watching him, maybe they would think he was still sleeping. He pushed his brain to remember. There had been a morning that was different. Two days ago? Three?

His father had come in with the woman who brought breakfast. There was no injection that day. When they took him to the courtyard, he walked in circles as his head slowly cleared. With clarity came anger. Tom could remember the rage the way he could remember reading about cheetahs back on Earth. Wonderful, but so far out of reach that it was only a myth.

Still, he remembered the events. Nev had come. Tom had yelled. The man had asked him about Cara. Tom could barely feel her, just a knot of anxiety buried under his own fury. When Nev asked why Cara was anxious, Tom punched him in the face. Two men held him down while Nev gave him another injection. There hadn't been any more mornings without needles.

Tom tried to think of what he wanted to happen, but he didn't really want anything. He remembered wanting things. Wanting people to believe him. Wanting them to begin the search. Wanting Cara back. And Lin.

The thought of Lin stirred something that was almost a desire. Tom tried to reach for it, but it slipped away.

The door opened, and a woman came in. She had the usual breakfast on a tray. Tom sat up automatically.

While he ate, she prepped his shoulder and slid the needle in quickly. As usual, it was over before he could swallow the first bite of food.

She waited in the room, making his bed while he used the bathroom. Then she led the way to the courtyard.

Tom began to walk his usual circuit around the outside edges. Someone had planted gashi under all the trees. They had no blooms at the moment, but their vivid green stood out against the brown. Tom looked away, beginning to count the windows as he passed them.

After a while, a door opened, and Nev entered the courtyard. He wasn't alone today. An old man followed him, his shock of white hair curling around his head in disorder.

"Uncle Max," Tom said.

"How are you, boy?"

Nev stood to the side while the old man embraced his great-nephew. "I've been told that you had some strange experiences but now they're taking care of you. How do you feel?"

Tom wasn't sure how to answer, so he didn't.

"Would you like to tell me about what happened?"

Again, Tom remembered the events of the last few weeks, but putting it all into words seemed like a lot of effort. He shrugged.

The old man's eyes narrowed. "Why isn't he talking?" he asked.

"He can talk," Nev said. "He often does not cooperate."

Max grunted. "He looks drugged."

"The medication is exactly what I described. It should only dampen emotion. All other mental processes function normally. His actions are still his choice."

Max grunted again.

"When we took him off it, he was violent. It may take time for him to adjust to this, but I assure you it's for the best."

Max didn't answer, just looked at Tom for a long time.

Tom noticed the dark brown of his uncle's eyes. They were almost black, just like Bree's. His oldest sister had inherited the same curls, too. This fact, like others, seemed like it should carry some significance that Tom couldn't find today.

Abruptly, Uncle Max turned away. "Tell the governor that I'll get those charts to him by this afternoon," he growled.

"You've seen what you needed to see?" Nev asked.

"Yes."

Max walked with a slight limp, but his steps were still firm as he crossed to the door. When he had opened it, he paused. "I'll see you, boy."

Tom didn't answer. Either they would see each other or they wouldn't. He didn't know, so what was there to say?

When Max was gone, Nev led Tom to their usual bench and began his daily round of questions. Tom answered when he could summon enough interest, which wasn't often. Nev made notes on his tablet. Tom watched without curiosity.

After an hour or two, a nurse came and led Tom back to his room for a nap. The nurse was young, clearly still an apprentice, but he was big. His shoulders stretched his simple uniform. Tom remembered him from school. His name was Mat.

When Mat left, Tom lay still again, not sleeping but willing to let his body rest. They always dimmed the room during nap time. There was just enough light to watch the outlines of the ceiling tiles. Tom had already counted them. Forty-six.

Outside Tom's door, voices approached. Someone was talking loudly, nearly shouting. The door burst open.

Tom's mother hurried in, followed by Mat with a scared look on his face.

Jul came to the bed and sat down on the edge, pulling her son into a tight hug. "They told me you were consulting with scientists, that you were being observed. No one mentioned drugs."

Tom could hear the anger in her voice. Again, he recognized it like he recognized the shape of Dua in the sky. A fact. Nothing more.

Still, his mother's hug felt good. He put his arms around her shoulders. She squeezed him even tighter.

When she pulled back, her face was tight with a mother's worry, but her voice was all doctor. "I'm going to find out what dosage they've been giving you. I expect it will take hours or possibly even a few days to leave your system. You may have side effects as that happens. I'll be monitoring you myself, and we'll deal with each symptom as it occurs. But I promise you, I will not be allowing any more injections."

Tom nodded.

"Go and fetch Dr. Ginopolis," she said to the lurking nurse. "Tell him I expect him to bring my son's file when he comes."

"But...."

"Mat," her voice was kind but firm. A mother's voice now. "I have known you as long as you've been alive. I am the one who told your mother to expect you. I've seen your files. You are a good nurse, just like your mother, and I respect you enough to talk straight. Under no circumstances am I leaving my son's side. Do you understand me? I am staying right here. Which is why I need you to ask the doctor to come to me. We have things to discuss, and I promise that once you've relayed my message, I'll see to it that you are left out of this. It's not something you want to be involved in."

"No, ma'am," said Mat.

"So go now and do this one simple task, and then you're free to leave when things get complicated."

For a big man, Mat could scuttle pretty quickly.

"Can you get up?" Jul asked.

Tom nodded.

"How is your energy?"

"Fine," he answered. "I walk in the courtyard every day."

"Good," she said, looking into his eyes. After a moment she nodded. "We won't leave here until I've spoken to Nev, but let's get you up. The more you move about, the sooner your head will clear."

She pulled him to his feet.

"Thank you," he said, "for coming."

Her eyes glittered but no tears fell. "I should have been here sooner."

"You didn't know where I was?"

"I knew where, just not what." The anger was back. "If your uncle hadn't come to see me, I still wouldn't know."

"You're here now."

"Yes. I am. And now we're going to get to the bottom of this."

Tom didn't hear most of the conversation between Nev and his mother. The minute the psychologist arrived, Jul marched him into the hallway and shut the door. Only twice did she raise her voice enough for Tom to make out the words.

"…not science…beyond your understanding…right this minute…."

When she came back in, Nev did not follow her, but five minutes later, the governor arrived.

That argument was not moved to the hall.

Tom let the words wash over him, trying to grasp hold of the emotions that he knew they should carry. He couldn't quite do it, but he did feel something familiar tugging at the edge of his consciousness.

*Cara?*

It was her. It was the first thing he had been sure of for days.

*I'm here, Cara.*

Her presence was too faint for an answer, but knowing she was there was like having an amputated limb reattached.

Something tickled his face, and he reached up a hand to find a tear running down his cheek.

His parents' voices suddenly fell quiet, and his mother come to sit beside him again.

"She's still there," he whispered.

Jul took his hand. "We're going to get you home," she said. "Get your head clear again."

"But Cara...."

"We get your head clear," she said. She pulled him to his feet, nudged his shoes closer.

Tom slipped them on, still too numb to summon any resistance. Cal stood aside and let Jul lead Tom out the door. He didn't follow them down the hall.

"Dad...."

"He'll be home when he's finished talking to Nev. He has some things to smooth over. You aren't to worry about any of it."

Worry was just a word anyway.

Jul reached the outside door, held it open for her son, but as he passed her, she stopped him with a hand on his shoulder. "When you talk to her, tell her I love her," she said. "Tell her we're coming as soon as we can."

She released his shoulder and let him lead the way out into the sunshine.

# Chapter 27

# *Life*

Ann's painting was the turning point.

For days, the group had worked to turn the caves into a suitable base of operations. They built up defenses at the opening, gathered grass for softer sleeping areas and rocks for a more permanent fire ring. They explored the underground tunnels and found several smaller caverns, which they designated for sleeping and storage, not that they had anything to store yet.

Oz turned his mechanical skills to designing primitive weapons, and Jak set about becoming a fishing expert. Jem experimented with new foods and sent the kids to collect what he found useful. Bree and Syl did regular examinations of everyone, monitoring the effects of their new environment. With the fish as the staple of their diet, no other doctoring was required.

When all their basic needs were met, Oz and Cara took to ranging far from the cave each day, exploring the terrain, gathering food and other resources along the way. The savannah stretched for kilometers on every side of the rocky outcropping that marked their cave. Though they could see mountains in the distance to the east, it would be several days journey to reach them, and no one wanted to split the group again.

Instead, each day they chose a new direction and walked as far as they could until midday. Everywhere, they looked for signs of animal life, but they never saw so much as an insect.

Back in Mayland, a quiet walk outside the fences would still have included the hum of flitting pennifins or the occasional grawp of a krona. Here the silence was absolute. At first, the stillness felt unnatural and oppressive, but as the days passed, Cara found the quiet soothing.

Whether it was the steady diet of healing fish or just her body naturally acclimating, breathing came easy now. She and Oz fell into a comfortable rhythm, exploring, gathering, sometimes talking, but mostly not.

The one shadow that hung over everything was Tom's continued silence. Cara hadn't felt him since the day she first ate the healing fish. She wanted to believe that was a coincidence, but the longer he was absent, the harder it was to convince herself. She had managed to put off telling the others but only because everyone had been so busy. Routines were beginning to be established. Soon someone would ask.

On their fifth day at the new camp, Cara worried over it all afternoon. She and Oz walked in silence, and she caught him watching her as if he knew what she was thinking. She made up her mind to tell him and Lin that night. They deserved the truth, and they could help her break it to the others.

Back at camp, Cara let Oz deliver their gatherings to the store room while she went to clean up in the cavern where the women slept. The second she stepped into the room with her torch, she stopped.

# TWIN

One whole wall was painted with the red, green, and gold of gashi flowers.

Cara sucked in a breath. Her mother had always grown gashi outside their door. Every year she picked the blooms and used them to decorate the table for Tom and Cara's birthday.

Footsteps echoed behind her and a small hand grabbed hers.

"Do you like it?" Em asked. "Ann painted it for me!"

Cara willed her heart to stop racing. "It's beautiful," she said. "How…where did Ann get paint?"

"She made it from mud!" the little girl giggled. "And leaves and berries and stuff. She showed me how. She's going to do one for Hal in the boys' room. She says she'll make stars on his. Hal loves space."

"That's wonderful," Cara said. She squeezed Em's hand.

"I can't wait to go to bed," the girl said. "I'm going to go ask Lil if she'll tell us our story in here instead of outside tonight. She's going to tell us the one about Rajish and Cassandra and the spaceship built in space."

"That's one of my favorites," Cara said.

Em skipped off, and Cara stood for a long time staring at the flowers done in Ann's signature bold style. It transformed the room. The neatly stacked grasses were more than just sleeping places; they were beds. Cara noticed that each one now had a small pile of possessions that identified its owner. Scraps of cloth to tie back hair, plants or rocks they found beautiful, the latest project they'd been working on.

It looked less like a base and more like a home.

The flowers on the wall condemned her. *We are home,* they said. *Not this place.* There were no gashi here.

Was this how Rajish and Cassandra felt when they said good-bye to Earth and looked out to the stars?

Cara shook herself. It wasn't the same. Her great-great-grandparents had left behind a dying planet and a corrupt society. They had nothing worth returning to. Una was fresh and beautiful, and her people had proven themselves worthy of their new planet. She was meant to live her whole life in Mayland, to make it grow and thrive.

No. They had enjoyed their safety enough. They had recovered from their arrival, and their base was established. It was time to get serious about going home.

*I'm sorry, Tom. If I can't hear you, I'm going to have to find a way on my own.*

Instead of listening to the answering silence, she went outside to make plans.

Most of the group had already eaten dinner, but they still hung around, talking and playing a rock-throwing game the kids had invented. Only Bree and Jak were missing. Likely they'd already gone to bed. Bree was in good health, but her pregnancy exhausted her, and Jak wouldn't leave her side.

Next to the fire, Ann was showing Oz the paints and primitive brushes she had made. Cara sat down next to Lin, accepting a roughly chiseled stone cup that Pol handed her. The steaming water had a pointed leaf floating in it, and a sweet smell wafted toward her.

"The painting is beautiful," she said, sipping the strange new tea. It was delicious.

"I didn't know how much I missed it until I started working. I haven't gone this long without painting in twenty years."

"You made Em happy."

"She hasn't been sleeping well. She misses her mother."

Cara nodded, feeling the weight on her shoulders press in more. "Do you think you could paint a map?"

Ann looked thoughtful, and for some reason, Oz grinned.

"On the wall?" Ann asked.

"If that's the best place. Maybe in the main passage? We could find a way to measure distances, bring you the information, begin to piece together where we are."

"I don't have any experience with cartography," Ann said, "but I think we could figure it out."

"Lin has some training. All explorers do. She could help you."

"It's a good idea," Ann said.

Oz was still smiling into his cup of tea.

"What?" Cara asked.

"You saw that painting, and in five minutes you had a plan for how to make it useful."

Cara flushed. "Well, if it makes you feel better, I spent the first five minutes appreciating its beauty."

"I'm glad you think of practical things," Ann said. "A map is a good idea. One I wouldn't have thought of."

"What about the stars?" Wyn asked. She had been sitting quietly on the other side of the fire listening.

"I'll have time to do Hal's stars, too."

"No, a map of the stars," Wyn said.

Cara's heart thumped. Of course. That was the map they really needed.

"Could you record their positions? On different nights? From that, I could identify them and calculate a rough location."

"You could do that out of your head?" Ann asked.

Wyn didn't answer, but Cara knew that she could. The woman had a genius IQ and near-perfect memory. If it hadn't been for the trauma that had stolen her voice, she would have been the head of her team.

Ann squinted up at the sky. "You would have to help me to make it accurate. And we'd probably have to do it on an outside wall, so I could see them while I work."

"Well, I don't think any rain will wash it away," Oz said. They hadn't seen a drop of rain since arriving here. Jem said all the plants had abnormally long roots, which he conjectured meant the water was all underground. Like their pool of fish.

"We might get another windstorm," Cara said.

"Not until the next eclipse," said Wyn.

"When will that be?" Ann asked. "Dua has been out at night since we got to the cave, so it should switch back to day soon, right?"

"It will be dayside in two days, but full eclipse will be at least a week beyond that," Wyn said.

Cara was grateful she didn't say more or tell Ann that it was actually Una she saw in the sky.

She still hadn't told the rest of the group about Wyn's theory of interplanetary travel. If the star map confirmed her theory, she'd have no choice, but until then, she didn't want to take away their hope.

*Any day now, Tom.*

Her hourly messages to her brother had started to feel like talking to herself, so she was surprised to feel an answering surge of confusion.

*Tom? Are you there?*

No words came back but her own sense of relief was magnified in a way she recognized.

Tears formed in her eyes before she could stop them.

# TWIN

*We're working on that map, Tom. I just need you to open the gate.*

His presence in her mind slowly faded away, but the last impression she received was determination. Whatever had happened, he was back and he hadn't given up on finding her.

A hand on Cara's arm made her eyes snap open.

"Tom?" Lin asked softly.

Cara nodded.

Lin's shoulders sagged, and her eyes closed. "Thank the stars."

So she had known.

"What does he say?"

"Nothing yet, but it's him."

Oz was watching them, his dark eyes reflecting the flames of the fire. He raised one brow, and Cara tipped her head slightly in response. His smile made something shift inside her chest.

He had known, too. Of course he had. If she had been communicating with Tom, she would have been reporting new developments. Her silence had been obvious.

She had been wrong not to tell them the truth. It hadn't protected them. It had just told them she didn't trust them. And it had left her alone.

"I'm sorry," she spoke to Lin but her eyes were still on Oz. "I should have talked to you about it."

"You didn't have to," Lin said.

"No, but I should have. My father taught me the principles of full disclosure, but he also talked a lot about picking your time and method of communication. It made sense at the time, but now I wonder...."

"If it's just a justification for keeping secrets when it suits you?" Lin said. "That's what Tom always thought."

Cara remembered Tom's arguments. She had always taken her father's side, mostly because he laid out his reasons so calmly. Calm wasn't really Tom's style. Or rational, for that matter.

But now her brother's willingness to be irrational was what was going to save her. It was like her whole history had shifted when her body did, and now she saw it all from a different angle.

And what about Wyn's theory? Who was she really protecting by not telling the group about that?

"I think we need to have a gathering tomorrow," she said. "It's time I stopped holding back. Time to let go of secrets."

"I'll spread the word," Lin said. She knew what secret Cara meant. There was only one that mattered. "They can handle it. And our best chance of getting home is to have everyone working on the problem. The real problem."

"Yeah. I know. It's just...." Cara struggled to find the right words for the dread that filled her. "I guess it was easier to only have my own fear to deal with."

Lin studied her face. "I'm sorry," she said.

"For what?"

"For your empathy. It must really suck to care about how other people feel."

Cara laughed. "Yeah, sometimes it does. And then sometimes what I imagine people are feeling is worse than what they actually feel. Which isn't empathy at all. Just fear, I guess."

"Tom always says, 'Fear is never a good reason to do anything.'"

"It was one of my grandmother's sayings."

"Well, she was right."

"Didn't I already say I would call a meeting?"

232

Lin laughed. "I was just being affirming."

"You are terrible at affirmation."

Lin stood up and stretched, arching her back like a cat. "Good thing I don't care, then, isn't it?"

Cara shook her head, a half-smile on her lips. Lin could talk about not caring all she wanted. She'd give up her own life to protect anyone here. If that wasn't caring, nothing was.

# Chapter 28

# Gathering

*Cara?*

*Tom!*

Her relief flooded the connection. Tom was glad he had waited until he was alone in his room to reach out. Sudden bursts of unexplained tears weren't going to help convince anyone of his sanity.

*Are you there?*

*I'm here.* He struggled to get his emotions under control. To make his thoughts clear.

*Thank the stars. It's been days. I thought....*

She was in his head, so he knew what she had thought, even though she didn't put it into words.

*It wasn't you. It was...me.*

*Are you okay? Were you hurt?*

He wanted to shield her from it, but his newly returned emotions were too out of control to keep hidden. Rather than drown her in mysterious angst, he told her the story as briefly as possible.

*They can do that with a drug?* He felt her fear. Her connection to him was her connection to home.

*I won't let it happen again,* he said. *And Mom. You should have seen her.*

*She made them stop.*

*Yes.*

Her fear was subsiding, being replaced by that thoughtful calculation that was Cara's resting state.

*I'm so sorry for what happened. I think I know why he did it, though.*

Tom's fury was sudden and complete. *Don't.*

*I'm not defending him, Tom. Those drugs could have damaged you forever, could have ruined everything. And I would never have forgiven him for that.*

*You would never have known about it. You would never have heard from any of us again.*

He regretted the thought instantly. Her grief and fear, so carefully controlled most of the time, bubbled up with an intensity that made Tom press both hands to his head.

*I'm sorry.*

*No,* she said, masking her own pain under concern for his. *I'm the one who's sorry. You…. It must have been so awful.*

*It wasn't. That's the terrifying part.*

He didn't have to explain further. She shared his horror. To be cut off from each other forever was unthinkable. In spite of all the years they had tried to ignore the connection, neither would be fully themselves

**236**

without the other. The thought of that happening painlessly, of not even being able to miss it....

*How's Bree?* he said, not wanting to linger on the thought of their separation.

*She's fine. Since we found the fish, everyone is in perfect health. As far as we can tell, that includes the baby.*

*Is she worried about the pregnancy?*

*She has to be, but you know Bree. If she's scared, no one will know except maybe Jak. She wouldn't want to burden me. She thinks I have enough to worry about.*

Bree had always tried to protect the two of them from the weight of being the governor's children. Not that Cal would ever let her succeed in that.

*How is Dad?* Cara asked. *What did he do when Mom took you home?*

*He's hardly been around. Mom says he was going to put an end to the medication himself, but he thought he needed more time to get things ready. She won't say what things, but he's called a gathering to tell everyone that I can talk to you. He already had two gatherings while I was out of it, to report the scientific findings. I guess the families of the disappeared were happy when he cancelled the memorial service, so they haven't pushed for more yet.*

*When is the gathering?*

*Tonight. He'll let me explain, but he also told Nev he can present his conclusions when I'm done. I'm not sure I can be more convincing than a scientist, but Cal is weirdly calm about it.*

*He has a plan.*

*No doubt.*

*Are you afraid?*

*No,* he said. She was, though. He could feel it. He sent her all the anger-fueled confidence he had.

*But what if....*

*Either they'll believe me and agree to help or they won't. If they don't, I'll find you without them.*

*But if they....*

*There will be no more drugs. I cooperated the first time. I won't cooperate again. The charter says no one can be drugged against their wishes. You know Cal. He'll never break the charter rules.*

*He's never faced anything like this before.*

*Yeah, but he's got rules for that, too.*

*There are some situations beyond the reach of any of the old rules.*

Tom smiled. *Who are you, and what have you done with my sister?*

She was surprisingly bleak. *I have no idea where that girl is.*

That hurt him.

*The gathering is tonight,* he said. *Tell me everything that's happened in the last week, and I'll pass it on. Then trust me. I will convince them. I will find a way to you.*

*I trust you.*

She didn't really, but she wanted to. He'd take that for now.

Tom had been to dozens of gatherings in his life. They held them for celebrations, community updates, and legal proceedings. He'd seen the colony excited about the future, worried about a newly discovered disease, and angry over a thief in their number.

He'd never experienced anything like the way the room felt today.

Tension crackled in the air. Every face was tight. Even the children who had been allowed to attend looked subdued and uncomfortable.

The meeting hall shared a building with the kitchens and the vast dining room. It was set up like a theater, with three sections of chairs divided by two aisles, all facing the low stage. With more than 900 seats, it could hold the entire adult population of Mayland.

Tonight it was full.

Tom walked behind his father toward the small podium at the front of the room. As they passed, the mutters and whispers of the crowd fell silent. By the time they were in their place, everyone was waiting quietly.

"Thank you for coming," Cal said without preamble. His steady voice carried easily throughout the hushed room. "There are no words to describe the difficulty of the last two weeks. The disappearance of fifteen of our best and brightest is a loss that we can't begin to calculate. The fact that we do not know how or why they are gone only adds to our grief and uncertainty. Before anything else, we want to take a moment of silent recognition of what we've lost. We recognize the pain of the families and friends of the disappeared. We recognize the strain on those who have lost coworkers and are continuing to meet the colony's needs without their help. We recognize the fear we all experience at the unknown future these events represent."

He paused and briefly closed his eyes. When he opened them again, he radiated resolution.

"We also recognize our strength. Our community has banded together in these last days. We have surrounded the bereaved with love and comfort. We have put in hours of work to study what occurred. Our understanding is growing and while it does, our regular work continues. New crops have been harvested. New children born. We have carried on, and we will keep carrying on."

Cal looked around the room. "Tonight we are gathered to share information about the disappearances. Some of what you hear will be confusing. Some will be shocking. Some will be difficult to understand or even to believe. All of it will be the truth, at least as understood by the speaker, and though there is still so much we do not know, nothing that we do know will be omitted. We are committed, as always, to full disclosure. No secrets. No lies.

"Whatever you feel about what you hear, we would ask, as we always do, that you listen fully before drawing conclusions. We would ask, as we always do, that all discussion remain calm and reasoned. And we would ask that you be patient. The Charter taught us to prepare for the unexpected, and the events of the last few weeks have taken us further into that territory than we ever dreamed possible. Navigating our path will not come without false starts and stumbling. As long as we continue in our commitment to patient progress, we will find our way together as we always do."

Tom saw his father's words take effect. Some of the tension left the room. People sat back in their chairs, reassured.

Wait until they heard what Tom had to say. They'd be sitting upright again in no time.

Cal began by presenting an update on the studies that had been run on the healing water and its connection to the disappearances.

They had discovered that if an altered animal–as they called those who had been given healing water—disappeared, it took any inanimate object it was touching along with it. Anything alive, plant or animal, would be left behind. They had also found that only rainwater collected in metal cannisters reacted with the healing water. Any rainwater that had touched the earth or had been collected in clay or ceramic containers was somehow neutralized and had no effect. They still didn't understand how the disappearance was taking place, but they were almost at the end of their supply of both healing water and rainwater, and they had concluded that there was no need for further testing. There would be no human trials. They couldn't afford any more losses.

Tom tried to be patient while his father slowly led up to the information they were really here to share.

Dr. Nev Ginopolis sat in the front row, waiting his turn. Tom avoided looking in his direction. Tonight, of all nights, he had to stay calm.

Finally, Cal introduced the topic of communication with those who had disappeared. He chose his words carefully, managing to make it sound like anything was possible while still being clear that he maintained a healthy skepticism.

With that ringing endorsement, he signaled Tom to begin.

Tom stepped forward and took a deep breath. He looked out at the sea of faces, saw his teammates sitting together several rows back. A few of them smiled. Most looked worried sick. Lin's parents were off to the left near the front, flanked by her older sisters. All of their faces were drawn and pale. Tom swallowed hard.

Jof Harson was in the front row. He leaned forward, eyes fixed on Tom.

Tom realized the silence was stretching out, but he couldn't look away from Jof's steady gaze. Slowly, the older man nodded, and Tom found his voice.

"All of you know me," he said, "and you know my sisters. You know that Bree is one of the best doctors in Mayland. You know that Cara and I were born six minutes apart and because she was that much older, she became my father's apprentice. You've all seen her at her work. You know she'll be a wonderful governor some day. You know that both of my sisters are missing." His voice cracked, and he stopped for a moment to steady it. "What you don't know is that since they disappeared along with the others, I have been in communication with Cara."

He saw the wave of surprise pass over the room, but this community was nothing if not disciplined. No one spoke.

Starting with the discovery of their connection as children, Tom explained everything, right up to the update that Cara had given him just a few hours before.

"They have been down the road to death, but they're still alive," he said. He wondered where Hy's family was sitting and Zyk's. He was glad he didn't know. "They are lost, but they can be found. They are surviving, but they need our help to make it home. They are waiting for us to reach out. Tonight, we have the chance to begin."

He stepped back and nodded to his father. Cal raised his hands against the murmur of voices that had begun to rise.

"Before we open discussion, I would like you to hear from Dr. Ginopolis, who conducted Tom's psychological evaluation. Nev is an expert in his field. Many of you have been helped by him in the past. He has his own educated interpretation of what you have just heard, and I've asked him to share that with you all, so that you may consider another point of view as we decide how to move forward. Nev."

Nev stood and thanked the governor for the introduction. He presented his clinical analysis with a scientific precision that somehow managed to project warmth and compassion even while he made Tom out to be delusional.

Tom didn't dare look around to see if the colony was persuaded by Nev's words.

Cal stepped forward. "One point of clarification, Doctor. Is there any precedence for the kind of mental communication Tom claims to have with Cara?"

"While a high degree of sympathy has been observed between children of multiple births, nothing of the clarity that Tom describes has ever been recorded. If the mental communication is what he has claimed, it is unique, the first of its kind. As such, it is much more medically likely that one of the conditions I have described is responsible for the symptoms Tom has experienced."

"Thank you. Continue."

Nev explained the effects of the drug he had given Tom and gave background on its development. When he mentioned Ny Lee's name, an audible hum passed over the crowd.

Tom was losing credibility fast, and Nev knew it. After only a few more pointed comparisons between Tom and the murderer, he took his seat with smug serenity.

Cal raised his hands one last time, but instead of speaking, he gestured at a young man and woman seated in the third row. The pair stood and made their way to the front where they turned to face the room.

Tom recognized Jorg Blackly and his sister, Mal. Jorg had been an apprentice teacher when Tom was in school. Now in his mid-twenties, Jorg had his own classroom.

"Governor Mayland asked if we would be willing to share our experience," Jorg said.

Something in his voice made Tom sit up straighter.

"With respect to Dr. Ginopolis, he's wrong about Tom's case being unique." Jorg paused long enough to meet Tom's eye. "Mal and I can do the same thing."

Mal nodded, and fireworks began to go off in Tom's head.

Mal. Not just Jorg's sister, his twin.

Nev put on his professional smile, but Tom could see the strain underneath. "That is an interesting claim, Jorg, and one we should discuss, but…."

"We've always been afraid to tell anyone, but what Tom is saying…it's how it is for us. When the governor first asked, we didn't want to admit it." He gestured at Nev. "We didn't want anyone to think we were crazy. But Tom…we didn't know anyone else could do this, but I know you're telling the truth."

Tom's mind raced. All this time. Why had they never talked to other twins?

On the far side of the room, a slender teenage girl stood up. Her voice shook, but she said, "Hen and I can do the same thing."

Her twin rose from where she was sitting three rows up. She had tears in her eyes. "We thought we were crazy."

A thirty-something woman stood up next. "Zan and I, too," she said. "Never words but feelings. We've never spoken to anyone about it. I never knew…." She broke off for a moment, then lifted her chin. "He's on childcare duty tonight, but he'll tell you the same."

The room was silent.

Tom stared at these other twins, overwhelmed. Nev had gone white, eyes on the floor.

Cal's plan had worked perfectly. Any chance that some would be convinced by the psychologist disappeared when he stood and hurried out the door.

Jof pushed to his feet. "We came here to talk about the disappeared. If we take these people at their word, that means that Tom has been speaking to Cara, that those we lost are alive and waiting for us, as he said. So how do we find them?"

His words brought Cal to life. "You're right. Our purpose tonight is to focus on those who are missing. The question of whether or not to accept Tom's story is merely the first step. What do the people of Mayland say? Do we believe the psychic communication between Tom and Cara and begin discussions based upon the information he has received?"

The vote was unanimous.

# Chapter 29

## *Disclosure*

"Right now it's only a theory. We're working on ways to test it, and hopefully we'll know more soon. But even if we are on Dua, there's still hope for getting home. Somehow we were sent here. It has to be possible to be sent back."

Cara wanted to pour out reassurances, to cover their looks of horror with positive words, but she forced herself to stop talking. She took a deep breath.

"Our grandparents and great-grandparents traveled through space to make a life on Una. If we have to do the same, we will."

Pol made a little choking noise and buried her face in her hands. Lil put an arm around her friend and whispered something in her ear.

"It might not even be true, though, right?" Syl said. "We might just be on a different part of Una."

"Yes, that might be. That's why we're making two maps: a land map and a map of the stars. And everyone at home will be working to find out how to travel to where we are."

"Can they get the old spaceship working?" Lil asked. "My Mom always said most of it is still floating up there."

"Only the heaviest structural pieces are in space," Jak said. "They brought everything else down to build Mayland."

"And we're generations away from producing the fuel it would take to break out of the atmosphere again," said Jem. "Landing on Una was a one-way trip."

His last words hung in the air.

"So what has Tom told you?" Ann asked. "What ideas do they have?"

Cara swallowed. Full disclosure. "Honestly, until last night, I hadn't heard anything from him in several days. But last night we talked. They were going to have a gathering to discuss what to do next. I'm sure they will have a plan soon."

Their faces said they did not share her confidence.

"I'm not saying this is going to be easy or that it will happen quickly," Cara said. "There's too much that we don't understand. But the good news is that we are safe now and fed. We have all that we need to survive until we get things figured out."

"We've already experienced at least five miracles in the last few weeks," Bree said. "It's not so hard to believe in one more."

Cara wanted to hug her sister.

"My grandmother always used to say she would move heaven and earth for her children," Jem said. "When my kids were born, I thought I knew what she meant, but now I guess I'm going to find out if I can actually do it."

"So what do we do?" Lil asked. She still had her arm around Pol.

"Ann and Wyn will work on the star map. You and Syl and Pol can be Ann's assistants. Gather what she needs for paints and brushes. Learn to make the paint. When you've done all she asks, you can continue food gathering."

Lil nodded, nudging Pol. "Pol is really good at drawing. Fashion design was her hobby. She could help with that."

Cara threw a questioning glance at Ann, who nodded.

"Good," Cara said. "Pol, will you be Ann's apprentice map-maker?"

Pol looked up, her eyes red but holding a hint of hope that hadn't been there before. She nodded.

"Thank you. Lin and I will work on surveying for the land map. Oz, can you help us make the tools we'll need for that? Then you can plan for a longer journey. We'll need containers for food and water. Would you be able to make a cart of some kind for carrying things?"

"I'll figure it out," Oz said.

"And there are probably other things that could help us. I'm counting on you to think of what they are. Jem, you'll keep working on the food stores? The twins can be your assistants."

"We've already got a good system down," Jem said.

"Bree, Jak, how are things coming on testing the fish?"

The two had been working the last two days to design ways to study the effects of the fish. They knew the healing water had somehow brought them here. The fish healed the same way, though their effect was even stronger. Maybe, if they could understand the fish, they could find some connection. Maybe they could find a way home.

"We don't have any equipment to study the chemical makeup, but we've been using plants as test subjects with some interesting results. And I'm designing a way to calculate the population of the species. It's going to be a few more days before we have anything to show for it," Jak said.

"If we ever do at all," Bree added.

"Okay. Stay on it. Those things are keeping us alive. It would be nice to know how."

"I think I've found a way to press the fish to extract oil," Bree said. "It would be more efficient to transport and last longer than dried fish."

"That's brilliant. You are all brilliant. That's why we're going to make it home," Cara said.

She almost believed herself.

Surveying, it turned out, was incredibly boring.

Counting his arm length as roughly a meter, Oz made them a rope of braided grass that was five meters long. While he worked on it, the twins helped Cara and Lin fill their pockets with dozens of tiny pebbles. Bree fashioned a bag from a scrap of material torn from the bottom her pant leg and some woven grass cords. The plan was to drop a pebble into the bag for each rope span, and so measure the distance to certain landmarks.

"It won't hold a lot of weight," Bree said, "So you'll have to use lots of landmarks."

When they set out, Cara felt confident. They were taking control of their environment. Measuring it. Mapping it. Understanding it.

After several hours of slow progress, the feeling wore off.

Cara held one end of the rope while Lin walked forward with the other end until it was taut. Then Lin stood still while Cara walked up to join her, dropped a pebble in the bag and walked on another 5 meters. Cara waited for Lin to join her, dropped another pebble in the bag, walked five meters more.

Over and over.

When they reached a tall tree standing all alone with its lowest branches crossed, they counted the pebbles in the bag. Lin used her knife to scratch the number onto the flat piece of bark she was carrying. Then they emptied the bag and started over.

The goal for the first day was to measure the distance to the edge of the forest. Creeping along like an inchworm on old Earth made that goal seem insurmountable.

"Please tell me we're halfway there," Cara said when they stopped for lunch under a set of half-dead trees that had grown around each other in a twist.

Lin studied the distant tree line. "I think we're more than halfway, but I can't really tell. That's why we're measuring."

Cara forced herself to swallow the bland root that had gotten a little mushy during the walk. "At least the trip home will be faster."

"I'll race you," Lin said, flopping down and casting a dirty look at her own lunch.

They made it to the forest by midafternoon. While Lin scratched out the measurements, Cara built a big pile of rocks and sticks to mark the spot. Then they took a long drink of water and turned back toward home.

They didn't race. Walking side by side felt good enough. They did retrace their route, making sure they recognized all the markers they had left and adding piles of stones and sticks to point the way. At each landmark, they paused and marked it as distinctively as possible.

It was almost dark when they made it back to the camp. Lin hurried off to show Ann her bark record. They would be making several more of them before the artist would transfer the information to the cave walls, but Lin had a better idea of scale now and wanted to discuss it.

Cara intended to make the rounds of all her people, checking in on their day, but a burst of emotion from Tom made her turn away to find a more private place.

At first it was hard to sort out what he was feeling. Confusion. Wonder. Hope.

Cara clung to that last one. They must be believing him.

A few minutes later, Tom's voice broke through.

*Cara, I can't... This is... The other twins... That was Cal's plan. He talked to other twins. Several of them stood up and admitted they could do the same thing we can.*

A million thoughts raced through Cara's head. She should have known. *Hal and Em. It was a pattern.*

*Hal and Em?*

*The kids who are here with me. They're twins, too. They can do it, too.*

*Why didn't you tell me that before?*

*I didn't know until we lost communication. And then last night...there was so much to tell you, I just didn't think of it.*

*I wish I had asked. But I never thought of other twins.*

*But Dad did.*

*He did.*

*I'm sorry I didn't tell you about Hal and Em. I could have saved you so much worry. I feel like I'm constantly reeling these days.*

*And here I thought nothing ever knocked the unflappable Cara Mayland off balance.*

*Being magically transported to a field full of monsters was pretty destabilizing.*

# TWIN

*And I'll bet you just calmly picked up a weapon and took care of the problem anyway.* He was only half joking.

Cara shuddered, thinking of the terror of those first hours, and Tom was instantly contrite.

*Sorry. This is just...we were never the only ones. There were other twins doing the same thing all along.*

*Yeah. It's my fault. I wouldn't let you tell anyone. If I had, we could have known sooner. It would have helped.*

*None of that matters now,* Tom said. *I'm just thankful everyone knows, and now we can get you home.*

*How many?*

*How many what?*

*How many other twins can do this?*

*I haven't talked to them yet. Three sets stood up in the gathering, and they mentioned more. Honestly, Cara? I think it's all of them.*

Cara couldn't answer.

*This changes everything,* Tom said.

*We say that way too much these days. I feel like I don't know anything anymore.*

*Now you know how the rest of us feel. Let's get you home, Six. Then we can be confused together.*

# Chapter 30

## Allies

The dining room was empty, and only a small pool of light illuminated the table where Tom sat. Jof Harson sat next to him, while Bea Demar and Ming Vance nursed cups of tea on the opposite side.

Bea had capable brown hands, a neat black braid, and a steady expression. Only the dark circles under her eyes told of what she'd suffered recently.

Ming was Bea's polar opposite. Small, pale, and intense. She fidgeted with her teacup and was the first to break the silence.

"It's been almost two weeks. How can they be content to say they'll study the situation more?"

"We were never going to see action from a full gathering," Jof said. "Gatherings are for talking. Action will happen when the governor decides it will."

"It's not his decision," Tom said. "I promised Cara I'd get them home, and I intend to keep my promise. Like I said before, the fastest way to find them is to let the water send us to them. If it all works the way we think, I just need to touch a few drops of it, and I can be transported with the next rain. If I'm carrying a tracking device, you'll be able to pinpoint our location."

"But didn't transport disable their tech?" Bea asked.

"They were rain showering, so they only had one watch among them. It may have died for other reasons. But even if transport affects all tech, I can take tools with me, make repairs, get it up and sending a signal again."

"Unless the place you arrive is on a different planet," Bea said. "I don't think our tracking devices cover that kind of distance."

"That's just a theory," Tom said. "I know they're somewhere strange, but there's no possible way it could be Dua."

"You can talk to your sister in your head," Ming snapped. "I wouldn't go on too much about what's possible."

Bea put a soothing hand on Ming's arm. Since Jem disappeared, Ming had been managing not only her own grief but also that of her two children. She was understandably on edge.

"It's still a good plan," Jof said. "We can go prepared with...."

"Let's get one thing straight," Bea interrupted. "It might be a good plan, but it can't be Tom who goes. There are two hundred ways this could go wrong, and he's our only connection to the disappeared. If we lose you, Tom, we've lost communication with them."

Of course she was right, but Tom felt a mild sense of panic at the thought of staying behind while others went to find the disappeared. He tried to think of a logical reason but found nothing.

Jof shook his head. "If we send someone and the tech works, we're lightyears closer to bringing them home. If it doesn't—if we can't get something as basic as a tracking signal to function on the other side—

there isn't going to be any way to transport them either. Most likely, we're talking about a one-way trip."

There it was. What was really at stake.

Bea's mouth was a straight line. "So we're not talking about rescuing them. We're talking about joining them."

"If we can't get them home," Tom said, "I'm going to them. I have to."

"So am I," Jof said.

"Me, too," Ming added. "And the boys."

"That's not what you promised your sister, though," Bea said.

"Right now she needs to believe that coming home is possible. And I still have hope that it is."

"So this isn't about running away from home?"

That stung. "No, it's not. I'd do anything to see them again, but I swear this isn't about me."

"So you'll let someone else go first? You'll stay here and provide a link to Cara until we know if the tech works?"

Tom hesitated, but she had backed him into a corner. There was only one answer. "Yes. But if it doesn't, then I go."

Bea set her tea down with a thunk. "Fair enough. And Kane and I will go, too. I wanted to use that healing water on his hands anyway."

"The first step is to convince the governor to send someone with the tech, and we won't do that with talk of one-way trips," Jof said. "We can work out the details once he's given the go ahead. If everyone at this table is in agreement, we can write up a proposal, ask the other families of the disappeared to sign it, get it to the governor tomorrow."

Proposals. Signatures. More people to convince. More protocols to follow. Tom understood the reasons for all of it, but the fact that everyone accepted the necessity of paperwork even in a crisis felt slightly ridiculous.

A little tug at the back of his head told him that Cara was waiting to talk.

"If you write it, I'll sign it," he said. "And I'll go with you to see my father when it's ready." He touched his head. "Cara wants me."

"Tell her thank you for the message," Ming said, "and to give our love back to Jem. Make sure he knows we're all okay. He worries."

Tom took in her anxious face. "I'll tell him your food is better than ever." Ming was one of the colony's master chefs.

"Go ahead and lie if you think it will motivate him to get home faster," she said. "The truth is I can't even cook an egg properly these days. My apprentice is doing all the work."

"So I should tell him she's the one who really needs him to come back."

"She does. The kids do. I do. Nothing works right without him."

"I'll let you tell him that yourself when you see him."

Her smile was forced, but it was a smile. He'd take it.

"Your proposal is thoughtful, and I appreciate the hard work you've put into thinking through a plan. Unfortunately, it isn't possible."

Tom stared at his father. He hadn't expected an immediate reply. The governor was nothing if not deliberate and thorough, but Cal had only briefly skimmed what Jof had written before giving his answer.

"You're making a unilateral decision?"

"In this case, there is nothing to decide. As I said, your proposal was well thought-out, but you did not have all the information." Cal squared his shoulders, always a sign that he was about to deliver bad news. "Last night the water sample you brought back from the lake was destroyed."

So many words whirled through Tom's brain that he couldn't grasp any of them long enough to speak.

"Destroyed," Jof said. "This was some kind of accident?" He sounded almost conversational, but Tom didn't think he was imagining the edge in the old man's voice.

"Not an accident. An unfortunate necessity. After the gathering, the lab techs detected evidence that someone had tried to gain access to the storage unit where the water sample was being kept. We still don't know who that was, but if they had succeeded, if more colonists had been exposed and transported without careful consideration, the results would have been disastrous. It's too high a risk. On the advice of the heads of the relevant teams, I had the sample destroyed."

"So you're abandoning Bree and Cara," Tom said.

Cal didn't flinch. "Don't be dramatic. We will still pursue other avenues of reaching them, your connection to Cara being the main one. I freely admit that the decision to destroy the water was not easy for me to make. I don't enjoy the idea of closing down even one potential avenue for bringing my daughters home. But my duty, all of our duties—our sworn oath, in fact—is to put the needs of the colony above our own personal needs. The girls understood that. They would want us to protect our people."

"The disappeared *are* Mayland Colony."

"They are a part of it, yes, but not the whole. The hard truth is that we cannot guarantee their survival and return. But we can guarantee our own."

The cold assessment left Tom reeling. He stood up, speechless, and headed for the door.

"Tom." His father's voice carried a command he couldn't ignore. Tom stopped and turned around. "Take some time to accept this reality, but then I need you back here helping us communicate with those we've lost."

The words Tom tried to say came out as an inarticulate noise. He turned away again.

"Tom." This time the word was softer. Tom stopped with his hand on the door but didn't look back.

"Don't make the mistake of believing that you love them more than I do."

Tom walked away and pretended he hadn't heard.

# Chapter 31

# Map

"We're going to put labels on everything anyway. We might as well give them real names," Ann said.

The adults were standing in a semi-circle around the land map on the wall of the main tunnel, studying Ann's latest work.

"It's not necessary," said Lin, "and it makes it all feel too...permanent."

"Maybe, but it helps," Jem said. "The kids and I already started coming up with names for the food. Things feel less foreign when they have a name."

*Another way of taking back control*, Cara thought. *Measure. Map. Name.*

No one else objected.

"We should start here," Ann said, pointing at the spot on the map that marked the cave where they stood.

"Incannu," said Wyn.

Everyone turned in surprise. Wyn never spoke without someone speaking to her first.

"It means 'unknown' in old Earth French." At their continued stares, Wyn shrugged. "My grandmother used to call me that sometimes because I didn't talk much."

"Unknown," Cara said. "Yes. That sounds right."

"If no one objects? That's where we live, then." Ann dipped her brush in a little clay pot of red paint by her feet, then wrote *Incannu* next to the cave on the map.

*Yes,* Cara thought, as the others began to discuss names for the landmarks they had found. *Incannu. The unknown. That's exactly where we live.*

A sudden surge of rage made her heart pound and her skin flush. *Tom? What's wrong?* She turned and hurried from the cave.

At first, he didn't answer in words, just radiated anger in incoherent surges. Cara made her way around the edge of the rocks, past the star map and into a little cleft where she could be alone. She crouched down and tried to take deep breaths.

After a few minutes, Tom began to curb his anger, and the raging subsided to a dull bitterness.

*He destroyed the water,* he said finally. *There's none left.*

*What? Who?*

*Who do you think? It's going to rain again soon. I told them your theories. We proposed putting a tracker on Jof. Then he'd use the water, be transported to you, and we could find you all.*

*Tom, that's....*

*Brilliant? Obviously.*

*Dangerous. The beasts....*

262

# TWIN

*We don't have a lot of options, Cara. And he could come prepared. Anyway, it doesn't matter now because Cal destroyed the water sample. Apparently, there was some security breach, and they got panicked that a bunch of people would be exposed and transported.*

Tom's rage was back in force. Cara was thankful that his emotion didn't leave room for her to feel her own yet.

*But....*

*He hasn't even informed the colony yet. I didn't know he'd done it until he told us our plan was impossible. As usual, he's not sorry at all. Says he wants to find you, but his responsibility is to the colony, that we can't afford to lose any more people.*

*He's not wrong.*

*He IS wrong. We can't afford to lose YOU. Lin. Bree. Jak. Getting you back is worth the risk.*

*We'll find another way.*

*There already is another way. There's a whole lake full of that water. He can't destroy it all. I'm leaving as soon as I can. Jof is coming with me. But we won't get to the lake before the next rain. It's going to be more than a month before we can get to you.*

Cara couldn't mask the sinking of her heart. She understood her father's decision, but it still felt like a betrayal. Even if it would be wrong, some part of her wanted to be her father's first priority. Sternly, she quashed the self-pity. *We knew this was going to take time. We're preparing for it. We'll be okay. And this way we can plan more carefully for his arrival.*

*It won't just be him coming. I was prepared to let him go first, to try the tracker while I stayed back to communicate, but not after this. I'm coming, too.*

*There's time to decide all that.*

*Ha. Too much time.*

*Is Jof really up for a trip to the lake?* Cara was pretty sure Ann's husband was nearly 70.

*He's in good shape for a man his age, but I'm not sure that even matters. I've never seen anyone with so much determination.*

"Cara?" Lin's voice sounded worried.

*I have to go. Lin is looking for me. We have another surveying trip today.*

*Tell her I love her.*

*I always do.*

*Tell Bree, too. And tell yourself.*

"Cara?"

"I'm here," Cara answered.

Lin came around the rocks. "You okay? You looked furious when you walked out of there."

"Tom's the one who's angry."

"Is he okay?"

Cara forced a smile. "He's fine. He said to tell you he loves you." She sighed. "I'll tell you the rest on the way."

As she expected, Lin shared Tom's anger toward their father. Being Lin, though, she quickly moved on to planning their next moves.

"So they're expecting rain in five days," Lin said as they inched their way across the savannah toward the west. "It will be another 20 or so before the next one comes. That gives us less than four weeks to prepare for his arrival. We're assuming he'll come through at the meadow where we did, right?"

"That's the theory. Jem says that's probably why the beasts live there. We've seen no other animal life. They must wait for prey to come through."

"So Tom and Jof need to bring weapons. And we can go meet them with our own."

"And the fish," Cara said.

Lin nodded, dropping another pebble into their measuring bag. "This will work. I know it will."

"But getting him here is only one step. If transport breaks the tracker and they can't fix it, we're no closer to getting home."

"Or if 'here' is on the other side of the vacuum," Lin said.

"Wyn needs a few more days for the map, but she doesn't have much doubt."

It was Lin's turn to carry the rope forward, but she stopped and squinted off toward the horizon. "So maybe Cal is right. Maybe they shouldn't come. If there's no way home anyway."

"We both know that's the real reason they're coming," Cara said. "If we can't get home, they want to be here with us."

"Is it terrible that I'm glad?"

"If it is, then I'm terrible, too."

Lin sighed. "Okay. I'm all right then. We all know you could never be terrible."

Cara wanted to believe that, but as the days dragged on, each with its creeping trip across the savannah, she found an anger growing inside that she was pretty sure no good person would feel.

With each passing night, Wyn's map was more complete, and her confidence in her theory stronger. Knowing that they were probably out of reach on another planet should have made Cara more sympathetic toward her father's choices. Instead, she felt abandoned. It was illogical, but she wanted him to come and rescue her, and it cut deep that he wouldn't even attempt it.

Cara tried to keep her anger from spilling over toward the others, but her answers to Lin got more snappish by the day.

Her friend never complained, just talked less and less. Cara couldn't blame her. She knew she was terrible company.

Cara told herself it was fine. She told herself that destroying the water sample hadn't really changed anything. It was only a delay, a safeguard for the colony while they made a careful plan. Of course her father loved her. Of course he was working to bring her home.

She reminded Tom of that every time she talked to him. It was the truth.

But it didn't remove the hole that had opened inside her chest or the simmering bitterness that bubbled out of it.

Cara struggled on, measuring, mapping, naming, but she had never felt less in control.

# Chapter 32

# *Division*

"How soon could you leave?" Ming sat on the small bench, her hands tightly clenched in her lap.

"Within an hour, but it will take at least a week to get to the lake, and the rain will come before then."

"Sometimes the rains come later than predicted," she said.

"Not that much later," said Bea. She had been leaning against a tree, but now she came and sat next to Ming. "We have to prepare ourselves to wait another month for the next rain."

A small choking sound escaped Ming's throat, and Tom's anger surged again. His father had no right to drag out their torture like this.

"You shouldn't travel alone. And you should prepare for the journey. Rushing doesn't help at this point," Bea said. "What do you need for the trip?"

"He won't be alone," Jof said. "I'm going with him."

Tom had already tried to talk Jof out of the trip, explaining the dangers and difficulties of trail life, especially at the rate they would be traveling. The old man wouldn't be talked down.

"My father won't give his permission," Tom said. "We should assume that we're going to have to find all the food and other supplies without his help."

Bea nodded thoughtfully. "That won't be difficult. Ming can get you food, and I have access to a wide variety of tools, not to mention that I maintain the machines that make all of our textiles and building materials. We can get you what you need."

"I already have the supply lists from your last trip," Ming said. "I can have the food ready in a couple of hours."

"It would be better if we didn't hide," said Joff. "We should ask the governor for permission. He might surprise you."

"Why would he give us permission to go get more of the same water he just destroyed?"

"Because it buys him time," Jof said. "He knows that the lake is out there; he knew all along this was only a delaying tactic. More than anything, he wants time to make a careful plan. You and I are an unpredictable element. This would get us out of his way and give him a few more weeks. I think he'll agree to it."

"And if he refuses? If he finds a way to prevent us from leaving?"

"He can refuse, but he can't prevent us, not if we've planned ahead and are prepared to do what's necessary. He's not going to break charter rules, at least not publicly."

"He already broke them when he destroyed that water without a vote!"

"That's not how he sees it, and he's technically right. In his eyes, this wasn't a major decision about the future of the colony but an administrative decision. It wasn't permanent; we know where the water can be found. He consulted his key advisors and took action based on their advice. That gives him space to convince the colony of his point of view. It's the same thing he did when you found the water. He always toes the line of full disclosure, but the timing is at his discretion."

"How can you defend him?"

Jof's grey eyes were steel sharp. "I'm not defending him. I'm understanding him. He's not evil, Tom, or even unfeeling. He's afraid, and he's doing what he thinks is best to protect what he loves."

"Well, so am I, and I don't need his permission to do it."

"This is not just about you, though, is it?" Jof's voice never raised, but the anger was there. "These women will help us on our way. Then they will stay here. If they've acted without the governor's approval, they will be the ones to face the consequences when we're gone."

Tom sagged.

"This isn't a time to work against each other," Jof said. "It's a time to work together. At heart, you and your father want the same thing."

"I don't trust myself around him. I don't know what I'll say."

"Then don't say anything," the older man answered. "I'll do all the talking."

"I know the pain you are feeling, but you're pushing too hard," Cal said. "Patience is more effective."

"Waiting gains us nothing," Jof said. "As it is, the trip to and from the lake will take weeks. We will miss the next rain. If we wait, we could miss the next month's as well."

"The whole colony is on edge right now. People are reeling from too much that can't be explained. First the water, then the disappearances, and now this new revelation about twin communication. This water is a dangerous element, and though I agree that we'll likely need to use it eventually, our people need time to process."

"They'll have three weeks. In the meantime, we'll be traveling."

"There's other work to be done. Everyone has accepted Tom's connection to Cara. That was a big step, and we need to build on it. He needs to be here to communicate with her."

For a moment, Tom thought Jof would agree to leave him behind. It was the easiest way to convince Cal to let him go.

Jof laughed. "You've just said that we are too impatient. How do you think keeping us locked up here is going to help that? Tom's communication with Cara comes and goes. How often do you speak to her, Tom? Once a day?"

"At most."

"And what is he going to do with the rest of his time? How else can he be useful here? He led the team that found the lake. He's the most qualified to take us back there. The information he already passed on from Cara will keep our people working for weeks. At the end of that time, Tom will be back, and communication can resume with all the new information gathered while he was busy being useful."

Cal shook his head. "You're talking about the potential to alter the Plan completely, without nearly enough thought. Our great-grandparents studied Una for months before changing course to come here, and for months after that before choosing this location. We've sent out exploration teams for the past year trying to find the right location for our next settlement. And now in a matter of weeks, we want to make changes to the Plan that far outshadow either of those things. No one is denying that we have decisions to make in time. But this is too much, too fast."

"I've been thinking about that," Jof said. "Some of these new developments shouldn't have been as much of a surprise as they are. In reality, anomalies have been occurring for a while. The birth rate of twins has doubled every decade since the day we landed on this planet. A completely unexplained phenomenon, and yet we've ignored it."

Tom sat up straighter. He hadn't known that.

"It wasn't ignored. There are several possible explanations, and none are particularly alarming."

"It's a sign that something is fundamentally different here. But we didn't choose to see it that way."

"Our priority has always been survival, both immediate and long term. Until now, the twin rate appeared to have no bearing on that."

"I understand. I'm not criticizing. I'm saying that we haven't adapted quickly to new information, and that's making this more difficult. But we need to change that. We have no choice but to react more quickly now than we have in the past."

Cal sat silently for a while, his face an unreadable mask.

"You have my permission to travel," he said at last. "Make a list of supplies, and I'll approve the requisition order."

Tom exhaled.

"Thank you," Jof said.

"Only the two of you will go, and I'd ask that you don't talk about this trip to anyone outside of your immediate families. I will announce it to the whole colony, but I want to do it in a way that will minimize alarm."

"As you like," Jof said with a warning glance at Tom.

Tom bit his lip to keep the words in.

"While preparations are made, Tom, I'll need you to make yourself available to any of the scientists who have questions, even if doing so delays your departure. You don't leave until they have what they need from you. And you'll carry a communication device. It will only be in range for the first day, but I want you available as long as possible."

Tom nodded tightly.

The governor held out his hand to Jof. "Get me the list when you have it, then."

Jof shook his hand without hesitation. "I'll send it this afternoon."

Without a word, Tom followed Jof from the governor's office.

"You were right," he said.

"It was close," Jof answered. "I think he was going to say no before I brought up the twin birth rate."

"What difference does that make?"

"I suggested that this world makes even less sense to us than he's admitted. I suggested we've been burying our heads in the sand. It made him want to get rid of me."

"Won't someone else notice the connection between twin telepathy and birth rate?"

"Of course. But not today. I told you, all of this is about buying time. You heard him say there are decisions to be made eventually. He sees what we see. It's possible to travel to where they are, even if we can't return. He knows the families are going to want to do that. He knows he can't stop us, and he knows if too many people leave with no way back, those who stay behind may not survive. He wants time to help people see what's at stake. Time to convince them of a rational plan. To regain control of the situation."

"How can he still think control is possible?"

"We're all trying to control our lives in some way."

"But we can't. If the last few weeks have shown us anything it's that we've been in over our heads this whole time. You just said so yourself. Since we arrived on this planet, we've been floating in an ocean that goes deeper than we can imagine. And we keep acting like it's a swimming tank."

"Believe me, your father knows that better than anyone. That's why he wants time to build a boat."

"Cara and the others may not have that kind of time."

"I know. So a hastily built raft is going to have to do. But rafts are easily sunk. Your father isn't wrong to be afraid."

"We don't have a choice."

"That's the part he hates most."

# Chapter 33

# *Light*

On their sixth day of mapping, they turned toward the mountains.

Cara was in her worst mood yet. She had barely slept the night before, and when she did, her sleep was filled with nightmares. She hoped at least some of them had been Tom's. Especially the one that featured her father turning into a krona and trying to attack her.

The morning had brought another meeting to review the maps, which gave them a later start than usual, so they didn't stop for lunch until midafternoon.

"Back home after this?" Lin asked, eyeing the slab of leaf-wrapped root with distaste.

"Back to Incannu," Cara muttered. She only called it by its name now, taking perverse pleasure in thinking of it as *unknown,* though in reality it was starting to feel disturbingly comfortable.

Admitting that made her hate it more. She didn't want to be comfortable here.

"It feels weird for it to have a name."

Cara grunted.

"You could try an actual answer, you know," Lin snapped. "Everything you've said today has been a mumble or an inarticulate noise. It's like traveling with a krona."

Cara was about to give a scathing reply when Lin opened her mouth and let out a loud and surprisingly accurate imitation of a krona *grawp*.

At Cara's startled laugh, Lin cocked her head and grawped three more times. She butted her head against Cara's shoulder just like the giant lizard would.

"Okay, okay," Cara said. "I get it. You're right. I'm a beast."

"No, you're not," Lin said. "You're just in a bad mood, and I don't blame you, but you've been there for days, and I can't stand the silence anymore."

"You're right," Cara said. "That's fair. I just...."

Lin held up a hand. "No need to explain. Just have a conversation with me, okay? I'll start again. It feels weird for the caves to have a name."

"I'm getting used to it," Cara said. She pushed herself to add, "And it seems to help everyone feel better."

"Maybe that will help with this, too," Lin said, holding up her food. "Jem says they're calling the roots 'pamata.'"

"'Pamata in an herbal wrap.' Sounds tasty."

Lin wrinkled her nose. "Yeah, but it's not."

"That's probably why I hear everyone else calling them 'blurgroots.'"

Lin laughed.

Cara nibbled one corner. "I think the leaf helps a little."

Lin gagged down a bite. "I think you have a really good imagination."

*276*

# *TWIN*

They rested for a while, leaning back against the scrubby bushes that marked their stopping point. Cara was surprised to find that two minutes of small talk had actually improved her mood. She needed to make more of an effort. She needed to stop moping.

She stared at the sky, trying to think of things to talk about with Lin, trying not to let her thoughts cycle back around to self-pity.

It was time to get up and walk home, but they didn't.

Cara was bone tired. Everyone in the camp ate fish for breakfast each day, and for a few hours, the rush of well-being that came from their power held her up. But the fish weren't the same as real sleep.

Cara closed her eyes and drifted for a few moments.

When she opened them, the shadows were long.

"Stars! We fell asleep. Lin! Get up!" she said.

Her friend was stretched out with her face shaded by some branches. When she bolted upright, she hit her head on one and cursed loudly.

"Sorry," Cara said. "Didn't mean to scare you. We fell asleep. It's getting late."

Lin scrambled to her feet. "The others will worry."

"Nothing to be done about that now."

Cara stretched, feeling the tightness in her back from sleeping on hard ground. She looked out at the mountains, still so distant. Her hope that they were the Silangan Mountains and that Mayland was on the other side was all but gone.

Something caught her eye, and she leaned forward, squinting for a better look. In the fading light, something glowed against the backdrop of dark peaks.

"Lin?"

"You ready?"

"Just a second. Can you look at this?"

Lin came to stand beside her.

"You said I have a good imagination. Am I imagining that?" Cara pointed to the light.

Lin sucked in a breath. "If 'that' is something glowing where nothing should be glowing, then no, you're not imagining it."

"Is it fire?"

Lin squinted at it for a while. "Can't tell for sure, but it seems too steady."

"What else could it be?"

"I have no idea."

Neither of them wanted to say that it would take intelligent life to make light in the darkness.

"We should check it out," Lin said.

"Too dangerous. It's just the two of us. We didn't come prepared for a long trip, and the others will worry as soon as it's dark. We should get back, gather supplies, and check it out tomorrow."

"What if it's not there tomorrow? We've never seen light like that. We may miss our chance."

"Our chance for what?"

Lin raised one brow. "Our chance to find out what it is. Isn't understanding our surroundings the whole reason for these surveying trips?"

Cara bit her lip.

"We're not completely unprepared," Lin said. "We have extra water and fish."

Though they only ate fish once a day to avoid killing too many, anyone who left Incannu took some along in case of emergency.

"It doesn't look like it's too far away. We can still make it back tonight and they won't be more than a couple of hours more worried," Lin said, and when Cara didn't answer, she added, "Light is a sign of life. We need to know what's out there."

It was the right argument. Cara wanted answers more than she wanted safety. "Okay, let's go. But once we're close enough to see it, we keep our distance. No unnecessary risks. And then straight back to the others before they come looking for us."

"Of course."

Cara picked up her walking stick. Oz had sharpened one end to a wicked point so it could double as a weapon if needed. They began to walk as quickly as they could toward the glow.

Darkness fell as they walked, and as it did, the glow seemed brighter. Its light was rosy and soft.

Cara still couldn't tell how far away it was. Her stomach twisted into a knot as curiosity battled anxiety inside.

Fifty meters ahead, a tight cluster of short trees stood in relief against the glow. It would make a good place to stop and evaluate the situation.

Cara hurried to catch up to Lin. She was so focused on keeping up with her friend's long-legged stride that she almost fell when Lin suddenly stopped.

"There," Lin whispered. "Through the trees."

Between the dark trunks, Cara could see something on the ground. She froze.

Both girls stood perfectly still, barely daring to breathe as they listened for any sounds.

There was no movement, not even a hint of a breeze. The utter stillness of the savannah, so peaceful in the day, seemed menacing in the eerily glowing night.

Lin began to creep forward, and though Cara wanted to tell her to stop, she didn't. Instead, she followed as softly as she could.

Under the trees, the glow was bright enough to clearly make out her friend's face. Lin smiled.

She eased forward to the glowing spot and knelt down next to it. When Cara joined her, she saw that it was a mound of rock jutting from the dirt. A few meters away, another pile glowed, and beyond that a whole sea of stones, lit as if something burned crimson inside.

Cautiously, Lin reached out a hand and touched the rock. "It's not hot," she said. The light from the stone shone through her fingers, giving them an otherworldly look.

Cara shivered. "It's beautiful," she said. She reached toward the stone, felt its rough edges, so at odds with the soft light it cast.

"And useful," Lin said. "If we take some of these back, we can light up the caves without torches. We can explore the lake. We can see the maps at night."

"Speaking of the caves, the others are probably frantic," Cara said, dragging her eyes away from the rocks. "Let's find some loose pieces and take what we can, but quickly. The sooner we're back, the better."

As she followed her own advice, she reached out to Tom, automatically looking up at the crescent in the sky, though she still hoped it wasn't Una.

*We found something new. Rocks that glow. They're beautiful. I wish you could see them.*

*Soon,* he answered.

Cara picked up a chunk the size of her fist and weighed it in her hand. *It's not heavy like a normal rock. It may be hollow.*

*Are you sure they're safe? Alien rocks?*

His use of the word alien should have spiked her fear again, but it didn't. She stared at the stone in her hand. It was beautiful. And useful, as Lin had said.

Weighed against useful and beautiful, alien didn't seem so bad.

A small part of her gut unclenched. Standing under unclassified trees with a glowing stone in each hand, she finally accepted the truth. She was on another planet.

No one had abandoned her, but no one could rescue her either. This was beyond their control.

She lifted another shining rock and thanked the stars that she couldn't explain it.

The unexplainable was now their only hope.

# Chapter 34

# *Understanding*

Tom was terrible at waiting. He organized his travel pack in the first hour after Cal's decision. Then he was forced to stare at it with increasing frustration each night as their trip got put off another day, and then another. Each new reason was perfectly valid and perfectly maddening.

At his father's insistence, Tom submitted to dozens more tests of his brain. No more drugs were used, and his mother monitored every step, but the long hours in the lab were grueling. Other sets of twins had volunteered to be studied as well. The colony had one doctor who specialized in neuroscience. He and his apprentice hadn't slept since the gathering, but their enthusiasm to advance their field wasn't dampened by exhaustion.

Each day Tom checked in with Cara and got a full description of what her team had discovered the day before. Her evident depression weighed on him, and he felt powerless to help her. The colony's artists and biologists were working together on maps and sketches of the unknown flora and fauna. Slowly they were putting together a profile of the ecosystem of their unknown location, but the news wasn't encouraging. It was increasingly difficult to imagine that the disappeared were anywhere on Una.

With that in mind, Ming had her kitchens working overtime to prepare food, not only for Tom and Jof, but also for the longer trip they now hoped would come after. Bea put together tool kits and worked to boost the signal on their communication devices, which currently only reached a kilometer or two outside the fence. They didn't have the ability to build what it would take to stay connected all the way to the lake, but she wanted to maintain communication as long as possible.

Between tests and consults, half a dozen members of Tom's exploration team came and asked to go with him. It hurt him to turn them away, but Cal had been very clear that no one else was to leave Mayland yet, and Jof and Tom had agreed to play the long game. This was only a trip to gather water. The real journey was ahead.

Finally, with the next rain only two days away, there were no more questions from the artists, no more tests to endure, no more preparations to make. They would leave the next day at first light.

Tom's impatience, kept under the surface for so long, now itched along his skin. All of their talk hadn't helped anything. It was time to act. There was no predicting what would happen until they did.

He was up before dawn and had just finished his third supply check when his mother knocked on his door. She came in without waiting for an answer.

Tom paused halfway through securing his pack. It felt strange to have his mother in his room, like the space was suddenly so much smaller than it had been a few minutes before.

She echoed his thoughts. "It's been a long time since I came in here. I like what you've done with the place." She gestured at the brightly colored painting that hung over the bed, as if it masked the tangle of covers under it and the piles of specimens and tools and broken tech that filled every other available surface. Tom liked to collect what interested him, and he was interested in a lot of things.

He laughed. "I admire your ability to focus on the positive."

"I like to think that if you have the good taste to hang an Ann Harson painting on the wall, maybe there's something in this that I'm just not seeing yet." She held up a roughly rectangular lump of dry river clay. A few pieces crumbled off the end.

"It was an experiment," Tom said. "A failed experiment," he added as another chunk fell. "It was supposed to be a brick, but…." He trailed off. Enough trying to avoid the real subject. "It's time, isn't it?"

She nodded.

"Bea's new signal booster will keep us in contact for the first day or two, and we'll be traveling a lot faster than we did when we were mapping. I expect to be at the lake in a week, maybe less. Once we've gathered the water, there shouldn't be any need to stay. We'll be home in another week. So really, only out of communication for ten days or so." Tom knew he was babbling and that none of it was reassuring. He only had to think back over the last ten days to realize how much could happen in that time. "There's no need to worry. Cara and Bree are in a safe place for now. And there isn't anything that can hurt Jof and I along the way."

"I hate waiting, and of course I'll worry," Jul said, "but it's for the best. Things have been moving too quickly lately."

"You think destroying the water was the right choice?"

She sighed. "I'm not sure if there are any right choices. I'm not sure our choices are making any difference at all. It's a defensible decision, and that's about all we can ask for."

"I could ask for him not to eliminate options."

"Look at you now. The options weren't eliminated, just delayed. He saw a danger to his people and protected them the best he could. He's only a man, Tom."

"Believe me, I know," Tom said.

"Do you? You may not worship him like your sister did, but you hold him to a superhuman standard anyway."

"He's the one who sets himself up to be superhuman."

"We're his family," Jul said. "It's our job to see past that."

"I do. I'm the one who has been calling him out this whole time! I'm the only one not blindly following his benevolent commands."

She raised a brow and said nothing.

"I'm sorry," he said. "I know you stand up to him. I just…everyone follows his lead like he can do no wrong."

"He's earned that trust."

"I get that."

"I'm not sure you do. You want people to listen to you? You want your father to listen to you? You have to show them that you'll put their needs ahead of your own. That's what your father has done all along. And that's what he did when he destroyed that water. You don't think he wants to go to your sisters? You don't think he wants to save them? You've lived with the man your whole life. Do you not know him at all? He wants what you want, but he won't choose it because he doesn't think it's best for everyone else."

Her conviction made Tom feel small. He sat down on the messy bed, ran a hand through his hair. "I'm just not sure I see what gives him the right to decide what's best for everyone."

"No," Jul said. "That's not the problem."

He looked up at her.

*286*

"You aren't angry that he's deciding what's best for everyone. You're angry because he would choose their best over yours."

"Thanks. That makes me sound like a selfish child."

"Not a child. A son. Believe it or not, you also are only a man."

"We've never been his priority."

He was surprised that she didn't even try to deny it. "And I know that hurts you."

"Doesn't it hurt you?"

She took her time answering. "It's different for me. I chose him. I chose this. And I know he loves me, even while I know he'll never let that love interfere with his decisions."

Tom didn't know what to say.

"He loves you, too. And Bree and Cara. But he is who he is, and that isn't going to change. And soon it's going to be time for you to make your own choice. Just promise me you'll think about it and try to understand."

"I will."

She smiled and smoothed his hair back down.

"I'll see you at the gate."

# Chapter 35

## Change

If Cara had thought Oz's quiet calm had no limits, one look at his face in the flickering torchlight taught her different.

"What happened?" His voice shook as his eyes flicked back and forth from her face to the glowing rock in her hand. They had met him a few hundred meters from Incannu, coming with Jak and Jem to look for them.

"I'm sorry we scared you," she said.

"What. Happened?" he repeated.

"We fell asleep."

He closed his eyes for a second, summoning a peace that didn't come. "What is that?"

"We're calling them glowstones," Lin said.

Cara explained. "When we woke up, it was getting dark. We saw the glow in the distance and went to check it out. We found these."

Oz's eyes were open again, two glittering black knives reflecting two kinds of light. His voice was steady but carried an edge. "You went to check it out? The two of you? In the dark?"

Cara raised her chin. "Yes, and it was the right decision. These will make a huge difference for Jak's work, for all of us."

"A huge difference," he repeated. She had never heard bitterness from him before.

"What's wrong?" she asked.

He glared at her.

"This is more than worry. Did something happen while we were gone?"

"You could say that," he said.

Cara's heart constricted. "Oz. Tell me. Please. What happened?"

Jak took over. "Everyone is okay. We think. It's…you'll need to see it for yourself. The kids…their skin is different."

"Different?" It was too innocuous a word for the dread that came with it.

"The color," Jem clarified. "Their skin color has changed."

"Flushed?" Cara asked. "Pale? Jaundiced?"

"Blue," Oz said.

"Only slightly," said Jak. "It's a minor variation in tint."

Cara started walking quickly toward home.

"They'll be asleep by now. You'll have to see them in the morning," Jak said, hurrying along beside her.

"Just Hal and Em?"

"The young girls, too. Pol and Lil. Syl."

"Do they have other symptoms?"

"Nothing. Bree gave them a full examination. Other than being psychologically shaken, they're in perfect health."

Psychologically shaken. In other words, they were totally freaked out. Because their skin had turned blue.

Whatever peace Cara felt with the discovery of the glowstones was gone. Would this never end? Blue skin. How did she even start with that?

"Most likely this is a side effect of our new diet and environment," Jak said. "We don't know anything about the chemical makeup of our food and water, and the fish provide a wildly unpredictable element. A slight alteration in pigmentation isn't necessarily a problem."

"Why is it just the children?"

"Most likely because their bodies are smaller and their metabolism faster. I imagine it will happen to all of us in time."

"We're all going to have blue skin?" Something to add to the list of things she never thought she'd say.

"The change isn't really that radical. It's more of a cerulean color on those who had light skin and a slight violet tint on those whose skin was darker."

"Cerulean?"

Cara stopped walking and stared at her brother-in-law. The others stopped, too.

"It's actually quite beautiful," he said. "Different isn't always worse."

"Please tell me that's not what you said to the terrified teenage girls."

"Don't be ridiculous," he said. "I didn't talk to them at all. Bree handled that."

Cara let out a long breath.

"At least you know your limits," Lin said.

"I need to talk to Bree." Cara hurried on again.

The cooking fire was still burning outside the cave entrance when they arrived. Everyone over sixteen was gathered around it.

When Bree saw their lights, she stopped her pacing and ran toward them. "Cara! You're all right! Lin! When you didn't come back by dark, we thought...."

Cara hugged her sister, then stumbled slightly when Bree pulled Lin in, too.

"What happened?"

Feeling like a wayward child, Cara repeated the story again. Everyone passed around the glowstones in wonder.

"Tell me about the kids," Cara said. "How are they?"

"Scared. Lil and Pol noticed it first and came screaming to the rest of us. Then we saw that the same thing had happened to the twins. Their case is actually more advanced, but with their darker skin, it seemed like a trick of the light. Syl's case is very slight, only noticeable because we were looking for it. No one else is affected."

"So far," Jak said.

"He told you about his theory?" Bree asked.

"Yes. What do you think?"

"I'm not as resigned to it as he seems to be." Bree cast an exasperated look at her husband. "I can't dispute his reasoning, though. I did every test I could think of with our current limitations, and they appear perfectly healthy. The pigmentation seems to be the only change."

"But you don't have the equipment to test their blood or do scans. We don't really know what's going on inside," Cara said.

"True, but as long as there are no external warning signs, there's no point in worrying about possibilities."

"Blue skin isn't an external warning sign?" Lin asked.

"Not necessarily," Bree answered.

"I want to see them," Cara said. "I promise I'll be quiet."

Bree nodded and led the way into the cave. Lin followed silently behind Cara. The glowstones were much easier to use than torches, their light steady and warm.

"Pol's is the most obvious, since her skin was the lightest," Bree whispered. She led the way over to where the girl slept, one hand tucked beneath her cheek.

Both hand and cheek were sky blue.

"Cerulean," Cara said.

Bree gave her a look. Cara turned away and crept over to little Em. The girl slept on her back with her mouth open, utterly abandoned. Her skin had been a dark chocolate color but now it was distinctly purple-blue.

They made their way back to the fire and sat down beside the others.

Lin shook her head. "Could this day get any weirder?"

"Wyn finished the star map," Oz said, as if he'd been waiting for her to ask.

"It was a rhetorical question," Lin muttered.

Cara turned to where Wyn and Ann sat on the far side of the fire.

Wyn nodded. "There's no place on Una that the stars would be in these positions."

"So we're on an alien planet," Lin said. "And now apparently we're turning into aliens."

It wasn't a joke, and no one laughed. The fire cracked and popped as they all stared into it.

Cara tried to think of the next step, some forward motion. She felt frozen. There was little point in continuing their land surveys if they were waiting on magical transportation back home. They had no choice but to continue to collect food and eat it, even if it turned their skin blue. Besides that, what else was there to do?

Next to her, Jak was examining one of the glowstones, his blue eyes purple in its light. "With these, I can finally explore the lake. I'll need volunteers to help."

"I'm in," Lin said.

"We shouldn't stop exploring outside, though," Oz said. "It was a survey trip that brought us the glowstones. Who knows what other resources are out there. We need anything we can find."

"Fine," Lin said. "It's your turn to take a survey trip, though. I'm swimming in some caves tomorrow."

"You'll go with me?" Oz asked Cara.

She nodded. It didn't really matter where she went.

"The northeast route is still unmapped," Lin said. "Maybe you'll find us a flying saucer. Don't all aliens have those?"

This time a few chuckles echoed around the fire.

Cara didn't join in.

The next day, Cara was exhausted. Between worry about the children and stress dreams from Tom, she hadn't slept more than a few minutes all night.

# TWIN

In the morning, Una's prominent presence in the sky felt like a taunt. *I am home*, it seemed to say. *You can see me, but you can't get to me.*

Even with her puffy eyes and foggy brain, Cara took time to talk with each of the children when they woke. The blue tint to their skin was plainly visible in the morning light. She had forced herself to look at it steadily, to listen to their fears without flinching, and to reassure them that they were still healthy and beautiful. She wanted to promise that they would get home soon and that their blue skin would fade away into a memory, but she didn't want to lie.

When Oz was ready, she gratefully left the kids to Bree's care, but she brought her bitterness and doubt with her.

The silence, which used to be a comfortable part of their walks, felt heavy. She remembered the anger on his face last night. As if he had any right to be angry. She was doing the best she could in an impossible situation. If her choices made him panic for a few minutes, it was just a small taste of what she felt every second of every day.

"Are you worried that you're next?" Oz asked.

Cara was startled out of her inner diatribe. "What?"

He gestured at her bare arms. "You're young and have a small build."

He was talking about her skin changing. She looked down at the familiar caramel color.

"At this point being blue will just feel like a bad metaphor."

He stopped, one end of the rope in his hands.

"You're angry."

"Just tired," she said.

He didn't move. "Which is probably why you can't hide your anger anymore."

"I'm...I don't know what I am. In the last few weeks, everything I believed about the universe has been ripped away by a series of unfathomable events. Healing water? Magical interplanetary travel? Miracle fish? Stones that glow for no visible scientific reason. Blue skin, for stars' sake! One minute we had a plan to ensure the future of mankind, and the next minute we're at the mercy of every random whim of the universe. Yeah, I guess I'm a little angry."

His eyes were too understanding. Cara looked away. "But what's the point in being angry when there's no one to be angry with? You didn't make this happen. Neither did my father. Neither did I. It's just...happening. This is our new reality, and it's messing with us at random."

"That might not be true. Maybe it *is* personal. Maybe there is someone to blame."

"You mean there's some advanced civilization out there playing games? Yeah. It's occurred to me. And it's not exactly reassuring."

"It could be aliens. Or an even larger force than that."

"Like what? A god?" she laughed.

"Maybe." His eyes were thoughtful. "It would make sense of some things."

Cara stared at him. She knew that he had chosen philosophy as his hobby, but she hadn't expected anything like this.

"Working on machines gives you a lot of time to think," he said, as if he had read her mind. "This is a question I've had for a while."

She shook her head. "Our great-grandparents rejected the religions of Earth for a reason. Belief in different gods only caused fighting and war and pain and death. They decided to stop blaming humanity's problems on supernatural beings and put the blame where it should be: on humanity. That's how they were able to find a different way."

"I know, but look around you. Our training vids didn't have all the information quite right."

"So you're saying that there is a real god out there, and he or she saw us trying to build a good and happy future for ourselves and thought it was time to put us in our place?"

"I'm saying that's one possibility."

Cara wanted to laugh, but right now it didn't feel quite as ridiculous as it should have.

"Well," she said. "If that's the case, then I do have someone to be angry with. Because that's a dirty trick for a powerful being to play on someone who never did anything to him."

"Except tell everyone for generations that he didn't exist."

Cara stared at him. "You actually believe this, don't you?"

"I don't know. Philosophers talk about God quite a bit. And after what's happened, it doesn't seem like just a philosophical exercise anymore."

"Would it make you feel better to think there was someone out there to be blame for everything?"

"Honestly? No. I find the idea terrifying. But we weren't talking about my feelings."

Now Cara did laugh. "So you're trying to make *me* feel better? By offering up an idea that terrifies you?"

He raised a brow. "It doesn't terrify you, does it? If you knew it was true, you would just accept it and figure out what to do next. It's not knowing that terrifies you."

When had he started understanding her so well? "I appreciate the attempt to make me happy," she said as lightly as possible. "It was worth a try."

He didn't look away from her eyes. "There are other things I could try."

Cara's breath caught.

Before she could think, he closed the gap and touched his lips to hers, soft and sweet. Cara felt her muscles tense, then slowly loosen.

She leaned into him. The kiss intensified.

When he lifted his head, she was breathing hard.

He watched her face with a searching look.

Cara couldn't stifle her smile. "Um, yeah. That…that was more effective."

That brought a grin that lit his face. "Good. Now we can get back to our map."

"Yes. Right. The map. Um…your lead still, right?"

"My lead," he said. He picked up her end of the rope where it lay forgotten at her feet. "You'll need this."

"Right."

Before she could decide if she was more embarrassed or happy, he pulled her close and kissed her hard again. Then he walked away without a word.

Happy. It was definitely happy.

At the tug of the rope, she hurried forward to meet him, waited while he dropped a stone into the bag, then took the lead.

There was no more talking. When they stopped for lunch, they sat side by side on a rock, legs touching as they chewed the bland blurgroots, but even then, neither of them said anything. Cara didn't mind the silence. She felt peaceful for the first time in…maybe ever.

It was only as they approached Incannu at the end of the day that she began to wonder what this meant going forward. Anything the two of them did would affect the whole group. They couldn't afford to let things be awkward.

"So," she said finally. "About what happened…."

"Our discussion of philosophy?"

"That…and the other thing."

They were walking side by side now, and he didn't stop, but he did look over and catch her eye before answering. "That's going to happen again."

Cara bit her lip. "Right."

"There's a lot of philosophy left to discuss."

She smiled. "And I do get sad really often these days."

"Exactly." Suddenly he stopped, his tone changing. "Someone's coming."

Cara squinted at the figure racing toward them across the savannah. Her chest clenched.

"Something's happened," she said.

Jak skidded to a stop just before he slammed into them. He was out of breath, but his eyes shone. "You have to see this," he said. "We've been waiting for you to come back."

"What is it?"

"The lake–" He sucked in another breath. "There are tunnels."

Suddenly he broke off and cocked his head, staring at her strangely.

"And…?"

"Your skin," he said.

Cara looked down. Her arm was tinged with purple.

She hadn't thought she would care, but a knife struck her heart at the sight. *If there is a god out there*, she thought, *there had better be a hell, too. Then I can wish him there.*

She looked back up at Jak, saw the pity on his face. "Not important," she said. "What did you find in the caves?"

Jak's excitement was back immediately. "Yes. The tunnels. One of them is special. I'll show you as soon as you're ready to swim. There's...it ends in some kind of window."

"Window?"

"A barrier, but you can see the other side."

"What's on the other side?"

Jak took a big breath.

Cara's stomach did a slow flip, as if she already knew the word before he said it.

"Una."

# Chapter 36

## Journey

The riverbed was nearly dry this close to the next rain, but Tom managed to find a patch of mud that was still soft under one of the larger rocks. He stuck his hand in, feeling his usual delight as it squished up between his fingers. When he felt a cluster of tiny spheres, he carefully scooped up a few, leaving the rest behind.

"Flik eggs," he said, holding them up with a grin.

Jof was unimpressed.

Tom looked down at the handful of mud. "Once I wash them off, you'll see. You spread them on the bread, and for once you can forget it was baked a week ago."

"How much water will that use up?"

"Most of what we have left." Tom shrugged. "But it's going to rain tonight. We'll refill our bottles and then have river water for days. These eggs are nearly ready to hatch. That's when they taste the best."

Jof still looked unconvinced.

"Tell me you aren't sick of dry bread and protein packets."

A grunt was Jof's only answer.

Tom smiled to himself. After two days of travel, he was getting used to Jof's mostly nonverbal communication. You had to be patient if you wanted to hear his voice. The man could go hours without saying a word. Then when you least expected it, he would ask a question or make an observation that led to useful and interesting conversation.

Only when he was ready, though.

Tom poured a small stream of water from his bottle over the handful of muddy eggs, careful to wash away the dirt without dissolving the transparent shells. On his first exploration, he had ruined several dozen eggs before perfecting the technique.

When the eggs were clean, he used the flat of his travel knife to spread them across the surface of the stale bread. He handed the first piece to Jof.

"Trust me," he said.

Jof eyed the brown goo with distaste, but he didn't hesitate to put it in his mouth. Two seconds later, his eyes closed in appreciation.

Tom grinned. This was the reason he hadn't given up on learning to clean flik eggs. Their taste, salty but delicate, was pure bliss. Quickly he spread the rest of the eggs on his own bread. He nibbled one corner, then sighed happily.

Jof raised a brow as Tom took another nibble. His own bread had already disappeared.

"I like to make it last," Tom said.

Jof shook his head. "It's going to be cold after the rain tonight," he said.

"There are heated blankets in the packs," Tom said. "We should each have three, so using one tonight will still leave us more for emergencies."

"Whenever you finish eating like an ipit, we'll get moving, then. With any luck, we can cover a lot of ground before we get soaked."

Tom sighed and ate the rest of his bread in two big bites. He wasn't embarrassed—he had perfected his eating technique with as much pride as his cleaning—but he was in a hurry.

It was late in the afternoon when the sky darkened with crimson clouds. Soon after, a soft rain began to fall. Roh was the first month of autumn, so Una's naturally chilly air carried an extra bite. Even though the water itself was tepid, both men were soon shivering.

As the rain increased in intensity, they paused out of long habit and pulled soap from their bags. Tom washed his hair in the rain, feeling more miserable by the moment.

It wasn't the cold that bothered him, so much as what the rain represented. Here he was, rain-showering as he had always done, when he should have been traveling to meet Lin and Cara and Bree. A wasted month, that's what this rain was. A month of the people he loved most facing unknown dangers too far away for him to help.

Thinking curses about his father wasn't satisfying enough, so he muttered them under his breath. Though he had kept his promise and thought about what his mother said, understanding his father didn't take away the bitterness.

Jof glanced over and gave him a nod. Tom's anger eased just enough to make room for gratitude that he wasn't alone.

When the rain stopped, the men huddled inside the heated blankets while the cold wind slowly dried their hair.

Tom's fury, now reignited, burned dangerously in his chest. He hunched over, warming himself around that core of heat.

*What's happened?*

He hadn't felt Cara's presence before her voice broke through his thoughts. Guilt rose up at the anger that had distracted him.

*Nothing,* he told her. *The rain.*

*We knew you would miss traveling with this rain.*

*Yeah. Knowing didn't make me feel better.*

*Yeah.* He had never felt so much brooding angst from her before. *Trust me when I say that not knowing is worse.*

He struggled against an unexpected resentment. Yes, her situation was awful, but he had his own emotions. Hadn't she started this by trying to comfort him? Guilt followed the thought instantly. It shouldn't be her job to comfort him. Not now. He needed to get his thoughts straight before she heard them.

*I know you're sick of being in the dark, but you've done well. You've got the caves. You're safe from storms. There is a whole lake of water, and fish to feed you. Heal you, too. You can survive however long it takes for us to find you a way home.*

He felt her struggle to care about what he was saying.

*You've been through incredible stress and trauma, Cara. It was bound to take its toll.*

*Great. Glad to know feeling this way was inevitable.*

Something in her tone pricked at him. *Is there something else? Did something happen?*

*There's always something else. Every day is something else.*

*Cara.*

*My skin is blue.*

*What?*

# TWIN

*My skin. It's blue. The kids, too. Probably everyone soon. Bree and Jak thinks something in our diet is doing it.*

*Are there other symptoms? Is it a disease?*

*No. They say it's probably harmless. If you call being blue being unharmed.*

*I don't care if you're neon pink, as long as you're going to be okay.*

*I know. I know it shouldn't matter. Mostly it doesn't. But....*

*I know. I'm sorry.*

*It's like I'm not even myself anymore.*

*Don't believe that. I can see you on the inside, remember? You are still you.*

*Right.* He could tell she didn't really believe him, but he felt her pull herself together, put the worry away.

*That's not even the real news,* she said. *The real news is that Jak found what he thinks is a window to Una.*

*WHAT? Why didn't you say?*

*Because I only had about ten minutes to myself before I'm supposed to learn how to swim in an underground lake. I was indulging in some very well-deserved self-pity when I felt your temper explode.*

*What kind of window?*

*I don't know. I haven't seen it yet. He says there is an invisible barrier at the end of one of the tunnels, and they can see underwater plants and animals on the other side. He's convinced it's Una.*

*This changes everything. We can get you home. You just need to find a way through.*

*We keep saying that. "This changes everything." It probably does, but it won't be in the way we think.*

*Okay, I get it. I won't jump to conclusions. But this is good news, Cara. You know it is.*

*It's hope. Which I'm thankful for. But hope isn't the same as reality.*

*It's a start.*

*Maybe. They're calling me. Time to go swimming.*

*Be safe, Six. Don't take any unnecessary risks.*

*Now you sound like me.*

*Everything is backwards these days. Everything but one.*

*What's that?* she asked.

He sent a flood of love toward her.

*Some things don't change,* he said. *Some things never will.*

# Chapter 37

# *Hope*

The lake was a smooth dark mirror reflecting the steady light of the glowstones Jak had placed around the cave walls.

Cara looked through the clear surface to where the curious fish were gathering around her toes. Though Jak and his helpers had scooped out dozens of them in the last weeks, the lake seemed just as full and the fish just as unafraid of their visitors.

"It's not too deep," Jak said. "It'll hit your shoulders, but you can still wade most of the way. There's only a small distance at the head of the tunnel where you'll need to swim."

Cara nodded and tried not to let her nerves show. Lin had shown her the principles of swimming, but they had only practiced for a few minutes. It was her first time. Even after a rain, the Vita River back home didn't have enough water for swimming.

"Don't worry," Lin said. "I got Jak through it. I'll get you through it, too."

Explorers were trained for lakes and oceans. Cara had been jealous when Tom told her about the tank of water they used for swim lessons. He had promised to sneak her in to try it out, but of course Cara had refused. It was only filled when absolutely necessary, and afterwards, the water was recycled. Water was a valuable commodity, necessary for survival and not for entertainment.

Now she was waist-deep in the most water she'd ever seen in her life, feeling its cool fingers slip over her skin as she followed Jak across to the far side of the cavern. The ground under her bare feet was rock, but something had smoothed its surface so that it felt polished.

As they approached the far wall, Cara saw the opening to the tunnel. It was a jagged triangle, its tallest point twice Cara's height, its width at water level just enough for one person to easily pass through.

"There's a drop-off right here at the beginning," Jak said. "You'll have to swim for about two meters before you'll feel rock beneath your feet again."

Cara glanced at Oz. He was studying the entrance like it was a puzzle he could solve.

"Just stay calm," Lin said. "Go one at a time. Kick your legs and push the water back the way I showed you. I'll be right behind you, and once we're a few meters into the tunnel, it widens so we can walk side by side again."

Cara slid her glowstone into a pocket. Its light showed dimly through the fabric. Lin held her stone higher to cast light for the others.

Jak went first, paddling awkwardly for a few meters before stopping and straightening up in the faint light from his own stone. "I'm across," he said. "You only have to make it to here."

"Ladies first?" Oz said.

"Sure," Cara said. "That way if I drown, you'll know not to attempt it."

"You won't drown," said Lin. "I'm here to rescue you in case of emergency."

"Right," said Cara, "that's what I meant. If Lin has to come rescue me, you'll have a chance to make your escape."

"Just go already," Lin said.

Cara took a deep breath and pushed off from the ground as Lin had showed her. She flailed for a second but soon found that she could move forward if she kicked hard enough and that the constant motion of her hands kept her head above water. She knew it wasn't pretty, but the feeling of water all around her was actually wonderful. It came as a surprise when Jak grabbed her arm and steadied her.

She put her feet down, felt solid rock.

"Your turn!" she called back to Oz.

Cara gasped when he plunged under the surface, but a second later he came up, cutting through the water with sure strokes until he pushed to his feet next to her. Water dripped from his hair. He grinned.

She glared back. "You've done that before."

"The swim tanks needed repair a time or two," he said. "Someone had to test them out."

"You could have said."

"I didn't want you to feel alone."

"You mean you wanted the chance to show off."

He grinned again. "Maybe. Fun, isn't it?"

"Probably more fun the way you do it," she said. "Plan to spend some time giving lessons after this."

"Gladly."

Lin joined them and punched Oz in the shoulder. "The next time you make me teach you how to do something you already know how to do, I'll choose a more painful location to punch."

"Sorry," he said.

"No, you're not," said Lin. "But only because I have chosen to be merciful this time."

"Could we move on?" said Jak.

Cara suddenly remembered what they were doing. "Lead the way."

It was slow going, pushing through the deep water single file. After a bit, the tunnel widened and Oz joined Jak up ahead while Lin walked next to Cara.

"It splits here," Jak said, gesturing to where a side tunnel opened up to the left. "We explored that one but found nothing."

They walked on for a while before another tunnel opened up to the right.

"This is our turn," Jak said. "The main tunnel goes further. There is another small cavern at the end with no external opening. This is the one that matters, though."

He held his glowstone high as they entered the side tunnel single file again. The floor sloped down, and Cara had to walk on tiptoes to keep her head above water. This tunnel was brighter. Their lights glittered off of something reflective.

"Put your stone under the water," Jak said, "and look closely at the walls."

Cara did, then gasped. Hundreds of thousands of tiny, glittering spheres clung to the rock walls underwater, covering them completely. They reflected back the rose-colored light of the glowstones in a rainbow of shades.

Unable to stop herself, Cara reached out a finger and lightly touched one. It was smaller than the tip of her pinky and the surface gave slightly under pressure, but the globe didn't pop.

"Beautiful," Oz breathed.

"Yes," Jak said. "But not as beautiful as this. Follow me."

Cara and Oz squeezed further down the tunnel side by side, careful not to brush against the delicate-looking spheres. The ceiling of the tunnel slowly sloped down to meet the surface of the water.

Jak stopped at the point where the rock met his head, with his chin just touching the water. Turning around, he held his glowstone at eye level, and gestured behind him. "It looks like the tunnel goes on further, but this is far as you can go." He reached back and pressed his hand against something Cara couldn't see.

"Try it for yourself," he said.

It took a bit of rearranging for Cara and Oz to squeeze past him, and Cara had to tilt her head up to breathe. The tight space and chin-deep water were beginning to make her feel a mild panic, but she kept a firm grip on the emotion.

"Oh," Oz said. He grabbed Cara's hand under the water and guided it forward until her knuckles met resistance.

It wasn't quite like a hard surface blocking the way, but no matter how much force she used, her hand couldn't move further forward.

"Go under and look with your light?"

"Under the water?" Cara asked.

"You can open your eyes under there, it won't hurt them," Lin said.

Cara shivered to think of all that water on her eyeballs, but Oz had already ducked under.

She took a deep breath and bobbed down. When she opened her eyes, the cool water was a strange sensation, but she was too busy with what she saw to worry about it.

Everything was slightly warped. The glittering globes seemed bigger under here, and Oz's face had an indistinct quality. He was holding up his light and staring intently down the tunnel.

Cara turned to look.

She stifled a gasp. Though her hand couldn't move more than a few centimeters forward, she could see beyond that, and the other side was a different world.

No tiny spheres lined the walls. In fact, the walls widened out and disappeared from sight, leaving an expanse of water that teemed with life. Grey-green plants grew from the bottom, waving gently with the water's motion. The rocks jutting from the ground were covered in algae.

And tiny brown and white fish darted around through it all. Not the silver-sided fish they had been eating here. These were fliks, the same fish the colonists of Mayland had been pulling from the Vita River for decades.

Cara pushed to the surface and sucked in a breath, coughing a little as water dripped down from her hair.

She backed away from the barrier and stared at Jak. His face glowed.

"It really is…."

"I told you. Now watch this." He let out a piercing whistle.

Nothing happened.

Cara looked around the tunnel.

"It doesn't do anything here," Lin said.

"It's the signal for Bree to net a few fish back in the main cavern," Jak explained. "Should be soon." He bobbed up and down on his toes while he waited. "Yes! There."

He pointed to the wall, where one of the tiny globes was swelling. Cara stared in horror as it quadrupled in size in a matter of moments, then suddenly burst.

Cara jumped back, colliding with Oz. A tiny fish swam out of the quickly dissolving sphere, headed straight for her.

Oz closed a hand around her shoulder, steadying her as the minnow swam past until the barrier stopped it. It began to wiggle around, its tiny nose pressed against whatever separated the two worlds. Two little bubbles formed at the spot and floated away on the other side. Then the fish turned and swam between them back up the tunnel and out of sight.

"What…?"

"We don't know what it's doing," Jak said, "but something passed through that barrier. To Una."

Cara struggled to make sense of it all. To think straight. "And you're sure that it's…."

"It's Una," Jak said. "Those are all recognizable plants and animals. None of which are in this cave. None of which we have seen anywhere here."

"But…."

"Somehow, those fish are connected to everything that's happened. My hypothesis right now is that the other side of that barrier is the lake the Thirds found on Una. It would explain the similar healing quality of the water."

Cara's head was swimming. She needed to get out of this water. Out of this cave. Into the open where she could clear her mind and think.

"Let's head back," Oz said.

Cara nodded gratefully.

"I told Bree to take three fish," Jak protested. "There will be two more."

"What do you mean?"

"One hatches for every fish we take out of the lake," he said.

"How do you…."

"We discovered it by accident, but we've tested it three times now, and it always works. Somehow, they know and they replenish their numbers. It's amazing."

"Okay," Cara shook her head. "And do they all…?"

"Yes, they all swim first to the barrier, release whatever that is, and then swim back up into the caves. There!"

Another globe had begun to swell. Cara watched in fascination this time as the tiny minnow emerged and made its deposit. Like the glowstones, it was beautiful and alien. She felt conflicting waves of hope and terror.

"It's been a long day," Oz said. "We could use some supper."

At last, Jak nodded his agreement. "Of course. I'll explain the experiments we've devised while we eat."

As Jak and Lin led the way back up the tunnel toward the main cavern, Cara focused on breathing steadily. Oz had released her shoulder, but she could feel his presence behind her. She was glad he was there.

This was the discovery they'd been waiting for. If the window really was some kind of portal to home and the fish had a way to breach it, then they could figure it out, too. Once she got over her shock, she was going to feel happy about this. It didn't matter that it was another unexplained mystery. All that mattered was getting her people back home.

By the time they waded up out of the lake, she had begun to believe it.

Bree met her with a grin and a hug and three fish in a homemade net. "Ready for some supper?"

Cara held on to her sister a little longer than necessary, but she was smiling when she pulled away.

"Bring it on," she said.

# Chapter 38

# Lake

The lake was exactly as Tom remembered it. The same water, so blue it was almost purple, surrounded on three sides by a pebbly beach. The same pale sun glittering off the dark surface. The same light breeze rustling the trees on the far side. Tom half expected to see a wounded yesela wading along the edges.

He half expected to feel Lin standing beside him.

She had urged caution with the water. He had put her in charge of collecting it, knowing she was better at caution than he was.

It had been his first mistake.

Tom pressed one hand to his gut, as if he could stop the bleeding inside. Then he dropped it, telling himself not to be melodramatic.

Jof was all business. His pack was already on the ground next to him, his shoes unlaced.

The night before, Cara had told them about the portal and their theory that it connected to this very lake. Tom and Jof had barely slept after that, waking early to cover the last kilometers as quickly as possible.

Jak's initial experiments on Dua had failed. Nothing they tried made a difference in the barrier. None of their handmade tools could break through, and no substance they found affected it.

His next ideas required their help on Una, and the first step was to find the barrier under the water.

Once their outer clothes were neatly piled with their packs, both men approached the lake cautiously. Tom reached out to Cara, letting his excitement flow through to her as he took his first steps into the water.

Her answering anticipation was laced with fear, but he hardly noticed it. The water was already having its effect.

Tom paused, knee-deep, and felt all the aches and pains of a week of hard traveling wash away. Even his sadness and worry faded in the rush of adrenalin.

*You should see Jof's face,* he said to Cara. *I swear he looks ten years younger.*

*I hope you taught him how to swim,* Cara answered.

*He already knew,* he said, wading in deeper. *He went through years of explorer training as a Third, and then his older sister died, so he took her job instead. I can't wait for you to get to know this guy. He's fascinating. When you can get him to talk.*

*Anyone Ann would marry would have to be.*

*Then I guess I can't wait to get to know her, too.*

*We're headed to the Hatchery now. Bree and Jak. Lin and Ann.*

*Then I'll see you soon.*

Ignoring her doubts, he took a deep breath and dived under the water.

The lake was clear, so Tom could see each pebble and waving plant that dotted the gravelly bottom. With sure strokes, he moved further out, angling down as the water got deeper.

*Be careful. Take your time.*

*I'm looking for some sort of barrier that's invisible. What could be easier?*

*Jak thinks it will be an opening in a rock formation.*

Tom's lungs were beginning to burn. He twisted in the water, looking every direction for rock, but his need for oxygen soon propelled him to the surface.

Jof was a few meters away, treading water.

He pointed to himself and then to the west bank of the lake. Tom nodded and pointed to the east.

Both men dived back under the water.

*We're here,* Cara said. *We have a glowstone. Light must travel through because we can see your side. If you see a pink glow, that's me.*

*Yes, I've always thought of you as a pink glow kind of girl.*

A brief image of Cara sticking her tongue out at him crossed his mind, but Tom was too busy swimming to pay much attention.

Two hours passed while Tom and Jof dove down and returned to the surface for air over and over. Though the water kept any pain away, Tom's exhaustion was beginning to return.

He began to wonder if they were wasting their time. What Cara saw on the other side of the barrier could be anywhere on Una, or not on Una at all. The healing property of the water could be a coincidence.

Near the south shore, the lake bed dropped at a sharp angle. Tom surfaced for one big breath, trying not to feel like this was their last chance. Under the water, he kicked hard for the bottom, deeper and deeper until the light from the surface was dim.

The bottom was increasingly rocky, and Tom felt a bubble of hope. He reached out a hand to the hard surface. A little further and his lungs began to burn again, but now he was at the opening of a rocky cave. The hope swelled.

*There!* A faint pink light, half out of sight. Tom's heart soared, but his body clamored for air. He turned and headed for the surface, letting his elation tell Cara what she needed to know.

In the world above the water, the sun was headed toward the horizon, and the air Tom sucked in was bitingly cold. A breeze laced icy fingers through his wet hair.

Tom ignored all of it. When a quick glance around showed no sign of Jof, he took in as much oxygen as he could and dived.

This time, he swam straight for the rocky opening, then let the pink glow guide him. The cave was deep and curved slightly as it angled down. Tom used his hands to push off the rocky sides, propelling himself forward.

When he rounded the corner, he saw her.

"Cara!"

The word came out in a rush, along with all of his air. Despairing, Tom took one quick look at his sister, then turned and pushed frantically backward.

When his head broke the surface, he gasped in water along with air, then spent a few minutes choking and panicking.

A hand grabbed his arm and lifted. With his head fully in the air, Tom coughed until all the water was gone.

"Thanks," he managed after a few minutes.

"You okay?" Jof asked.

Cara's worry echoed in the back of Tom's brain. "I'm fine," he told them both. "I found it."

*And then I wasted my air shouting underwater like an idiot.*

*I saw you.* Wonder had replaced her doubt and despair.

*I saw you, too. Hold on. We're coming back down.*

A few moments later, they were both underwater, staring at each other through a barrier neither could see and neither could cross.

Cara put out a hand. Tom held his up against it. For a second, he imagined that he could feel her touch.

*We did it,* she said, amazed.

*We always do.*

*You look exhausted.*

*Yeah, well, you're soaking wet.*

A bubble of laughter burst from Cara's lips. *I'll make way for the others.*

*Sick of me already?*

*Obviously.*

This time he was careful to keep his mouth closed as he grinned. *I love you, Six.*

She turned away, and a second later Lin and Ann took her place. Jof shot toward his wife, only stopping when both hands were pressed to the barrier.

Tom's eyes were only for Lin. She stared at him through the water, her red hair floating up around her like a cloud.

As he had with Cara, Tom put out his hand to hers. This time, he felt only frustration that he couldn't feel her hand. She was there, but he couldn't reach her.

She couldn't read his mind, but his face must have told her. Lin smiled, cocked her head to the side, and raised one brow. He knew that look. The one that said *Yep, there's a problem. So how are you going to solve it?*

He'd break down this barrier if he had to use his own hard head to do it.

His lungs were burning. Jof had already disappeared, but Tom couldn't take his eyes off of Lin. She turned sideways, listening to something, then made a gesture for him to go.

Cara had ratted him out. Reluctantly, he turned and headed to the surface for more air.

*What do we need to do?* He asked Cara. *Tell Jak we're ready to do anything.*

# Chapter 39

# *Action*

The morning light showed that Cara's skin had darkened to a dusky violet, and both Wyn and Lin now had a bluish tinge. Bree offered to do a full examination, but Cara shrugged it off.

Now that she had seen Tom, she just wanted to find a way home.

Even with Tom and Jof working from the other side, nothing had breached the barrier yet. The fish were obviously the key. Only their bubbles passed through to Una. Tom said they felt like drops of oil, but each one dissolved immediately on the other side.

Jak had a plan in mind, but he was still collecting data to finalize the details. The fish were keeping them alive. They couldn't afford to mess with them without a reasonable plan.

Cara was happy to let him take charge, volunteering for any job no one else wanted to do. In this case, that meant carrying dead fish up the tunnel.

Ann had fashioned a wide clay bowl and hardened it in the sun. Cara watched as Bree filled the bowl with water, then quickly netted a fish and dropped it in. The sisters waited. They had never taken a fish from the lake and kept it alive before.

"He says nothing is hatching," Em said. Hal had gone with Jak to observe the eggs.

"We'll wait the full ten minutes," Bree answered.

Cara watched the silvery fish wriggle in its bowl of water. It didn't have room to truly swim and kept tilting slightly. Its round eye stared up at her.

*Are you okay?*

Cara nearly jumped out of her skin, then scolded herself. It was just Tom, worried by her feeling of revulsion.

*I'm fine. We're running tests with the fish. They freak me out a little, that's all.*

She looked down at the fish, still unable to shake the idea that it was trying to tell her something.

"Still nothing," Em said. "Jak says to go ahead."

Cara steeled herself, but she still cringed when Bree lifted the fish out of the water and slapped it expertly against the cavern wall. It died instantly.

"Yes!" Em said. "He says one just hatched."

"So it's not removing them from the lake. It's only when one dies that a new one hatches."

"How do they know?" Cara said.

"Some kind of instinct, I guess," said Bree. "Tell him I'm taking another one."

They planned to repeat the experiment three times, each time waiting longer to verify the results. Cara couldn't look away from where the second fish lolled in the bowl. Was she imagining that it was watching her, too?

Of course she was. It was looking at her, not watching her. It was a fish. Alive, but not sentient.

But nothing seemed certain anymore. If a person could be magically healed, instantly transported, and speak telepathically with their twin, why couldn't a fish be sentient?

"What if they can communicate with each other? What if that's how they know when one dies?"

She hadn't meant to say it out loud, not with Em sitting right there, but the words slipped out.

Bree shot her a look. "The fish?"

Cara nodded, swallowing hard.

Bree looked at the fish in the bowl. "They probably do communicate in the sense that there is some sort of shared chemical reaction or other mechanism that's evolved to maintain this perfect population count. It isn't the same as actually thinking or communicating with language like we do."

That sounded reasonable.

Bree watched Cara with a look of concern. Cara made a point to look thoughtful and convinced.

Her sister saw through it. "I get it. We did just discover our own capacity for telepathy." She glanced down at Em, but the girl seemed preoccupied with kicking her legs in the lake water. "Jak did raise the question of sentience. We discussed it at length, actually, and our conclusion was that the extreme predictability of their behavior indicates that there's nothing here we would consider independent thought."

"So they're not...?"

"They're animals. Nothing more."

Before Cara could respond, Em laughed loudly. "Hal says it's got to be past time, and since he's hanging on Jak's back to keep from drowning, they want you to get on with it."

Bree quickly went to work, killing the fish with one blow again. Cara forced herself not to flinch.

When they had finished the third repetition of the experiment, Cara carried the dead fish up the tunnel and outside.

Wyn and Jem were in charge of preserving fish and of bringing as much of their camp inside as possible. They expected eclipse by late afternoon, and a windstorm would most likely follow. Ann was busy painting something transparent over the top of the star map.

"It's sap from those scrubby trees," she explained. "I want to see if it will protect our paint from the storm." She looked at her creation. "It's not my finest work, but it would be a shame to lose it."

Cara stuck a finger in the sap. It was thick and sticky. "If it works, this could be useful for a lot of things," she said.

Ann gave her a smile and a pat on the shoulder. "Almost makes you want to stay here forever and see what we can discover, doesn't it?"

Cara was surprised to realize that was true. She looked down at her blue skin and tried to summon the anger she had felt yesterday. Instead, she thought of what Jak had said. *It's actually quite beautiful.*

Maybe once they found a way home, they could begin to travel back and forth. The resources of a second planet would be at their fingertips. Maybe some good would come from all this after all.

Two hours later, the storm hit with all its fury. Dua did not like being overshadowed by her sister.

Jak gathered everyone in the main tunnel around a pile of glowstones, and while the raging wind echoed down to them, he outlined his plan.

They would take out and kill seventy fish all at once, triggering seventy new minnows who would approach the barrier at roughly the same time. With so much of the oil passing through, Jak hoped the barrier would be temporarily weakened, and they would be able to break through as well.

Everyone was assigned a task. They scattered with grins and backslapping. Hopes were high.

Cara swam through the underground lake, following the light of the small glowstone attached to Jem's arm. She was thankful that her place was in the Hatchery. She knew it was cowardly to avoid looking at the fish they were destroying, but when Jak said he needed her to communicate with Tom, she was embarrassingly eager. The fish were a renewable resource, and this was a justified risk, but the thought of killing that many made her slightly sick.

Bree was in charge of fishing back in the main cavern, and Oz had taken the job of preserving as many fish as possible. Most of the group was assigned to help the two of them.

Only Cara and Jak would be at the barrier, with Jem prepared to attempt the crossing and Hal to communicate with the main group.

Everything had to be timed as perfectly as possible. Tom and Jof could only stay underwater for a few minutes, and Jak wanted them there when the fish breached it, to make observations on their side and hopefully receive Jem.

They waited in the deep water, breathing as normally as possible, until Bree sent the signal through Em that the nets were ready.

*Tom,* Cara said. *Ready to dive?*

*That would be a yes. I've been floating for a half an hour waiting on you all.*

Cara nodded at Jak. Jem took his place by the barrier. Jak squeezed Hal's shoulder, and the boy closed his eyes.

Two minutes later, he opened them wide. "73," he said.

Jak grinned. "Those are some good nets."

Cara stared at the egg-lined walls, holding her glowstone high. She held her breath.

It looked like an optical illusion at first. The walls warped slightly as 73 of the tiny globes swelled up and then burst. A flurry of minnows wriggled toward the barrier. Jem stood perfectly still as they passed him and pressed their tiny noses against its invisible surface.

Cara knew Tom saw them, even as she saw his dark shape on the other side. Jem reached a hand forward to where a group of minnows wiggled side by side. He pushed through them and against the barrier. A few fish, disturbed by Jem's hand, found a different spot to release their bubble.

Frantically, Jem tried another place. Then another. The barrier held firm.

On the other side, Tom's hands reached forward.

*I can feel the water pulsing! Whatever they're sending through, there's a lot of it!*

*Can you get your hand through?*

In the dim light, Cara saw him make a few sharp motions.

*Nothing. No give.*

Now the minnows were turning away, their tiny deposits delivered. In a glittering swirl of bodies, they swam together up the tunnel and disappeared.

## *TWIN*

The experiment had failed.

"It didn't change anything," Jem said. "Whatever they're sending through, it doesn't alter the barrier."

"Not at these quantities, at least."

Tom had disappeared when the fish did, back to the surface for air.

*It didn't work,* she said. *This isn't the way.*

*No,* he insisted. *I felt it. It felt different when the bubble came through. A powerful blast. It just wasn't enough.*

Cara's heart sank. *So we need to take more.*

*We have to try. I think we're on the right track.*

Jak, Hal, and Jem were watching her face. She forced a smile.

"We'll keep at it until we succeed," Cara said. "Go ahead. Tell the others we start again."

# Chapter 40

# *Reaction*

"Stay here this time. You need the rest."

"I'm okay. Just give me a minute, and I'll be good to go."

Jof fixed Tom with a piercing stare that made made Tom feel like he was five years old.

"You've been at this since dawn, and that's after putting in ten hours yesterday. You're exhausted, and eventually that's going to make you do something stupid. We can't afford stupid."

Yesterday, they had made five separate attempts to breach the barrier, each time taking more fish and increasing the pressure the minnows sent through. Tom and Jof could feel the pulse that flowed into the water on their side, but so far, they hadn't been able to get anything else through.

After three more attempts today, Tom felt desperate. If this didn't work, they needed to get back to the original plan. He and Jof were exposed to the healing water, and then some. They would travel with the next rain. To keep their promise to the other families, they needed to get water samples back to Mayland before then. Which meant leaving in two days at the latest.

*Okay, we're going to do it,* Cara's voice broke into his thoughts. *If this doesn't work, though, we need to take a break for a while and reevaluate.*

Tom sighed with relief. They had been increasing the number of fish they took in slow increments, trying to be cautious about the effect on the barrier as well as the fish population. He had argued for a more forceful approach. They didn't have time for this much caution. They needed to start doubling their numbers.

*We're working on the practicalities of taking out that many fish at once. We need some new nets. It will be another hour at least.*

Tom passed on the information to Jof. "An hour's rest is all I need. I'll be good to go by then, especially if I hang out in the water."

Jof raised one brow. "The water heals. It doesn't make you invincible."

"I'll sleep on the raft. I swear."

Tom took Jof's inarticulate snort as agreement.

While the others had spent days experimenting, the two men had rounded up as much fallen wood as they could find and lashed it together with rope to form a floating platform. Using a long vine and some rocks, they had anchored the raft above the cave opening, giving them a place to rest when they came up for air.

Tom lay on it now, dangling one arm into the healing water. All the aches and pains that should have come with exhaustion were missing. His mind, though, was fuzzy, feeling the fatigue that his body no longer had a way to express.

He shivered in the cold air. He should get back in the water where he wouldn't feel the breeze. He should....

# TWIN

Tom fell asleep.

*We're ready,* Cara said. *We'll pull the fish as soon as we see you at the barrier.*

Tom fought his way back to consciousness.

"They're ready," he mumbled.

"I'll head down," Jof answered immediately. "Follow when you're fully awake."

*On our way,* Tom told Cara. He tried to push himself up, but his body felt like it was made of lead. He heard the splash as Jof dove in.

Tom thought again about sitting up. He thought about it for several minutes before realizing that he was still lying immobile on the raft. He decided he didn't really need to sit up. Instead, he rolled over into the water.

When his head submerged, he finally came awake. For a minute, he floated, letting the water warm him and his senses sharpen. Then he surfaced for the deep breath he would need to make it to the cave.

Jof had been the first to point out that the healing water was giving them extra time below the surface. It didn't take away their need to come up for air, but it optimized their bodies' use of oxygen and must have also been dealing with the carbon dioxide in some way. They could last more than ten minutes and had learned that if they breathed purposefully for a couple of minutes before making the descent, they could stretch it to twelve.

Tom had just taken his final deep breath when the ground rumbled. The lake heaved, and the raft was ripped out of his hand.

*Tom!* Cara's call was a scream in his head.

Panicked, Tom dove.

The water was choked with mud, and bits of debris floated everywhere. The further down he swam, the more the filth hurt his eyes. Tom blinked them rapidly. He needed to see.

Still searching for the cave opening through the clogged water, Tom crashed into rock. His shoulder took most of the impact, and for a second, blood mixed with the mud. The sharp sting faded quickly as the water healed his wound.

Tom felt around, frantically trying to see an opening of any kind. Where was Jof?

The rocks shifted slightly, and Tom seized the opportunity to lift several away. He couldn't see what he was doing. His lungs were already burning. How long had he been down?

Where was Jof?

*Cara, what happened?*

*Tom! You're alive! I...It...exploded.*

*Jof. I can't find Jof.*

Her wordless horror clawed at him.

Tom shifted more rocks, digging down, trying to fight despair even as he fought lightheadedness.

He reached into the small hole he'd made and cut his hand on a jagged rock. This time the bleeding barely started before disappearing. He stretched out his hand more carefully.

Something soft brushed his fingers.

Tom strained further, pulling away more rocks until he could wrap his hand around what he thought was an arm. The rubble shifted, and Tom could finally see what he was holding. Not just an arm, but a shoulder.

Frantically, Tom dug deeper. Below the rocks was thick mud. Keeping a grip on his friend's shoulder with one hand, Tom scooped away the silt with his other until he had uncovered Jof's head and neck. Hooking his arms under both shoulders, he pulled with all his might.

The mud didn't let go easily. Tom's muscles were burning, and black spots danced in front of his eyes by the time he felt a slow sucking pop and Jof was free.

With all the strength he had left, Tom kicked for the surface, dragging Jof's body with him.

It was slow. Too slow. The world narrowed to a pinpoint as blackness took over. Then the pinpoint disappeared.

Tom's head burst through the surface, and he dragged in a breath. Then another. Then another.

Slowly, his eyesight returned, along with rational thought. Jof was floating facedown in the water next to him.

Tom had no strength left, but he also had no choice. Floating on his back, he heaved the older man's limp body until it rolled. Now Jof's face was up, but he wasn't breathing.

The raft was nowhere in sight.

Tom guessed the direction of the nearest shore and kicked feebly, propelling himself backward and dragging Jof with him.

It could have been minutes or hours before Tom felt the ground under him. Trembling uncontrollably, he pushed to his knees, pulling Jof onto the bank.

Tom started chest compressions, not considering how long it had been, not thinking about anything but the steps that had been drilled into him in his training. He pinched Jof's nose, breathed into his mouth, resumed compressions.

He focused on counting. Only the numbers mattered. Eight, nine, ten. Pinch and breathe. One, two, three.

Jof's body slipped, and the water lapped his face. Suddenly the old man jerked. He snorted and bolted up, knocking Tom back as he coughed and then vomited into the water.

Tom was weak and shaking. A few minutes passed before he realized that he was laughing. Nothing was funny. Nothing was anything. He just couldn't stop the spasms of laughter. Tears were rolling down his cheeks.

When he finally calmed enough to speak, he shook his head. "Sorry," he said weakly. "Welcome back."

Jof turned a furious glare on him, those blue eyes burning. "What did you do?"

"Wha…?" The sense of unreality was returning. "I don't…."

Jof looked away, and Tom followed his gaze to where the older man's legs were stretched out in the water.

One of them ended at the knee.

# Chapter 41

## *After*

There were voices all around her, overlapping and frantic, but the one she wanted to hear, the one inside her head, was silent.

She could feel him. He was alive. He was looking for Jof. He was in pain. He was staying underwater too long.

Cara closed her eyes, blocking out the sight of the others desperately examining the now solid rock barrier.

Her mind supplied its own images. A blast of color. Falling rock. Jof being crushed. Tom's body drifting in the water, unmoving.

She didn't know what was memory, what was telepathy, and what was imagination. She couldn't stop the images.

Someone was saying her name. Not Tom.

*You have to breathe, Tom. You have to breathe. I need you to breathe. I need you.*

He was lost in his own fear and struggle. She knew he didn't hear her.

The images replayed. She begged again for him to live.

Someone shook her. They had a hold on her shoulders. Her eyes snapped open, saw a face too close to distinguish, snapped shut again.

Something shifted. Was that relief? Hope? It was gone as soon as it came.

*It's been too long. Tom. Are you still there?*

The silence was unbearable.

Cara waited. She held the connection in her mind, straining for a sign. Dully, she felt pain, but even that was fading.

She was losing him.

An arm around her shoulders. Someone lifted her in the water. She was being carried.

It didn't matter where she went. She was alone now.

A burst of...something. *Tom? Are you there? Please be there.*

A faint sense of life. Life was good. A surge of desperation. Desperation was better. Desperation was survival.

She poured her own determination into the connection. *Don't you dare leave me, Tom Mayland. Don't you dare.*

She was floating, being tugged along. Grateful that she didn't have to decide anything. The arms lifted her again. She was out of the water. Shivering. Then held close to something warm.

A burst of triumph from Tom made her suck in a breath. *Thank the stars. You're okay.*

It was followed by confusion, then horror, then finally...finally, his voice.

*Oh stars, Cara. I can't....*

# TWIN

*You're alive!* Vaguely she realized that now someone was holding her. She let the sensation of safety and warmth bleed through her into her brother. *You made it. You're not alone. I'm here.*

*Jof....*

*There was nothing you could do.*

*But he...his leg.*

Understanding dawned slowly. *Did you find...?*

*I found him. I got him out. He's alive, but....*

Cara snapped back into her physical reality with a suddenness that made her stomach churn. Her eyes opened, and she bolted upright.

She had been leaning on someone, and the fire was right in front of her. All around it, her friends watched her with looks of terror. Immediately, her eyes fell on Ann, sitting with an arm around one of the girls.

"He's alive," she said.

Ann burst into tears.

Lil pulled her close.

"Tom?" asked Bree.

"They're both alive. They made it out."

She could still feel his panic and horror, but she didn't say that.

*Breathe, Tom,* she told him, still reeling from the relief of knowing that he could. *Just breathe. You did well. You did so well.*

*He wants to know what happened. His leg....*

*What's wrong with his leg, Tom? Can't the water heal it?*

*It's gone.*

Cara's heart stopped for a second, then remembered its job and started up again in double time.

*Okay. First things first. Have you stopped the bleeding?*

*No. Yes. It's...not like that. The water. It's already healed. But it's gone.*

Cara tried and failed to keep her face blank.

"What's wrong?" Ann asked.

As plainly as she could, Cara told her.

Ann stopped crying. She nodded, stood up, sat back down, allowed Pol to hand her a cup of tea.

The arms that had been holding Cara tightened a little. She could feel Oz's heart beating against her back. She was grateful for its steadiness.

"He'll be angry," Ann said. She was gripping the stone cup tightly, but she looked at Cara firmly. "Tell him to stow it for now. It will still be fresh later."

Cara stared at her.

"Just pass on the message for me. Please."

Cara did. She waited. After a minute, she felt Tom's relief.

*He says she needs to stop stealing his lines. He smiled when he said it, though. A little. He says we need to talk about what's next, but...Cara, what happened? He won't say.*

Cara pictured it again in her mind. The swirl of fish jostling for position. Jem straining to keep his hands against the barrier as they crowded him out. A sudden pulse and the tunnel shaking. Jem's shout. More chaos of frantic fish. The sight of rocks tumbling and a blast of heat.

Briefly, she told Tom everything.

After a few minutes, he said, *Jof says the pulse pushed him back up the tunnel just before it started to collapse. That's what saved his life.*

She could feel him carefully avoiding thinking about the leg.

*Cara, it's blocked now. The way is closed.*

*It can be unblocked, reopened.*

*You don't know that. And we're out of time. They are waiting for us back in Mayland. Everyone's families. We tried this, but it failed.*

*We can't just give up. This is our way home! Probably the only way! Believe me when I say that my people are ready to move heaven and earth to get there. A few rocks and some mud won't stop them.*

*Even if we moved those, how would we get you through? We can't risk another blast like that.*

Stubbornness fought with resignation. *I'm not asking you to do anything. Just wait while we examine the damage on our end.*

He thought she was being unreasonable. He thought she didn't understand what had happened. He was wrong. She knew how bad the blast had been. She was there.

She had also seen her brother and her home just on the other side of that stars-cursed barrier, and she wasn't letting go of the chance to get there until she had no other choice.

"Jak, we need to go back and evaluate things. We need to figure out the next step."

Jak had his head in his hands, and Bree was leaning into his shoulder, arms wrapped around him.

Bree shook her head. "Not now, Cara."

"Clearing away the rubble will take time. We'll need to start as soon as possible."

"It won't work," Jak mumbled into his hands. "It's over."

There was a long silence.

"So that's it," Lil said. She was looking at her pale blue hand. "This is it."

"This is it," Pol whispered. "This is where we die."

"No," Cara said. "We'll pursue every available option before we give up. And if the worst happens, this still isn't where we die. This is where we live."

"I'll take you down there," Oz said.

She turned toward him. "Thank you."

His face was unreadable as he helped her to her feet.

They were knee deep in the lake when Cara heard a splash behind her. Jak and Bree were following.

At Cara's glance, Bree shrugged.

"I should face my failure," Jak said.

"This isn't on you," she said.

He looked away.

Oz carried the only glowstone as they swam across the gap and into the tunnel. When he turned into the Hatchery first, the light disappeared with him. Cara took a deep breath in the dark. Then she followed.

The second she rounded the corner, she wished she hadn't come. Not only did a pile of rubble completely block the far end of the tunnel, the walls near it were charred black. Tiny fleks of grey floated in the water, and with horror, Cara realized they were dead eggs. They had been blasted off the walls. A rotten fish smell wafted up from the water.

Stomach churning with guilt and despair, Cara made a slow circle where she stood. At least half of the eggs had been destroyed. The
*342*

other half seemed okay, but who knew what the long-term effects would be for them.

Behind her she heard a choking noise. She turned just in time to see Jak stumble back out of the Hatchery. She could hear him retching in the darkness outside.

"I'm sorry," Cara whispered.

"It's not your fault," Oz said.

"I shouldn't have made you come here."

"You had to see for yourself."

"You knew?"

"I saw when I came for you."

"I'm sorry."

"It's not your fault," he said again.

"It's mine," Jak said from the doorway. His face was drawn, his blue skin darkened to purple under the eyes.

Bree stood next to him, holding his arm. She looked at Cara pleadingly, but there was nothing Cara could say to make it better.

There was no reassurance to give.

# Chapter 42

## Adapting

They would stay at the lake one more day.

Though he agreed to let the group on Dua decide, Jof made it clear that he didn't think there was a choice left to make. The passage under the lake was no longer an option. Probably it never had been.

Tom knew he was right. He also felt Cara's anguish and the guilt that went with it. This decision couldn't be taken away from her. She needed to accept this on her own terms.

It would take them a day to prepare for the trip anyway. Jof refused any plan for travel that involved Tom carrying him or even helping him walk. Instead, he drew up designs for simple crutches, and set to work making them from the branches and other materials Tom brought him.

Tom had too much time to think.

Once Jof had what he needed and the samples of lake water were secure, there wasn't much for Tom to do. He dove under the water a few more times to examine the collapsed tunnel, but he could barely even make out where it had been under the mud and debris.

Cara and the others would see the same thing soon. This was no longer a way home.

Maybe there were other tunnels out there, other windows between the worlds. Maybe they would find them someday. Or maybe it was time for them to make a new home.

On dry land again, Tom watched as Jof tried out his new crutches. He moved slowly, but determinedly went up hill and down, on stones and on grass, until he finally collapsed from exhaustion.

Tom handed him a cup of lake water. Jof swallowed it down and sighed as the pain dissolved.

Apart from his request for materials, the man hadn't said a word all day. The silence weighed on Tom, but he was determined not to be the one to break it.

Instead he began to make a circuit of the lake, looking for running water. Under the trees on the far side, he found a narrow creek bed. It was dry now, but probably after a rain a small stream of water ran through here from the Vita River.

Tom followed the dry stream back into the forest until a cracking branch brought him up short. A few meters away, he saw two yesela munching on feathery leaves. From their size, he guessed it was a mother and her calf. He froze as they perked up their pointed ears and stared at him. After a minute, the calf went back to his meal, but the mother continued to watch the intruder.

*I won't hurt you,* he thought, wishing she could read his mind. *And even if I did, the lake could heal you. Do you already know that? Is that why you stay so close?*

He thought of the yesela that had first brought them here. What instinct told the creatures that this was a place of healing? And why

*346*

didn't it warn them that the healing would only be temporary? Did they know that one drink condemned them to be transported into the jaws of waiting predators on a distant planet?

Maybe they didn't care. The biologists believed that yesela didn't have much long-term memory. Maybe when each day was new, having one more was the only thing that mattered.

A sudden thought occurred to him. Cara said they had found no animals on Dua apart from the predators waiting at the meadow. If he wounded these yesela right now, they would go to the lake to be healed. In the next rainfall, they would all travel together. They would arrive prepared to fight off the predators, perhaps even well enough that the yesela could also escape. Yesela bred quickly. In time, they would be a new source of food for the settlement.

The mother yesela had finally given up on watching him. She stepped leisurely through the trees, feasting on the low hanging branches.

Slowly, Tom eased his arrow gun out of its holster. He would injure the mother first since she was faster. Inch by inch, he raised it, taking aim at the hindquarters, trying to judge the spot that would do the least damage. He squinted down the sight. She raised her head, twitching her antennae as if she sensed her danger.

Tom held his breath, stilled the tremble in his hand. He wasn't killing her, he told himself. He wasn't even capturing her. He was just starting a chain of events. She would run to the water of her own choice.

If she couldn't grasp the consequences of her choice, how was that his fault?

Somewhere in the back of his mind, he felt Cara's troubled dreams as she slept.

"Fine," he said out loud. "I get it."

The yesela jumped at the sound of his voice, darted away under the trees.

Tom holstered the arrow gun.

Back at their camp, Jof was still practicing with the crutches. Tom sat down to wait.

When Cara finally made contact, he was ready for her.

*We agreed to sleep on it,* she said. *But now I'm awake, and reality is just as bad as it was before.*

*It's hard to let go of yesterday's hope, but this isn't the end of everything, Six. A week ago, we didn't know that tunnel existed. Who knows what we'll find in time?*

*No. This was the way. The lake water that brought us here was made by these fish in that tunnel. This is the loop. How can we just let it close?*

*It's not a matter of letting. It's a matter of accepting. It's closed. It's out of our control.*

*Ha. Of course. Everything is out of our control. I keep thinking I've accepted that, and then....*

*You get a chance to make things right, and you take it.*

*I see a way to regain control, and I stupidly believe it's possible.*

*Hope isn't stupid.*

*Depends on what you're hoping for.*

He searched for the words that would help her.

*I'm sorry,* she said. *I'm trying to find hope again. Trying to believe we'll find another lake of fish, another portal. Another way. I just can't bring myself to believe.*

*So maybe it's time to hope for something different. Maybe getting you home is impossible, but we can make a new home. Together. We can still come to you.*

# TWIN

*You can't all leave Una with no way back. You'd be abandoning everything we've built over three generations.*

*We won't abandon anything. Some will stay, but some will go. Some of us were going to anyway. Dua can be our new settlement, just slightly farther than planned.*

*But don't you see? That distance is everything. It's never seeing Mayland again. It's never seeing the people you leave behind, and it's probably forever.*

*Yes. It's not an easy choice, but it's a choice we can make. A life we can make.*

*A completely separate life. No ability to share resources. No way to give aid in times of need. Probably not even any way to communicate. In time the two settlements will grow apart. We won't even look the same.*

*Blue skin isn't such a big deal.*

*It's more shocking than you think. Tom, if you do come here, you should prepare yourself. Lin....*

*Would be the most beautiful woman on any world in any color.*

*Well, yes. And I'll tell her you said that.*

*I'll tell her myself when I see her.*

*I hope so. But Tom, it's...hard to explain. Something so frivolous shouldn't matter. But when it's your own skin....*

He tried to imagine how it would feel to find yourself fundamentally changed.

He looked over at Jof, stumping along on his crutches with his face set in a tight mask of determination and discomfort. Moving from one radical change toward the next as fast as one leg could carry him.

Tom was determined to keep up.

# Chapter 43

# Twin

Wyn was sitting in the middle of the women's room, only one small glowstone on the floor next to her. In the faint illumination it cast, the gashi flowers on the wall looked like ominous faces. Wyn stared at them, unmoving, even when Cara came and sat beside her.

"The others are outside rebuilding the fire ring," Cara said. "I noticed you never came out."

Wyn didn't answer.

"I'm sorry if I'm intruding."

"You aren't intruding." Wyn's voice was hoarse. She had been crying.

"We have to decide what we're going to do next," Cara said. "I'd like to hear from everyone."

"Clearing the tunnel will be a lot of work," Wyn said, "but everyone has families. They want to get home to them."

"Yes."

Wyn didn't answer, and they sat quietly for a while. Cara wanted to ask questions, but she didn't know where to start.

"I'm not going," Wyn said. "Even if we find a way through, I'm not going back."

Cara turned to look at the older woman's profile. The glowstone cast dark shadows under her eyes, their purplish hue underlining her sadness.

"You…."

"I'm staying here. I've studied this planet from a distance my whole life. Now I can study it up close."

"But…."

"I can survive here. Food. Water. Shelter. Eventually others will come back to study. I wouldn't be alone forever."

It sounded like a rehearsed speech. Logical. Convincing.

Incomplete.

"What about your daughter?"

There was a long pause. "She'll understand," Wyn whispered. "You'll tell her…everything. She'll understand."

Cara studied those dark circles again. "I'm not sure I understand."

Wyn was silent.

Cara waited.

When Wyn did speak, it was in a whisper. "How did you know?"

"How…?"

"How did you know it was really him?"

In a moment of clarity, Cara understood. Wyn's brother, Ny. Her twin. He had tried to poison her for stealing his work. Work she had believed was her own because she had thought up the ideas in her own head. Oh stars, this poor woman. Unable to live with being banished from his work, which was his sentence for attempted murder, Wyn's brother had taken his own life.

Cara picked her words carefully. "I didn't at first. I thought I was just remembering him, imagining what he would say to me."

Wyn's breathing was jagged.

"If we hadn't come here, if I hadn't been put in a situation where I couldn't imagine what he'd say, where it had to be coming from him... I don't think I ever would have realized."

Now Wyn's shoulders began to shake.

Hesitantly, Cara put a hand on the woman's knee.

"He said I stole his ideas," Wyn choked out. She started to go on, but a sob interrupted her words.

Tears came to Cara's eyes. She put her arm around Wyn's shoulders as the woman's usual stoicism gave way to open sobbing.

When she finally calmed a little, Wyn sucked in a breath. "He was right. I stole from him."

"They felt like your thoughts. There was no way you could have known."

"I should have," Wyn said. "It was his voice. He always had all the good ideas."

"I don't know how it was for you," Cara said carefully, "but for me...When you are with someone every day for your whole life, you think in their voice all the time. It doesn't mean.... It doesn't mean every time it was really them. And we all thought... I mean, telepathy wasn't supposed to be possible."

"I should have known," Wyn said again.

"We can't help what we don't know," Cara said.

"It destroyed him. 'I didn't know' isn't much of an excuse."

"Your using his ideas is not what destroyed him," Cara said. "It was his choice to obsess over that. To let bitterness take over. He did that."

"You don't know what his work meant to him."

"It shouldn't have meant more than his sister's life, Wyn."

Another small sob slipped out. Wyn choked it down.

They were silent for a long time. Then Wyn pulled away, and Cara let her arm drop.

"I wish he was still… I wish I could tell him I'm sorry," Wyn said.

"I'm sorry you lost him," Cara said.

"I thought we were like two arms working together, that if one was gone the other would have to work harder." Wyn's voice was almost impossible to hear. "But it wasn't like that. It was like we were two sides of a flipping coin, and then one was erased. Without it, there was no way to choose, no way to win. I was just a face."

*Yes*, Cara thought. She understood that now. Tom wasn't just a part of her. He was her counterpart.

"I can't go back," Wyn said. Her voice was firm again. "I can't live there anymore. I always told myself it was something wrong in his brain that made him think that about me, that he was sick, and it was unavoidable, and I could honor him by continuing our work. It wasn't until here…until you…now I know I was lying to myself all those years. He wasn't sick. And our work was deprived of all the best ideas. The ones he would have had."

"You've been brilliant on your own merit," Cara said.

"It was never my own merit," Wyn said. "Even after…when Ny was gone. My daughter was already there, nearly fully apprenticed. She's the real genius. She'll carry on without me."

"And what about what you've done here? The star map? Finding us in the universe?"

"That's why I want to stay," Wyn said. "This is the first work I've ever done all on my own."

Bree and Jak passed the doorway on their way to the lake. Cara heard the murmur of their voices.

"I've thought a lot," Wyn said. "I know why everyone else wants to get home. I'll help you as much as I can if that's what you decide to do. But I'm starting new. And you can tell everyone that Ny was right. It's all I can do for him now." She lifted her chin. "There's so much to study here. This entire system we've stumbled into: the fish with healing properties that can send healing oil through a membrane that crosses worlds, the water that not only gains the healing power but also transports those it heals across space, the animals waiting for prey…the only animals in this whole world, maybe. None of this is random. It could not have developed naturally. It has to be an intelligent design. But who? Or what? And the technology being used is…beyond us, to say the least."

"The answers to those questions could be dangerous," Cara said. "Even asking them has been dangerous."

"Science is always dangerous."

"Is this science, though? Or is it magic, like everyone keeps saying?"

"Science. Magic. They're twins, too. Opposite sides of the same coin."

Cara hugged her knees in silence.

"We may have already destroyed the system." It was a confession, and her guilt echoed from the stone walls.

"All the more reason for me to study it while its pieces remain."

"All the more reason for us not to risk destroying it further."

"You would choose to stay?"

"I'm afraid the system isn't really giving us a choice about staying or going. I'm afraid our only choice is between accepting where we were sent or burning down our new home in anger over what has happened to us."

"Could you really give up the chance to go home? Could the others do that?"

"Yes. We've all already considered it. We all knew the odds of us making it home were slim, that we had a better chance of bringing our families here."

"We're well beyond the place where any of us can accurately calculate the odds of anything," Wyn said.

"Says the woman who used the stars to mathematically calculate our location."

"Why do you think I became an astronomer?" Wyn said. "Stars are the only thing you can count on."

"Stars burn out eventually," said Cara, hating how bitter she sounded.

Wyn looked down at where her hands were folded in her lap. "They do," she said, "but the universe is infinite. Even when a star has burned out, its light travels on forever."

# Chapter 44

## Choices

The people of Mayland came to meet them.

Tom had contacted his father as soon as they were in range the night before. Cal had a lot of questions, and when Tom saw the reception waiting for them, he was glad he had answered them in full.

No one commented on Jof's leg or offered to help him. Instead, the crowd outside the gates parted as Jof proudly hobbled through. Only a handful of people ran toward them. Jof's daughter lifted his grandson up to give him a hug. Grish slapped Tom on the back. Two apprentices from the dining hall held out fruit juice and sandwiches. Next to the fence, the governor was waiting to welcome them home.

Tom held out his hand, but he didn't resist when Cal used it to pull him into a hug. It felt good to have his father's arms around him for a moment, no matter what the motive.

When he pulled back, Cal looked into Tom's eyes, nodded at what he saw there.

"We brought the water," Tom said, loudly enough for everyone standing nearby to hear.

"Good work," his father said, shaking Jof's hand. "There is a lot to discuss, but it can wait until you've rested. A meal is waiting in the dining hall."

"The rains will most likely come tomorrow," Jof said.

"Yes," said Cal. "Preparations have already been made. We have more to do, but we have time to eat together first."

Tom and Jof traded a look. Tom shrugged.

"Lead the way."

They followed the tidy path that led to the dining hall. As soon as the door opened, Tom could smell something delicious. People were everywhere, bringing food to the tables, herding children toward their seats, streaming in through every door. Tom barely had time to think that the entire colony must be here before his mother was in front of him, wrapping him in a tight hug, telling him with a catch in her voice how glad she was to see him.

Tom's throat constricted, and tears welled up behind his eyes. He bent his head, buried his face in his mother's hair.

This wasn't just a meal. It was a good-bye feast.

When his mother stepped back, more people crowded in, shaking his hand or touching his shoulder. Jof was similarly surrounded.

Eventually they made their way to tables heaped with food, but even as Tom filled his plate, more people stopped by. Most only wanted to say good-bye and good luck. A few thanked him, some with tears in their eyes. Many of those, Tom noticed, were family of the disappeared.

When the visits tapered off, Tom finally turned a questioning look on his parents.

"We knew there wouldn't be much time after you arrived," Jul said. "It seemed important for us all to be together one last time."

Tom caught Jof's eye where he sat at the far end of the table. The old man slid closer to listen.

"We understand from your report that there is most likely no way home from that other place," Cal said. "It was devastating news for everyone."

"We can still go to them," Tom said. "We can found our new settlement there on Dua."

"Yes," Cal said. "We reached the same conclusion."

Tom was stunned. He and Cara had been preparing arguments for days now, assuming that the governor would need to be convinced to let more people go.

Cal smiled at the shock on his son's face. "You assumed I would be unreasonable," he said.

"No, I—"

Cal held up a hand. "You did. And I understand. I have always chosen the welfare of the whole community over the welfare of my own family, and I always will. I accept the consequences of that."

Tom had no idea what to say.

"You should know that even in this, my priority is the preservation of Mayland. Our people could never tolerate abandoning the disappeared to their fate. Their families would not allow it. That makes it easy for me to concede that a contingent of settlers must be sent to join them." He quelled Tom's interruption with a look. "However. We cannot send a full contingent of 100, as we would have to a settlement downriver. Without trade and resource-sharing or even communication, we cannot afford to lose so many. Instead we will send half."

"You'll send 50?"

"50. Including those who have already traveled."

"So only 35."

"37 actually. It's not a random number. We spent days on the calculations. If we send more, the risks to Mayland's future are unacceptably high. And while 50 would not be a viable colony under most circumstances, we believe that the presence of the healing fish make it so. We have arranged to send sufficient genetic material to ensure future diversity."

Tom was still struggling to process it all. "Who is going?"

"Family members of the disappeared were given first priority. Then Thirds. Everyone who is traveling chose to do so knowing the full import of their decision."

"Who?" Jof asked.

Jul handed Cal his tablet, but he didn't look at it. "Ming Vance, and her children, Cam and Lane. Fer and Li Rayson. Bea and Harm Demar, along with their oldest son Dom and his wife Nel and young daughter June. Moll and Ken Vargas. Wei and Mar Harambe, and their son Li. Paul and Lind Mondburg. Dan and Cher Savari, their daughter Sam and her husband Ror and two children, Kim and Bran. Sal Moreland. Grish Hanso. Pel Rune. Rik Koato. Barb Nasaki. Mat Jeshua. Jil Okeke. Marc and Fran Delaroso. Hap Vuittan. Ken Nzeo. Bel Imobuko."

Tom could barely breath. His team. That was his whole team. Even Bel, whose brother had died on Dua.

Next to him, Jof squared his shoulders.

"I'm sorry, Dad," his daughter was saying. Tears ran down her face. "Grey can't leave his research. We talked all night—"

Jof cut her short with a hand on her shoulder. "Of course you must stay. Your life is here. The children's lives are here."

She was crying hard now, and Jof wrapped her in a hug that made Tom's chest ache.

"I don't want the kids to grow up without their grandparents," she said into his chest.

Tom's tear-filled eyes met his mother's. Cal and Jul would also stay behind, of course. They would do their duty and lead Mayland and keep its people safe.

And they would never see their children again. They would never meet their grandchildren. They would never even see them in vids or photos.

"We'll still be able to hear from you," Cal said. He had taken Jul's hand, and she was clinging to it as if her life depended on it. "Ror Henderson has a twin brother, Jer. They have been practicing their communication."

The pain in Tom's chest eased a little.

"And maybe," he said. "Someday. When you are ready to retire…."

"No," Cal said. "Those who are staying have all signed a new contract. For Mayland to survive, our decision to stay must be permanent. You will take your samples of healing water with you. We will not seek out the lake again."

So that was that. Finalized before Tom could say a word. Even through his sadness, he couldn't muster any blame. Unlike the yesela, they knew the consequences of their decision. They had weighed the losses against the gains.

And they had made their choice.

# Chapter 45

# *Waiting*

When they left Incannu, Cara let Jem lead. She and Oz walked at the back, observing the others.

She hardly recognized them as the same people who had been transported here two months ago. Their clothing was tattered and torn, many patched with a combination of tree sap and thin strips of bark. Everyone carried long spears and packs made from woven grass. Somehow, though, the outlandish outfits looked impressive. Probably because the people wearing them stood tall and walked with energy and purpose. Their arms swung gracefully as they moved, their shoulders were straight and unburdened by pain.

"They look like they just stepped out of a vid about the ancient tribes of Earth," she said.

"Until you notice that their skin is blue," Oz answered.

"Didn't some of those tribes paint themselves blue when they went to war?"

"Hoping the color makes us more impressive?"

"Hardly. They did it to be terrifying, I think."

"Cara," he said, taking her hand and turning her to face him. He leaned close and whispered, "You were terrifying long before your skin was blue."

She laughed. Then she kissed him. "Don't think I didn't notice that you never kissed me before the day my skin changed."

"Nothing gets past you."

She tugged his hand, and they hurried after the others. The last few days of preparations had left them quite a bit of time for philosophical discussions, and Cara enjoyed those conversations as much as the kissing that inevitably followed. Oz had thought deeply about a lot of things. His mind was like a mountain full of buried treasure. Talking to him had quickly become the best part of any day.

There was a shout from the head of the group, and Jem lifted a laughing Hal into the air. Those two were nearly inseparable. Cara tried not to worry about how things would go when Hal's parents and Jem's own children were here. When she thought about the adjustments that would come when the newcomers arrived, she felt her old anxiety threaten to overwhelm her.

As if he read her mind, Oz asked, "How was Em?"

Em had cried for two days when Cara told her she had to stay behind with Wyn and Bree while the rest went to the meadow to receive her parents. Not only did they need a way to communicate with Incannu, the meadow would soon have enough children in danger from beasts without adding one who didn't need to be there. Still, Cara had felt cruel as she held the sobbing girl.

"She was calmer today. She even came and said goodbye to Hal. She wouldn't look at me, but I keep telling myself that once this is over and she has her parents again, she'll forgive me for these few awful days."

"She will," he said.

Cara didn't share his confidence, but she forced the little girl's tragic face from her mind, focusing instead on the women in front of her.

Ann walked with the three teenagers. Syl's spear was short – she only planned to use it for self-defense—but Pol and Lil carried full weapons and looked like they knew how to use them. It wasn't an act. Lin had been training them, and she said they were both surprisingly fierce. Their parents were in for a surprise when they arrived, but Cara hoped it would be a good one.

Jak and Lin walked together behind them. They were deep in some sort of debate, and from time to time Jak would raise his voice in frustration. Cara noticed that Lin was smiling. Everyone was happy that their loved ones were coming, but no one could beat Lin's good mood. She was so happy that it was getting weird.

*Tom, you don't know how lucky you are. That girl actually loves you.*

The connection was weak, so she doubted he could hear her. Something told her he already knew, anyway.

By midafternoon they arrived at the little grotto that had been their first shelter. No one wanted to linger in the place where Zyk had died, but they did stop for a few minutes at his grave. Cara gripped Oz's hand as the emotions of that day ripped through her all over again.

The fear that she had been keeping at bay rose up. Yes, they were coming prepared, and so were the new travelers, but they didn't really know for sure how all this would play out. The beasts still guarded the meadow. The transport itself was a mystery. There was a lot of room for things to go wrong.

*I won't lose any of you,* she thought fiercely to Tom. *I won't.*

His answer was faint but clear. *I know.*

After that, the group was somber. When they arrived at the far edge of the forest, they looked out across the flat rocks toward the meadow that haunted their nightmares. Cara was relieved to see that the grass had grown back, though it was only waist-high.

They made camp under the trees. As best they could tell, the travelers from Mayland wouldn't arrive until nightfall of the following day. The plan was to scout the meadow before they came.

Defending the newcomers wouldn't be easy. Their own group had appeared in random spots throughout the meadow. If 37 new people materialized in the same way, inevitably some would be alone in a vulnerable location.

They were taking every possibly precaution. Everyone who was coming, including the children, was bringing an arrow gun. The firing device was mechanical rather than electronic, so they hoped that the weapons would still function after transport. Each person was also armed with a knife just in case.

The plan was for Hal and Syl to stand in a central location and shout out a prearranged signal. Every new arrival knew to run toward the sound of their voices. The rest of Cara's people would be prepared to fight off the beasts while the group reunited.

Though there were no signs of the creatures, they set a watch that night.

It hardly mattered. No one was able to sleep.

# Chapter 46

## *Together*

They said their good-byes at the gate.

For a life-changing moment, it felt disappointingly ordinary.

His father shook his hand, then followed it with a brief hug.

"Anything you want me to tell Bree and Cara?" Tom asked.

Cal hesitated for a moment, then shook his head. "They already know everything they need to know."

Tom turned to his mother, trying to make himself understand that this would be the last time he saw her. It was beyond his grasp.

She pulled him into a hug, her hair tickling his cheek the way it had for as long as he could remember.

It was only when she finally let him go that he realized how much he would miss that.

She touched his chin with one hand. "Tell the girls…look forward, not back. You all…you'll be all right when you are together."

Tom nodded.

"I love you."

"I love you, too," he echoed, still feeling that he couldn't make the words mean all that they should.

The governor opened the gates and gestured for his son to lead the way out of Mayland. Tom's last picture of his father was him shaking hands with each person as they filed out. His mother had disappeared.

Everything felt unreal as Tom walked the short way along the river to the place they had agreed to meet the rain.

He felt numb. Somewhere inside, he felt Cara's joy and anxiety, but even that seemed distant.

The clouds gathered, faintly green-tinged in the cold air of Ehrde. They seemed too commonplace for the role they were about to play.

Bel and Rik stepped close, each taking one of his hands as the small group of travelers huddled together. Everyone had packs of tools and food strapped to their backs. Most were wearing extra clothing, and some had hats and coats as well.

"The rain is coming," Ming Vance told her boys.

*The rain is coming,* Tom echoed to Cara.

*We're here. We're ready.*

When the first drop hit his cheek, its cold shocked him awake. Briefly, he wondered if they had gotten it all wrong. If everything from that first day by the lake had been a dream.

The world went black.

He couldn't move. He couldn't breathe. He couldn't feel his body.

Panic clawed through him.

# TWIN

He fell to his knees on solid ground and gasped in a breath of air. It wasn't enough. He sucked in more. The panic was still with him.

So was the darkness.

He wasn't alone. Someone was yelling. That meant something. A sign.

A signal. Cara said there would be a signal. It had worked. He had traveled.

The thought broke through his fear, and he opened his eyes. It wasn't black, just night here. Stars shone overhead and he could see torches against the darkness.

His body still gasped for air, but now he pushed to his feet.

Above the yelling, a feral scream split the night. The sound sent adrenalin coursing through his body, and he spun in a circle, searching for the danger.

One of the torches bobbed toward him, and suddenly the person carrying it was in front of him, grabbing his arm.

"They're coming," the girl said. "You need to run. That way."

He let her push him along, though the effort made black spots dance in front of his eyes. He stumbled, but she pulled him to his feet. He couldn't look up or look around. It took all of his concentration not to fall.

Suddenly, they burst into a circle of light. A crowd of people stood, most of them dazed and confused, a few coughing and vomiting on the ground. Tom sank to his knees again.

"Your weapon," the girl said. "The arrow gun. You have it?"

Tom fumbled for the holster at his waist. When he managed to get the gun free, the girl snatched it away.

More people were arriving at the circle. A young boy brought a wooden cup of water and offered Tom a drink. Hal, he thought. This was Hal, the young twin.

The water was lukewarm and had a bitter tang, but it cleared Tom's head. He had made it. He was here. Where was Lin? And Cara?

Another scream erupted, this time somewhere close. Several people cried out as two giant beasts leapt out of the grass. One landed in front of the girl who had taken Tom's gun. She dropped it, snatching up a spear instead and using both spear and torch to attack the beast with a ferocity that took Tom's breath away. He picked up the arrow gun, but her vicious dance left no room to aim it.

He looked around. The group that had traveled with him was now huddled in the center of a ring of blue-skinned fighters carrying torches and other weapons. They were fending off eight lizard-scaled creatures, which shied away from the torches, but didn't break off their attack, even as one by one they began to fall.

On the far side of the circle, he caught a flash of what looked like red hair. Tom staggered toward it, saw Lin engaging a giant creature with a blackened eye. She was defending herself with the torch but couldn't get close enough to damage it with her spear. Two other fighters joined her, and the creature, seeing itself cornered, reared back and leapt over their heads.

For one suspended moment, Tom saw that it would land in the middle of the circle. Then he raised his gun and fired an arrow right into its heart.

The creature screamed and dropped. People scattered out of the way, then watched in horror as it thrashed on the ground.

Lin stepped forward and drove her spear into its brain.

Silence fell.

# TWIN

Tom stared at Lin, speechless. Her pale skin was now sky blue, her clothing torn and spattered in green blood. An ugly scratch ran down one arm, and her long hair straggled around her face.

She was beautiful.

"That may not be all of them, so we should move as quickly as we can," Cara said, striding through the group with her torch held high. "Do we have everyone? We need a count."

"Cara," he whispered.

She met his eye, took his hand, then turned toward one of the young girls.

"I have 36 new arrivals," Syl said. "We're missing one."

"It's Dom," said Nel Demar. She was clutching her young daughter and looked frantic. "He's not here."

"We'll send out four people to search. Oz, take Pol. Jem, take Lil. The rest of us will stand guard here." Cara took Tom's gun and pressed it into Oz's hands. "We're going to find him."

"No need," said a voice. Dom Demar staggered into the torchlight. His shoulder was shredded, his shirt torn completely off, but he bared his teeth in a grin. "The arrow guns work," he said. Then he passed out.

Oz grabbed his brother just before he fell.

"Fish," Cara said.

Syl was already kneeling next to the men, holding out a small bite.

Oz had forced Dom to swallow, and the man's breathing deepened. His wound began to knit back together. A few minutes later, he opened his eyes.

Tom sagged with relief.

Then everyone was hugging everyone else. People were laughing and crying. And Lin was in his arms.

Tom didn't notice anything else for a long time.

When Lin finally pulled away, she was grinning. "You'd better give your sister a hug."

Behind her, Cara was waiting. He could feel her worry and impatience.

"We'd better help her get these people out of here before she has a heart attack," he said.

She raised a brow. "No hurry," she said. "If the vicious predators come back, I can always save your life again."

"Hey, I took that one out myself."

"Yeah, you came through eventually."

"What can I say? I've been six minutes behind since the beginning."

Cara laughed.

*I can't believe you're really here*, she said. *I can't believe you're real.*

*This is as real as it gets,* he answered.

Then finally, he got to pull her close. Finally, he could feel her relax against him.

Finally, he was home.

"When our grandparents chose this planet to be their new home, they committed themselves fully to their choice. They dismantled the very ship that brought them here to build the systems that feed us, the computers that offer education to our children, even the structures that shelter us today. A life free and untainted by the plagues and wars of Earth was their gift to us.

That gift did not come without sacrifice. They left behind family and friends. They left behind the comfort of the known to face doubt and anxiety and risk. And still they made the journey without wavering. They pursued the dream of this colony with steady purpose.

That same sacrifice they made has now been asked of us. We also have chosen to let our loved ones go. We have chosen to accept the challenge of continuing our lives even while surrounded by unexplained phenomena. I'm sure by now all of you have heard the news of the birth of our first grandchildren on Dua, and some of you have asked if I now regret my choice to stay here and accept the separation from my family.

Tonight I say to you: NO. I do not regret. I do not look back at what once was or out at what might have been. I look around me, and I say: YES. This is the dream. This is the life my grandparents imagined. And this dream, this life, is worth any sacrifice.

Our sister planet now holds our sister colony, and we recognize the truth that it holds half of our heart as well. But Una holds our full purpose, captures our complete imagination, and contains the entirety of our life. We have chosen this planet to be our home, and we commit ourselves fully to our choice."

Governor Cal Mayland
Address to the full gathering
Colony of Mayland
L.D. 82

# *About the Author*

Deborah Dunlevy was born in Indiana and grew up everywhere else. Even moving every year or two couldn't satisfy her need for adventure, so she learned how to read and started taking trips into other people's lives. Eventually she grew up, went to college, and got a respectable job as a teacher. Then she ditched that to go live on the other side of the world, where she learned that everything can be upside down and still exactly the way it's meant to be.

Deborah now lives in Indianapolis with her husband, Nate, her three kids, and a mismatched pair of furry animals. You can find more of her work on her website, deborahdunlevy.com.

www.ingramcontent.com/pod-product-compliance
Lightning Source LLC
Chambersburg PA
CBHW050906250626
47155CB00001B/123